Can a Leopard?

Susana Cory-Wright

Can a Leopard?

As ever, for my wonderful Book Club for their unfailing
support and friendship:

Nickey, Jane, Marie-Louise, Fenella, Clare and Perry

And for

Georgina Wyatt

Always an inspiration

Can a Leopard?

1

Did you really fantasize about shops re-opening rather than, you know…?"

Carla glanced up from her book. She was reading *Sex Matters* by Mona Charen or 'not' as one of Les Girls had been quick to respond when Carla suggested they read it for book club. Carla had giggled but it was pointless trying to tell them that the insightful, fascinating polemic, with the by-line: '*How Modern Feminism Lost Touch with Science, Love and Common Sense*' was worth a discussion. It was enough at any rate, to initiate dialogue. '*Not during lockdown anyway!*' someone else had texted. '*Last thing on my mind!*' While yet another had quoted from Carol Ann Duffy's *Mrs Rip Van Winkle*. Carla remembered the words 'Viagra' and 'Niagara' rhyming in that one. Which had set them off on another tack entirely. Les Girls had met at their convent school when they were approximately eleven years old. Living dangerously, some had even gone on together to the same university. Their parents were friends, their brothers had also attended the same boys' school, if not always at the same time. Suffice it to say, they were closer than even the closest of friends usually were.

But Seb was waiting on her reply. His eyes were broody under dark brows that were prized apart like the bascules of Tower Bridge opening to allow tall ships through. He was scouring his phone for the latest lockdown updates and this being July, there were several. Pubs had opened earlier in the week and people from two households could now meet outdoors provided they observed social distancing measures. Deaths from Covid-19 stood at 44,198 in the UK falling below the average for the time of year, while those in India and

Can a Leopard?

Brazil were on the increase. But that's not what Seb was thinking about.

"Do you mean sex?" said Carla playfully. "'Course not," she said crossing her fingers. But her mind had drifted to the famous landmark and its extraordinary feat of engineering.

"Bascule," she said aloud.

"Come again?"

"French for 'sea-saw.'"

Seb's eyebrows were now doing just that.

"Y-es?"

"Tower bridge is a combined suspension and bascule - and you - your - oh, never mind."

Seb was used to her random, eclectic references. He took a sip of coffee pouring from the metal cafetière with a wooden handle that always reminded Carla of an old-fashioned diving helmet. He'd once said it came from the Conran shop in the days, (pre-Carla), when he'd had nothing better to do than spend a morning browsing for innovative (if not always practical) home gadgets. Later he confessed that he hadn't bought it himself at all but that it had been a present from an ex. Carla secretly hoped the coffee pot reflected the girlfriend: solid and squat and in need of a polish. They were sitting on their patio having breakfast basking in the glorious summer weather. It seemed to have been hot now for months and they'd taken nearly all of their meals outside during that time. The end of lockdown was in sight and there was excitement in the air.

"Don't worry," added Carla smiling into her book and stretching a foot so that it rested on Seb's thigh. "They'll be plenty of you-know-what in Italy."

Can a Leopard?

Carla said it lightly but her glibness belied her true feelings. The truth was, that she, who was used to hopping on a plane at the drop of a hat (or Manolo flat) was far from easy about their forthcoming trip. Long before anyone could possibly have dreamt up this pandemic, Seb had booked the three-day break to coincide with a school trip of their twelve-year old son, Alfie, when he would be in France visiting the war graves of Normandy. They could always visit the sick wards of Lombardy instead; she had muttered when the school trip was cancelled.

But the hotel in Porto Ercole hadn't cancelled their reservation which, as luck would have it, was for July anyway and BA had simply moved their flight a few days. And yet now, the idea let alone the reality of their travelling anywhere other than Sainsbury's seemed somehow illicit and fraught with danger. They'd been cocooned in their own cosy bubble, their world defined by trying to eat creatively (if not well), home schooling Alfie (before Google Classroom kicked in), ensuring they all took enough exercise, and trying to help out in their local community wherever possible. Carla had dreamed about escaping but now that the moment was upon them, she was apprehensive.

"We're not doing anything wrong," said Seb reading her thoughts. "It's completely legal. Italy is welcoming tourists again and there is no quarantine required by the UK on our return. It's all OK." He held her foot in his large strong hands. "The Majors have agreed to have Alfie. He'll love being with his friends. He'd probably rather be with them than with us."

"It's not that," she said.

"What then?" the bascule bridge was definitely on the rise again. "Aren't you looking forward to it just being us? After all this time?"

3

Can a Leopard?

"117 days. Or put another way: 3 months, 26 days. And" she glanced at her phone, "4 hours and 35 minutes. Actually 36. What do you think?"

"Well, then." He began massaging her foot like a pro. Carla had always loved Seb's hands. They were broad and tanned, the fingers straight and well-shaped. His right wrist was paler than the left, from years of wearing a glove for polo,

"What is it?"

She took a breath. "I'm not sure. I'm not sure I'm ready to see anyone, that's all."

Seb stopped massaging. "You? The most sociable woman in Winchester? Not *see* anyone?" But when he realized that she was being serious added kindly. "You won't have to. The hotel has half occupancy as it is - you can stick to the pool or sit by the sea. The dining is al fresco anyway. It'll be fine."

"We've got out of the habit, though, haven't we? Of being with other people. Of socialising properly. I mean Zoom get togethers just aren't the same thing. Besides if you're bored you can just cut out - leave the meeting."

Seb lessened the pressure across the arch of her foot.

"Is that what you do?" he said sounding vaguely shocked.

"N-no…" she lied. *Sometimes…*

"Look, if you just want to lie by the pool all day and read and do a Greta Garbo thing, then that's fine by me. As long as you're mine come the night."

Seb's eyes twinkled and Carla responded with a weak smile.

It would be heaven … but it wasn't that.

4

Can a Leopard?

It's just..." she swallowed turning her book so that its spine was splayed against her stomach and wriggling her toes to encourage him to continue.

"It's just what?"

"It's-" She sighed. Everything she'd said was true but there was something else. How to tell Seb, that after her great Covid purge, when she'd given away or sold her entire wardrobe to garner funds for the Hampshire Air Ambulance or to make PPE, she had nothing (well virtually nothing) left to wear? How to explain that it did matter after all, not having nice clothes? She was conflicted. She'd thought she wouldn't mind ever again, not shopping for pretty things. While there was nowhere to go much beyond a stroll by the river, she hadn't. Holidaying in Italy was another prospect altogether. Especially after lockdown. This should be cause for celebration. What was more, the prospect of a trip abroad awakened all those latent feelings in her of insecurity, competition and desire.

"Was that the doorbell?" Seb paused, his fingers cupping her foot.

"Was it?" Carla suddenly felt clammy.

"Yeah. Definitely."

Carla pulled her foot away abruptly. "I'll go!"

"No, I will," said Seb, already on his feet, his hand on her shoulder rooting her to her seat. "You're not dressed."

He'd leapt up, faster than she'd seen him move in their entire married life and that included the days when he could leap from horse to horse without dismounting- something she'd always found dead sexy. She swivelled her chair to so that she could see down the corridor, through the sash windows to the now open front door. And shrank back down. Kevin,

Can a Leopard?

the DHL driver (ex-army tattoo down one calf - New Wave cat-eye sunglasses perched atop his top knot) was social distancing, standing on the doorstop opposite and pointing at the package he'd left on theirs.

Kevin's arrival was bad timing. Pre-lockdown, Seb was generally out when Kevin delivered parcels from Net-à-Porter or Mytheresa.com or any of the numerous shopping sites, Carla frequented. There was usually plenty of time to secrete boxes into the house without Seb seeing. Not that any of that should even be relevant now. Carla needed no reminding that she'd promised to give up buying clothes for the foreseeable future - emphasis being on the word 'clothes.' Carla discounted the daily stream of packages that had arrived at the beginning of lockdown. Prior to then, she'd never have considered Amazon as a credible online site, but *faut de mieux*, Carla had found all kinds of weird and wonderful pieces. She'd bought: a rubber toe divider (to prevent bunions), multipacks of rubber exercise bands in NHS rainbow colours (5-10 kilos weights had sold out almost immediately), Imedeen tablets in bulk (for skin and nails) and a beautifully designed wooden paddle - a hole at either end in different sizes, for measuring pasta. It didn't matter at all that the Caves were not a pasta eating household. But buying stuff from Amazon wasn't deviating from her promise. The purchase of an article of clothing was. Now she was getting closer to the truth; guilt and longing all rolled into one.

She popped her head up like a periscope. Seb and Kev were still exchanging pleasantries - no doubt along the lines of Carla's shopping habits. Former habits, Seb could be forgiven for thinking. She picked up her book again, trying to find her place on a page she must have re-read several times already: *'relations between the sexes are ailing ...'* hardly seemed relevant in this time of Covid and turned back to the table of contents opting for a chapter on 'Family.' Apparently, the number of people in Europe reporting to feeling lonely was rising sharply and chronically lonely people had a rate of death twice that of the obese and higher rates of suicide. And that was before lockdown.

Carla could only imagine what it was now. She remembered an episode from the sitcom *To the Manor Born* where a lonely Penelope Keith determines to fill her day with visits from various handymen. You couldn't count Kevin social distancing on the pavement as 'a visit' though. It certainly wouldn't be enough to fill in the hours. She moved the book from her lap. It was already so hot that Carla's nightie was sticking to her lap, the book with it. Now that she thought about it, she had kept one Paravel packing case, but rifling through its contents had found nothing but a faded Stella bikini, a watermarked pareo and a once beautiful (now crushed and dis-coloured) Gucci sun hat. There was nothing remotely suitable for wearing at one of the most glamorous hotels in the world. And not just glamorous by English standards - Italian glamorous. *Oh, God…* The thought of going down to breakfast, filing past sultry Italian beauties who would no doubt start dissecting her attire as she sidled past with her cereal bowl, made her feel positively nauseous.

She felt a renewed, light sheen of perspiration creep over her skin.

"It's for you- hou!" called out Seb cheerily, the whole house shaking as the door slammed.

Carla picked up her book again quickly.

"Mmmn?" she said feigning a distracted air while her heartbeat increased incrementally with Seb's approaching footsteps.

"Voilà," he said placing a large package on the breakfast table with a flourish. "Or should I say 'ecco'?" She sat up slowly, tucking *Sex Matters* between cushion and chair, but made no move to rip open the package as she normally would. Seb looked from her face to the box.

7

Can a Leopard?

"You seem very thoughtful," he said surprised. "Is the book so good?"

"No - I mean, yes. It's so-so."

With a practised eye Carla glanced at the label. The shape and size and weight were all wrong for what she was expecting. She felt giddy with relief.

"Actually, darling. It's for *you*."

"Ah," said Seb as they both appraised the parcel.

"What's in the box?" said Alfie suddenly appearing and plopping into a chair bedside her. He wore shorts and his dressing gown. He was barefoot, his hair tousled.

"Bring me the head of John the Baptist," said Carla under her breath.

Seb shot her a 'not-now-to-weird-references' look.

"*Is* it a head?" said Alfie.

And Carla thought her boy was bright...

"No," said Seb.

"Maybe," said Carla.

"Can I check my messages?" said Alfie.

"Aren't you supposed to be in class?"

Alfie rolled his eyes. "It's my break!"

"Again?"

Can a Leopard?

"Sure," said Seb removing the box with unusual care from the table. It was Carla's turn to express surprise but Alfie's appearance distracted her before she had a chance to question Seb further.

"Couldn't you do something else instead?" said Carla irritated. "Violin practice for example? Or more of the self-portrait you're supposed to be working on? I thought the teacher said to spend at least five hours on it."

Alfie looked up. "I've finished it."

"No, you haven't," said Carla her tone sharp. "If you spent five minutes I'd be surprised. All the Year 8s' pictures are going to be displayed for the younger ones to see. I don't think you've done yourself justice."

"That's because I'm rubbish at art."

"No, you're not! You just haven't tried."

Tears sprang to Alfie's eyes. "Yeah, I am. Besides, what's the point?"

"How do you mean?"

"Well, there isn't, is there?"

"Come on big guy," said Seb alerted by the despondency in his son's tone. "Give it a go. And a start might be getting dressed."

"Yes," agreed Carla. "That's not at all what the school meant by 'appropriate attire.' Or 'dressing as if you mean business.' Do you know that I saw Julien in his whole summer uniform - I mean the lot - blazer and tie?" Alfie shot her a withering look. Seb's also seemed to imply that he agreed with Alfie. "OK, maybe that's going a bit far. But you need to feel good about yourself. It makes a difference being properly dressed."

9

Can a Leopard?

Didn't she know! "Go and shower and change. Now!" she added firmly.

"But it's my break! It's wasting time!"

"Yes, well maybe if you'd got dressed earlier, you'd wouldn't have to waste your break time now."

More tear droplets.

"Oh, really!" said Carla exasperated. "What is it?"

Seb made the pushing down gesture he often did when he thought she was overreacting or should be quiet. Preferably both.

"But-"

"Come on, big guy," said Seb calmly. "Time to march!"

Alfie banged the chair then scarpered throwing a "Sorry, sorry!" over his shoulder as Seb began a mock chase.

Carla sighed. It had been easier during the Easter holidays when she'd pretended to Alfie that the holidays were off and she'd taught him herself. When term began, his present school had made a valiant effort to offer distance learning with Google Classroom and the like but it just wasn't the same. Alfie was lonely, he missed his friends and he was becoming lazier by the day, hardly moving from his bean bag where with his iPad propped on his lap and the teacher muted, Carla was pretty certain he wasn't doing much course work. On the other hand, given how difficult the past few months had been for Alfie, they didn't like to nag him too much.

Seb made Carla a fresh pot of tea. These days, with no deadline, nowhere to go and hours of warm weather ahead of them, breakfast tended to be an extended affair. From time to

Can a Leopard?

time, Carla cast surreptitious glances at the box Seb had placed firmly on the ground by his feet. Seb was being as coy as Carla usually was when a parcel arrived.

"Aren't you going to open it?"

Seb had the grace to look sheepish. "I will, just not yet."

Carla felt a start of alarm tinged with gut-wrenching thrill. As long as he was out when hers came …

Carla lifted the mane of her hair off the back of her neck. It really was swelteringly hot; and not such a push at all to imagine themselves already in Italy. A couple of butterflies, pale and translucent shimmered in the sunshine, while elsewhere a bee buzzed and then fell abruptly silent as it disappeared into the bell-shaped head of a snapdragon. Against mellow stone, spindly stems of lavender made a cat's cradle crawling up through the grouting. They sat together in companionable silence, Carla's mind drifting to ideas for her garden. Well, 'garden' was a bit of an exaggeration. In reality it was a large walled space with two ridiculous herbaceous borders set bang in the middle. As it was though, they did divide the space into separate eating areas, one where they had breakfast with the morning sun, the other on the far side, which was larger, where they had supper as the sun went down. Carla dreamed of filling in the borders to make a proper courtyard, arranging olive trees in beautiful pots and building a pergola over which honeysuckle and a vine might grow. She'd keep the cherry tree in the corner. When Seb looked at the garden, he didn't see beyond the walls, marvelling at the brick and flint. The previous owners had restored it with exquisite care, randomly filling the cement crosses with Roman coins, tiny green glass bottles and whatever odd shaped stone they happened to discover in the course of their excavation.

"You do know it's our anniversary," said Carla flashing him a look that challenged him to remember.

11

"I know," said Seb.

"Soon,"

"Yes." He sounded perfectly relaxed. She cast him a suspicious look.

Ah, but do you remember the date?

"We'll be away." *On the day…*

Seb unfurled Carla's stiff fingers then turned her hand so that it was palm upwards.

"Sh!" he said quietly. "It's the second and yes, we'll wake up in Italy on our anniversary. Is that good enough?" He raised her hand to his lips. "That's why we're going."

was doing, he wouldn't reply at all, but whenever she said she was going out, his response was instantaneous. He would invariably say he was 'just chilling' for which she read 'just playing a computer game.' This once she didn't mind, replying with such a distracted 'great' that Alfie actually get off his bean bag.

"How are you, Mum?" he asked concerned, appearing at the top of the stairs in his dressing gown.

"Just rushing to collect something," she answered vaguely. Which in itself was strange as no one had been rushing anywhere recently, least of all to pick up anything from anywhere.

"Love you!" she called gaily over her shoulder.

"Love you more!" he replied worriedly, the 'more' swallowed by the sound of the door slamming. Theirs was a front door that didn't close quietly.

Thank goodness, they were allowed to drive again, thought Carla as she rushed past the newly re-opened Cornflowers Gift Shop, its front pavement brimming with artificial flowers and decorative household items. For a moment she struggled to remember where she'd last left the car. They'd only been on the road a couple of times since lockdown began. Once: to visit her daughter Sophie, the other when they'd taken Alfie for a swim at a friend's pool, breaking the 'all but essential travel' rule. Taking Alfie's mental health into consideration, they'd weighed up the pros and cons and decided that rousing him from his catatonic depression had been more important than not taking him to see a friend and worth the risk of a fine. But they'd been nervous travelling on roads post-apocalyptic in their spooky emptiness. Afterwards, Alfie had hugged and thanked her repeatedly. There was a time that playing a computer game was the acme of pleasure, now it was doing simple boyish things, going for a swim, climbing trees, building a den in the woods. But all the time, the adults

Can a Leopard?

had hovered nervously, whispering to each other and to their children, warning each other to keep their voices down in case neighbours snitched on them.

Carla almost twisted an ankle in her rush to get to her car. Trembling with excitement, motivated by one clear objective only, she couldn't leave the city fast enough. Out of practice, she drove badly and much too fast. Failing to indicate, zigzagging across lanes and driving in the wrong gear, she eventually careered to a stop right in front of Moda Rosa. No matter that it was a bus bay. *'So fine me,'* she muttered to herself, *'this is important!'* She was breathless entering the shop, the first time she'd visited since lockdown. She felt dizzy with emotion. The shop was quiet - it would have to be with only two customers permitted at any given time but still there was an air of luxe - the plush carpet sinking between her sandalled-feet, tuberose aromatizers competing with alcoholic spurts of hand-sanitizer and rails filled with the vibrant colours of the summer collection.

After the drabness of lockdown, everything seemed bright and fresh and new. She whisked out her face mask which she was told she could remove when trying on clothes in her cubicle. Just as well, thought Carla as she'd almost tripped going *up* the stairs not being able to see over the edge of the mask. Any unwanted items would be quarantined for 72 hours before being put back on the shop floor. It certainly concentrated the mind. Not that Carla needed concentrating. She'd come for the pale blue dress and the pale blue dress she would have. Out the window went any resolve to change. All she was aware of was the desperate thudding of her heart, the scratch of tissue paper as her purchases were wrapped, the tingle of excitement coursing through her entire body as she presented her credit card and she saw that delectable word: 'Approved' light up the monitor. And then, almost as quickly the pinprick crash of guilt because she'd not just bought the blue dress but the darling jumpsuit by the same designer as well. The matching kimono (perfect for cooler evenings) was

Can a Leopard?

coming from the flagship store in London. Along with a red bathing suit.

Driving home, she felt a great deal calmer. Except now, she was faced with the reality of how to explain all these purchases to Seb? When she'd been adamant that she'd changed, that she didn't need designer gear anymore? She parked the car carefully this time and managed to get home without bumping into anyone she knew. She virtually held her breathing letting herself into the house but there were no riding boots in the hall, no sign of life of any kind. She called out feebly thanking her lucky stars when the answering silence meant Seb was still out. She ran up to her dressing room hiding her shopping behind the door.

Taking a deep breath, she braced herself for a run-in with Alfie, calling to him several times to get ready for 'assembly' and tutor groups and when he didn't answer, tip-toed up to his attic rooms. She was astonished to find that he was actually dressed (shorts and a t-shirt being an advance on robe and pants) and was tucked into his beanbag. But he was wearing headphones and Google Classroom did appear to be running in the background. For a moment she was waylaid by the sight of abandoned Lego bricks, half-formed vehicles scattered beside him, board games he no longer was interested in, a pack of cards. She felt a pang of nostalgia for the loss of childhood - at least the kind of childhood her older children had enjoyed. It had been so much easier for parents of their generation not having to compete with the highly addictive computer games. She remembered the anticipation of birthdays and Christmas as being something wonderful. Now, they hardly rated.

Carla glanced at Alfie's screen. The school had endeavoured to make the final weeks of term (when the boys would have been on school trips abroad) as memorable as possible hiring a dynamic duo - Sharky and George (*'finding the fun in everything we do'*) - to offer party-type games remotely. The remnants of attempted experiments: bits of glass, sugar,

Can a Leopard?

biscuits, multi-coloured sand, Smarties, balloons and various sized flasks also lay discarded on the rug. But Alfie had become bored with that too. There was a time when children were used to being bored. Now, it was a dirty word.

Carla mouthed that she was popping out again and asked Alfie to answer the door to DHL. Retreating down the stairs she caught sight of the timetable that had begun taped to his desk and was now floating on the rug. She was close to giving up trying to distract him. He was tired of Zoom, tired of remote learning, tired of the effort of keeping his mental health in check. Alfie wanted his friends - to *see* his friends in the flesh and nothing else would do.

Carla understood that compulsion; she had also become used to her own company. She wanted life to resume around her without necessarily having to take part in it. But she was glad to see a busy High Street, with shops once again opening their doors. It didn't matter that masks would have to be worn inside - it was a small price to pay for choice, the opportunity to pretend they were back to pre-Covid times. When she'd first read that they'd have to wear masks, she'd been appalled. Now, it was second nature and the house was scattered with the cheap 5-in-a-pack variety from Boots. (She refused to wear matchy, fabric ones - they looked awful no matter what colour they came in.) The only distinguishing mark between hers and Seb's, was traces of her lipstick. *'You'd be worried if they were mine'*, he joked.

As elated as Carla was, at being 'out' again, she was wary of being caught up in the frenzy of social and cultural activities she'd once thought it impossible to live without. The flying here there and everywhere in the pursuit of ... what exactly? Purpose, she supposed. Covid-19 was, and continued to be, terrible, but combatting the pandemic had also provided a collective sense of purpose. They were surviving, they were shopping for loo paper, protecting the elderly, the NHS, teachers, their families. And now? Now that the worst-case scenario (the half a million lives that were purportedly at risk

20

Can a Leopard?

in the UK if this pernicious virus wasn't confronted) *hadn't* come to pass, Carla suspected that the advice of SAGE and other so-called experts was the least reliable evidence to be had. At the end of the day, theirs too was just opinion. Viruses had been consuming human life since it began and Carla believed they would also recede in their own good time. The world had watched with morbid fascination and in real time, the trajectory of a virus doing exactly what viruses had always done. But where would they all be when that common purpose was no longer unifying, no longer required?

Carla's, meanwhile, was clear. If only that morning she'd felt unleashed by a demon, she now felt unleashed in a different direction. She was consumed with an insatiable need to be out and about and shopping. She intended to check The Hambleden for new stock - just to *look* - and be back home by the time Seb had finished polo. She skirted the Cathedral - now open to worshippers although a neighbour had alerted her to the fact that she would have to give her personal details for contact- tracing. The neighbour hadn't wanted to have to self-isolate if some mug from Leicester came down on a day trip and was later to be found Covid-19 positive. Neither did she, not when they were off on holiday.

The green in front was wall-to-wall in people, mostly mothers with young children, their laughter a welcome novelty after months of silence. A short distance away, revellers drank beer from the pavement and consumers collected takeaway meals from coffee shops. Before entering The Hambledon, Carla paused to apply a dollop of the now customary sanitizer and whisk out her mask. She whipped through the ground floor with its displays of enamel cups, Brighton Rock-coloured candles, recipe books, cushions and glassware. The blocked arch on the ground floor led to a sunken floor showcasing men's cashmere and linen, the stone backdrop perfectly complimenting its edgy style. Carla looked again. It fascinated her that a labyrinth of tunnels had once connected the Cathedral to the Great Hall and other houses in the city.

Can a Leopard?

During the dissolution of the monasteries, monks had hidden from the King's men in these twisty, narrow passages. In her favourite Café Monde opposite, the basement eating area was also to be found under the arch to one of these former entry points.

Carla vaulted the sisal covered stairs. The first floor was empty. *You're only looking…* She didn't need anything more. But then again, when did 'need' ever come into it? As passionate as she'd once been about her clothes, shopping now seemed indulgent and spoiling, her recent purchases poleaxing her with guilt. Until that is, she saw the beautiful silk thigh-slit maxi dress - a delicate floral motif on an ivory background in the palest gold, ivory and taupe. Perfect for going down to breakfast at the hotel, wafting past all the Italian beauties. For the second time that week, she felt the familiar, uncomfortable, all-consuming do or die, heart to stomach, stomach to heart, lurch.

"Yes, I'll try it," she said to the girl belting past, and diving into the first available cubicle. A moment later, Carla pulled back the curtain having noted the girl's left hand.

"Poor you," she added.

The assistant carefully peeled back the gauze bandage revealing skin that was raw and blistered. She also removed her mask, leaving it dangling from an elastic loop around one ear so that she could speak clearly. "From all the sanitizing."

Carla recoiled. "Ouch! Looks painful."

She let the curtain fall into place and removed her own mask. She pulled her old dress over her head, her earring becoming entangled in her hair in the process, then hunkered on all fours to stop the pearl rolling into a corner. She was breathless when she stood up and couldn't get into the new dress fast enough. She peered at the mirror. She had definitely aged since lockdown - her skin looked sallow and

Can a Leopard?

her skin sagged. In fact, every bit of her seemed to be saggy. Re-fixing her earring she noticed how it hung lower than it usually did. God - even her *lobes* could do with a lift. Which was why the dress beautifully skimming her hip, billowing out behind her as she moved was perfect. Elegant and age appropriate but subtly sexy too. But she'd just bought the Alice Temperley... She wasn't supposed to be shopping any more. She was *supposed* to have given it up. She replaced her mask and went out to look at herself in the larger mirror. She'd send her daughter Sophie a selfie. She could always count on Sophie to give her an honest opinion. On everything.

Whaddya think? She texted.

You mean with or without the mask?

Carla whisked it off.

Better?

And this is for?

Oh, you know...

Are you going somewhere?

Just the library...

Oh, that kind of somewhere.

'Just the library' had become synonymous with absence - a kind of joke between them. When Alfie was about three or four, Sophie, who was fifteen years older than her little brother, had been corralled into looking after him for a couple of hours. Apparently (although she couldn't remember it now) Carla had told Sophie she was going to the library (she was completing a research degree at the time) when in fact she'd shot up to Harvey Nichols.

Can a Leopard?

Carla left the shop with the dress wrapped in a neat little parcel under her arm. Once outside, she removed her mask, now a crumpled mess from having blown her nose on it in the cubicle. Somehow, it was never the smooth, cool gesture surgeons in TV medical soaps managed. Not wanting to go home quite yet, she decided to walk the long way, down the High Street looping back by the water meadows. In front of Anthropologie, five, skinny, white youths, stood in a row. They had cardboard signs around their necks with the letters 'BLM' written in bold letters and invited passer-byers 'to take the knee.' She heard one older lady say that *all* Labradors mattered, even if black ones got a bad press and she had no intention of getting down for any dog.

Viewed from the top of the High Street, the bronze statue of King Alfred was imposing, his raised arm appearing not so much to brandish a sword, as to present it to the city. One hand rested on the large round sphere of his shield; as if in service, or in penance. Behind him, the hills sloped gently towards the horizon, trees and a line of houses forming a border beneath. Legend had it, that if a sixteen-year-old virgin walked around the granite base three times, Alfred would lower his arm. *'Don't!'* Carla had warned Seb when she'd told him. *'Don't go there.'*

Yellow markings and jaunty feet motifs spray painted on the pavement, endeavoured to ensure social distancing but no one was paying much attention. Except in front of the food stores where customers continued to adhere to the rules. In the time since lockdown began, staff at M&S had worn masks out of choice, then been told they didn't have to and were now wearing them again when masks in shops, had become mandatory. The schizophrenic about-turns on just about everything summed up government policy. She was beginning to think it was more difficult to come out of lockdown than it had been going into it. At least then, there'd been a clear premise and collective fear. And obedience. And the Brits were good at both; good at queuing, good at helping

24

for the greater good. It seemed to have brought out the best in people: all that clapping for the NHS and the painted rainbows displayed in windows.

But the hysteria of fear was something else entirely. Carla knew of some neighbours who'd not been out of their houses at all, since March. On one occasion, when she'd been shopping at Waitrose, Carla had been appalled to hear a woman of about her own age shouting at an older man who'd asked her to reach up for a tin of soup. He wasn't wearing a mask (they'd not yet become mandatory) and the woman was screaming (actually looking like Munch's): *'Do you want to kill me? Do you want me to die!'* Carla had been doubly mortified when she'd recognised the woman as an acquaintance of hers. When the coast was clear, Carla had helped the man with his shopping. She may have been mistaken, but Carla had been under the impression that lockdown was designed to protect the older generation. Not the other way around. But people - not helped by the government's mixed messages - were confused. And now, with restrictions being lifted, it seemed as if it was each woman, for herself.

Carla sidled past Tesco where the usual handful of drunks were having their daily tussle with security and arguing the toss as to whether they should be wearing masks at all. Moments later, in front of Mountain Warehouse, the same lads were using plastic Tesco bags to shoplift sweatshirts and water bottles. She then walked past Abbey Gardens to turn right at the Mill and follow the course of the river towards the Bishop's Palace. There manicured lawns were bifurcated by the chalky lines of 'Winkies' - that most primal form of football peculiar to Winchester College boys. 'Peculiar' was an understatement. In former times (like two hundred years ago), it was played along Kingsgate Street but too many broken windows had seen the game relocate to St. Catherine's Hill until that too had proved unsatisfactory when the ball repeatedly rolled down to the river.

Can a Leopard?

The weather was balmy; the bulbous flowers of rhododendrons barely ruffled in the heavy air. The branches of a weeping willow appeared more listless than usual, while badminton shuttlecocks barely cleared make-shift nets. Sprawled in deckchairs, making a day of it, older couples enjoyed themselves, drinking tea and prosecco. Bare-chested teenagers spun figures of eight on their bikes, others sneaking a cigarette threw away the butt, grinding the ash into the gravel. By the tennis courts, the odd couple canoodled on blankets.

Carla wondered how the young had fared when non-cohabiting singletons (who hardly knew each other at the beginning of lockdown) had been presented with the stark choice of either moving in together or shunning each other's company for the duration. How did you flirt on Zoom? Or cope with the inevitable lag to avoid both talking at once. Or talking too much? Revealing too much? Gone too, Carla supposed from the dating scene, was all the excitement of anything remotely clandestine. Not when masks and sanitizers were involved and no kissing. She wondered how she and Seb would have fared had they been dating now. Well, she knew how. They'd have carried on regardless.

Carla's phone vibrated in her bag and she fished it out, shifting her parcel, to read the messages from Alfie's year group. There was an ongoing discussion as how best to mark their end of term given that prize-giving was going to be carried out remotely. It seemed too sad to dismiss nine years - which many of the boys had spent together since nursery- by way of Zoom. But though the good will was there, it was becoming complicated. Boys in the final year were going to be allowed on site - well on Wolvesey anyway - that playing field in the ruins of the 12th century castle that had once belonged to Henry Blois, brother of King Stephen. Carla never heard Wolvesey mentioned that she didn't wonder if the boys batting a ball for six or forming a rugby scrum had ever brushed against the ghosts of jousting knights. Had they

Can a Leopard?

ever heard, however faint, the sound of trumpets announcing the marriage between Mary Tudor and Philip of Spain?

The boys took it all for granted. As they had, normal, everyday contact with each other, which is all they wanted now. And at last, it looked as if they were going to have some, grouped in their respective bubbles - with fun activities organised for them on the field. But the various bubbles were not supposed to mingle, which was why one of the parents had offered his farm for an impromptu reunion after the official end of term. Having been shopped by nosy so-and-so's in his village on other occasions, he wanted to keep the whole thing low-key. Some parents, quoting government directives (gatherings up to thirty people were still restricted by law), weren't happy with a get-together of any kind. The class rep suggested a picnic after the zoom prize-giving so that the boys (and their parents) could say good-bye to each other and then those who were happy to, could go on to the farm to continue the festivities. Carla was relaxed with all of that. Alfie was emotional as it was - she wanted him to have one last Valhalla.

Carla texted a 'yes' to everything - that she was up for it all - and shoved her phone back in her bag. Crossing a cattle grid, she walked straight into a cloud of midges. For a moment, she imagined she'd swallowed one and spent the next few minutes shaking out her skirt, her hair and her bag. Satisfied that she could no longer feel their feathery touch, she raised her head only to find herself looking straight into the doleful eyes of a huge white cow. Ever since a neighbour of hers had been killed by a heifer in the village where she used to live, Carla had been wary and so turned around slowly, to take the lesser-known path. In retrospect, it *would* make all the difference.

Hugging her new dress to her chest, she picked her way along the shaded, ever-narrowing river track. Gnarled, twisted roots rose up every which way. Although, in the summer it was difficult to see, Carla knew that on the other

27

Can a Leopard?

side of the bank, was the garden and orchard of the mill house. Through a gap in the trees, Carla had once glimpsed a girl sunbathing on a striped sun lounger. Surrounded by so many lavender bushes, it had looked as if she was floating on a giant purple Lilo. Carla had been transfixed, as though she'd stumbled on something magical, beguiling, and unknowable. She hadn't dared stop looking, afraid that if she did, the girl and the enchantment of the place would vanish, a mirage in the hazy heat. Carla pushed overgrown bushes aside now, seeking a bit of that wonder. A wrought iron gazebo, a bird bath, endless lawns evaporating into a hazy blur, did not disappoint, all enduringly romantic.

What was not in the least bit romantic, was the naked man she came across quietly, silently, now, as she rounded the next bend. Hidden by overhanging branches, facing away from her, he stood making an odd trance-like movement, arms jigging as though trying to gain purchase on uneven terrain. He was bald, naked, thin and white - his skin was surprisingly white given the months of heat they'd had - he looked as though he hadn't seen the sun in a decade. As though he'd been living underground. Or in prison.

Carla ran.

3

Carla had also run that day. At twenty-two years of age, she was as scared as a rabbit about most things. Chronically, pathologically shy, it wasn't so much that she was afraid of people *per se*, as afraid of what they might ask her. She just didn't seem to have an opinion on anything and more than anything, dreaded being asked to voice one. Keeping silent was by far the easiest option and so she shrank from gatherings of any kind. Supper parties with loud, sexually confident Sloane-types filled her with trepidation, parties where you wandered aimlessly alone, in darkened houses, bumping into entwined couples in the dark, was her idea of hell. (Had she lived in Winchester then, King Alfred would not only have lowered his arms but leapt off his plinth and done an eightsome reel.) She was as uncomfortable in her skin as it was possible to be. Given half a chance, she'd have assumed anyone's but her own.

Despairing of her monosyllabic daughter, Carla's mother Eugenia, had vented her frustration in vocal tantrums - *she* never had a problem expressing herself. Her diplomat father, equally perplexed, approached the problem of their daughter in a subtler fashion. In the course of an illustrious career, he was used to meeting strong, independent women and over the next few months or so, they were paraded before Carla. Some were more beautiful, more captivating, more effervescent than others but all were passionate about what they did. Most had fought to succeed in male-dominated professions and were at the top of their game. They too were puzzled by Carla's lack of ambition, that she wasn't capable of capitalizing on the opportunities she'd be given, by her apathy. Their drive and passion were something at which

Carla could only marvel and it left her feeling more inadequate than ever. She simply didn't know what she wanted to do, nor did anything inspire her.

Exasperated by the meals, teas, cocktails, coffee mornings Eugenia had been expected to provide in an attempt to motivate her daughter, but that had led nowhere, Eugenia took matters into her own hands. The minute her husband embarked on his next overseas mission she enrolled Carla in a secretarial course. This was only partially successful. Carla never really mastered shorthand. Only a couple of phrases stayed with her: 'bill of lading' and 'they', neither of which Carla ever used again. The only time she'd managed to transcribe an entire dictation she'd been unable to read a single word of it back.

By now, frustrated to the point that she developed high blood pressure, Eugenia took drastic measures. When a friend of hers let slip that her husband was being posted to Oman, Eugenia didn't hesitate to call in a favour. It didn't matter that women under the age of twenty-five weren't usually granted visas unless they were health workers. Those women, lived in compounds on the outskirts of the city centre and were bussed into work under strict supervision. But single-minded spouses of diplomats with missions of their own, are not easily deterred. Eugenia's diplomat friends had contacts in the diwan royal court. Carla, who found taking a taxi alone stressful, soon found herself not only on a flight bound for the Middle East, but to stay with people she had never met.

"What will I do there?" Carla had protested, astounded by the proposition. Actually, not so much a proposition as a fait accompli. She may not have known what she wanted to do in life but she was very clear as to what she didn't. "I can't even drive!"

"You won't have to drive," her mother had snapped. "That's not what you're there for."

Can a Leopard?

Which is how Carla found herself waiting to be collected by Mungo (sourced from the small pool of vaguely eligible, vaguely youngish bachelors in the vaguely British ex-pat community) who could, and had gallantly offered to show her the sights. He arrived at the embassy to collect her, dressed like Indiana Jones, in combat camouflage and desert boots. Unlike Harrison Ford however, he wasn't carrying a whip or machete but a roll of ... Carla blinked. Loo paper. Maybe he'd had a presentiment that Covid times lay ahead...

"You might need this," were the only words he said to her during the entire road trip out of the capital as they headed towards Jebel Shams, the highest peak of the Hajar mountain range and Oman's Grand Canyon.

Clutching her toilet roll ('*velvet comfort, extra strength*'), Carla wasn't sure whether to laugh or cry, whether to lay it carefully at her feet, toss it onto the back seat or joke. If she'd been able to, if she'd been one of those girls who joked with blokes and knew how to. Instead, she let it rest uncomfortably on her lap - casting uncertain glances at it from time to time, feeling it burn through her lap. She could hardly breathe she was so nervous, so uncertain, so completely out of her depth. She didn't know this man, didn't particularly like what she saw and wished for the hundredth time she was any place but in a car hurtling with him to god only knew where.

After an hour, Mungo decided to make a detour and show her Misfat al Abriyeen, a village renowned for its mud architecture and al falaj. Carla had read a little about falajes so that she wouldn't have to initiate conversation. It was an ancient irrigation system by which spring water was collected upstream and carried through a main channel to different levels. The capital Muscat, Carla was shocked to discover, consisted of a modern tangle of ring roads and an old souk difficult to locate. It was not the kind of place anyone could wander and given her age and gender, Carla wouldn't be wandering anywhere unaccompanied. But under the large

Can a Leopard?

plateau shadow of Jebel Akhdar, (or Green Mountain), Misfat was a taste of old Oman, the kind of village carved on rock slabs with adobe-like plaster dwellings. It promised verdant gardens, lush date groves, and a more temperate clime than the 40 C in the city.

After driving through desert, its arid sameness punctuated by crumbling watch towers and the odd long-haired goat, they alighted by peeling gates shaded in palm fronds. Already, it felt cooler, an oasis hugging the craggy hillside kept clean by fresh water funnelled through multi-layered terraces. A dusty turning place was the only indication that visitors to the region occasionally ventured this far. Carla felt clumsy in her mother's clothes. The only potential obstacle to Eugenia's scheming had been the last-minute realisation that Carla was going to have to wear demure, ankle-length, long-sleeved dresses. Which were not the fashion. The only solution was to have some of her mother's clothes altered. Carla didn't mind at all. Dwarfed in tops and skirts several sizes still too big, she felt as though she were play acting, hiding behind someone else's choice. But even so, there was no disguising that she was a Westerner and within moments she and Mungo were surrounded by a throng of children all clamouring for 'baksish.'

"Just ignore them," was Mungo's pithy advice. He seemed to find it amusing to be pawed by many small hands. When he offered a young girl a bic biro as a gift, she held it to her lips and blew on it, clearly uncertain as to what it was for.

And although there was a certain rustic charm to be found in the dusty rock-strewn paths, the wadis or dry riverbed that encircled the village, Carla felt uneasy. The place was too remote, a hundred hostile eyes peering through small slits in its helter-skelter stacked shacks. Arches led nowhere, the owners having abandoned dwellings to erosion, to build new ones amidst small holdings of pomegranate and apricot, all fertile from the steady supply of water from the falaj. It was deadly quiet and still and eerie, all contributing to Carla's internal uneasiness. For once though, her anxiety was external; she could feel the tension in the air. And because Mungo seemed so calm, so completely oblivious, her instinct was at odds with her reason, alarming her all the more.

The children soon dispersed when they realised, she had nothing to give them (well, nothing except toilet paper) but she suspected that wasn't what they were after. Without warning, Mungo began to walk and she followed him blindly placing all her trust in him, down a maze of cobbled passageways, glancing from time to time at the fragile exoskeleton of terraced buildings, nothing but sticks and stones and fig tree.

They'd reached an open space on one of the higher banana terraces with water cascading down the hillside. Mungo paused uncertain. And there, emerging from behind huge oil jars, as if they'd been waiting for them, two men appeared. Both were wearing the traditional (don't-call-them-dish cloths) dishdasha and small simple caps, not the elaborate embroidered turbans she was used to seeing in the capital. The older of the two, said something to Mungo, in Arabic. The younger held back, respectively. Or so Carla imagined.

"They're from the Al Abri tribe," Mungo translated rapidly. "He says we should split up. That I should go with this man and you go with him."

"Why?" said Carla bemused, confused by the monkey puzzle of stone bridges and walkways they'd begun slowly to climb. And then in a moment's bravery, heart thumping, said, "I really don't see why we should separate. I'd rather go with you."

"This is Khalfan," said Mungo by way of introduction. Carla viewed the man distastefully while he averted his eyes completely. There was further exchange in Arabic - not one word of which Carla understood.

Can a Leopard?

"They don't want that and we don't want to offend them," said Mungo impatiently as if she were obfuscating matters.

Later Carla would wonder why the hell, not. They didn't know these men from Adam. What did it matter if there was a misunderstanding, if their supposed offer of friendship was ignored? In the light of what later transpired, taking offence was the least of it.

Within moments it would seem, Mungo and the older man had disappeared from sight climbing high onto the upper terraces, edged by the stone channels of the falaj. Carla had no choice but to follow the younger man - Khalfan - as he picked up the corner of his dishdasha to expose dirty fat toes in leather sandals. Her unease grew by the minute. She barely noticed dusty exteriors, lush palm and fruit trees, carvings on faded walls in colours of the Omani flag, as the quiet and remoteness replaced any residual charm with something sinister. Khalfan began to skip along the falaj, his skirt dipping into the water as Carla struggled to keep up. It trailed mud along sandy paths, flapping against his skin. She was breathless as his pace quickened. From time to time, she lost her footing, while his was assured. He looked like a mountain goat with his little goatee beard and narrow ankles. Had she felt less tense, she might have giggled. But she didn't, unable to supress an ever growing feel of dread.

Her heart was thumping. She felt clammy and giddy, the cross fall ever steeper. She wanted to turn back but Khalfan mumbled something in Arabic which she couldn't understand, pointing above him. In the distance, triliths composed of stone monuments looked as paper-thin as a house of cards, as though in a single breath, she might blow them apart. And then they'd emerged onto a clearing, with breath taking views of the mountain range, a sea of palm trees below and a sheer drop either side. It was breath taking all right - hers strangled in her chest. Khalfan stopped abruptly, turning on his heel to look her straight in the eye for the first time. Her glance slid away from his, distracted by something else. The flash of his knife fished from under his dishdasha glinting in a sunbeam, silvery and slippery.

4

Carla managed to reach the turn-style in one breathless leap. A female jogger (headphones, Lycra and a pink racing t-shirt), looked irritated by the fact that Carla was blocking her path. She turned sideways covering her mouth.

"Er… you might not want to go that way," said Carla. "There's a naked man just a bit further down." And then to Carla's embarrassment, tears pricked her eyes. Her chest felt tight as it had that other time. "I'm sorry," she said. "Nothing happened. I don't know why I'm being so foolish."

The woman was instantly sympathetic, forgetting about Covid rules to touch her arm. "Are you sure, you're OK?"

Carla shook her head. "No, yes," she said. "I really am. It's ridiculous. I'm not one of those pathetic females…" *Not for a long time…*

"You should report it?"

Carla touched her bag and the woman misinterpreting the gesture was quick to offer hers.

"You can borrow mine."

"Thank you, it's fine. I will." *Report it I mean. Maybe. And say what? A naked man by the river. That was all and yet…*

The woman's face and voice faded as once again, Carla was assaulted by other disconcerting sensations and memories. She'd run as fast as she could that other time as well, losing her shoes in the process. She'd felt her left shoe slide off her foot as easily as if it had been a slipper. The other, she'd kicked off desperately, not wanting to be slowed down, adrenaline pumping through her body, propelling her forward. She'd vaulted up through terraced orchards, jumping across streams screaming all the time. But no one emerged from the houses, the palm fronds stopped swaying. It was as if everything was frozen in time. And then suddenly she wasn't sure how, she'd found her way back to the entrance to the village and there was Mungo standing absolutely still as though he too were petrified in stone. A hawk suddenly screeched above his head but still he made no movement. He made no move towards her; she'd ended up comforting him rather than the other way around. And although they were later married, if there was one good reason why she never should have married him, it was his reaction - or lack of - that day.

"You really should report it," the woman was saying now. "He might have Covid. You'd never forgive yourself…"

"Yes, yes," said Carla abruptly. She felt odd, tearful. "Thank you. You're so kind."

It was strange the way that other memory came to her now. She'd not thought of it once in nearly twenty years. Her reaction was exaggerated. All she'd seen was a naked man doing a strange dance. He was probably one of the homeless, of Winchester. She'd seen the guy who sold the Big Issue on the High Street sleeping on a bench in front of the Cathedral. There were night shelters but some chose to ignore them while others with addictions of any kind were excluded anyway. And yet all she could think of was that other encounter in Oman.

"It's OK," she said again.

"Think I'll run a different way," said the woman refitting her earphone and the band on her arm.

37

"Good idea," Carla mumbled and they'd parted, Carla to walk back slowly along the busier path that hugged the river - the woman on the other side, by the College grounds. Afterwards, Carla regretted not asking the woman her name, her responses dulled by shock. Countless people were walking their dogs and she was continually having to step onto the verge, her back to them and mutter 'sorry' or 'thanks'.

Alfie was in the kitchen scouring for snacks when she got home and she hammered that other memory firmly into its box. She could already see where he'd eaten several breaks. There was a trail across the kitchen of Colin the Caterpillar cake beginning at the breakfast bar. Empty packages were all that remained.

"Darling, do put things in the bin if they're finished," she said trying not to feel irritated. It felt as though she were always nagging these days but then they'd never spent so long together as a family. Endless tidying up from endless meals even if it was just the three of them.

"You weren't long," he said.

She drank a glass of water feeling calmer. "Really?" It felt as though she'd been ages. It felt as though she'd lived several lifetimes, experienced several emotions.

"Where's Dad?" Carla knew Alfie was asking because he wanted to use Seb's phone.

"Polo, he'll be back soon."

Alfie opened the fridge, his arms positioned either side of the door and leaning into it as if he were doing an imaginary push-up. That also annoyed her.

"What's for lunch?"

Can a Leopard?

"Um… chicken, salmon. What do you feel like?"

But Carla was distracted by the ping of her own phone. Les Girls no longer communicated so many memes, although there was the kind of recurring typo (*'keep your pubic areas safe'*) that still brought a smile to her face as did the one (she was waiting for the right moment to share it with Alfie) about the mother who had decided not to have children. So, she and her husband were preparing to tell their children that evening. Carla cast a glance in Alfie's direction. He was bouncing a ball around the kitchen. She winced every time it scraped the skirting board. Maybe now would be a good time. Another ping distracted her. Les Girls were wondering about travel now that restrictions were being lifted.

What did anyone think about Scotland?

The drive's off putting at the best of times

Agreed!

And what to do about comfort breaks?

At services along the way?

Forget Scotland!

Hope had pinged back. She'd had to queue at IKEA for three hours which had been boring as.

Ikea?

Yeah, Rob needs a soundproof cubicle for recoding his audio books.

Carla wasn't aware you could buy such a thing there. Hope sent through a photo of masked customers standing in boxes marked out on the pavement. And then the contraption itself. All Carla could see was hours ahead of self-assembly misery.

Can a Leopard?

Talking of masks, don't want to whinge - OK I do - I had terrible migraine.

Because?

The doctor in their group - her tight mask was causing a build-up of CO2. She'd already had eight negative Covid tests and negative antibody tests but wasn't sure how to improve conditions. She was given one mask for the morning, another for the afternoon. She wasn't supposed to touch them or remove them except to eat lunch.

Does anyone take supplements?

Why for?

To boost the immune system

I'm taking vitamin C with Zinc

D3 for me

Mine coming from sunny weather in Essex

No sun in Pembrokeshire

Carla didn't dare confess that she and Seb were heading to Italy for their vitamin D top-up. She changed the subject.

Anyone heard that Kanywe West is up for president?

Carla turned her phone to silent.

Alfie had taken his skateboard onto the patio and was trying to execute a three-point turn. One of the screws had come loose making the thumping noise excruciating.

"Darling," she began. "Please?"

Can a Leopard?

Alfie made a final skid and then carefully balanced the board against the wall.

"What class are you supposed to be in?" she asked making a concentrated effort not to show the irritation she seemed to feel all the time these days.

"Games," said Alfie shortly.

"Oh," said Carla instantly contrite. "And that's what you're supposed to be doing?"

"Yeah - it's the only thing I *can* do. Everyone else I know has a proper garden."

Alfie looked at her meaningfully. They'd had a proper garden once too. Acres and acres of one in fact. When they lived in the country before moving into town.

"Yes, well, now you have a whole city at your disposal."

"That's not true," said Alfie kicking a chair as he left the kitchen.

And of course, it wasn't. They weren't allowed to play cricket or football or meet in each other's houses. The closest the boys had got to seeing each other was on Facetime or Zoom. But it was all changing. Soon, they'd be meeting on site. And Alfie was going to stay with a friend. It would be just like before.

Carla switched on her Mac - she was still tense from the naked man incident - and would do a session of Jessica Smith dot TV. She'd stopped bouncing around Alfie's lair like a lunatic trying to follow Joe Wicks with his Spider Man poses designed to motivate children. Her knees for one thing couldn't keep up. Nor could his, by all accounts. She knew

Can a Leopard?

he'd damaged his hip. And then she put the mild-mannered, nicely spoken American girl on pause.

Alfie was lying face down on his bed when she went up to his bedroom.

"Darling?" she said all irritation evaporating at the sight of her soon-to-be teenager, his damp hair clinging to the base of his neck as it had when he was a baby.

"Oh, sweetheart," she said gently turning him to face her. He'd been crying and his thick lashes were heavy with more tears. "I'm sorry it's so hard. But you'll see your friends soon. Don't you want to?"

Alfie nodded unconvincingly.

"Are you...apprehensive?"

Alfie nodded and this time with conviction.

"I'm nervous," he said. He shrugged. "I don't know why."

Carla clasped him to her, his rigid body gradually relaxing. She glanced around his room. The toddler's piggy bank, the first edition print of a still from *The Snowman* that Seb loved and neither she nor he, would admit was perhaps a little babyish now - in amongst the other trappings of childhood: toy soldiers, pop-up books, stuffed animals in amongst the SAS handbook, and various A.I. based novels. How quickly the prep-school years had passed! She felt angry that Alfie had been cheated of the kind of send-off the twins had enjoyed when they'd left theirs. No trip to France or week away for a final bonding, no boys hanging out together as they should.

"Of course, you're nervous!" said Carla with feeling. She knew exactly what he was going through. "You've not seen anyone in months. You've forgotten what it's like to be with

42

people. But I think that after a day back with your friends, out of doors, you'll feel differently. You will."

Alfie sniffed. "We can take a bike into school next week. Hal says I can borrow one of his."

Carla considered this. Alfie hadn't ridden one since he was tiny. She wondered if he remembered how. It was something she'd always felt guilty about.

"Would you like that?"

Alfie nodded.

"OK, then. And if you like it. We'll get you one of your own."

Alfie's face lit up and Carla hugged him again.

"There," she said. "It'll all be all right. You'll see. This has been such a strange time and you've been such a good boy and so patient. It's just a little longer and things will be back to normal."

They both jumped as the front door slammed and the windows on the top floor vibrated.

"Dad's home," said Carla leaning over to pick up Alfie's dirty laundry from a sitting position and chucking it in the basket in the corner. She refrained from a further nag about doing just that.

Seb was standing in the hall looking very pleased with himself. His long hair was wet with sweat.

"Apart from having to wear masks while we play, it's pretty much back to normal," he said flushed with exertion. "And the fact that we're not allowed to tack up our horses."

Can a Leopard?

"When did you ever do that?" asked Carla. She was pretty sure Seb didn't know how and had never gone near a horse box in his life. He was more of the flown in by helicopter to play genre.

"No, you're right," he said. He sat down on one of her delicate, dwarf French revival chairs and began pulling off his boots.

"And you? What's been going on?"

Carla took a deep breath. "I saw a naked man."

"Lucky you!" Seb was grinning failing to notice the undercurrent, the fear in her eyes.

"Not really," she said casually.

5

Tingling with excitement, Carla perched on the edge of her seat as they sped towards the entrance to Heathrow's Meet and Greet. She was wearing the blue Alice Temperley (as copied from Olivia), old Gucci flats she'd bought on the fly (quite literally) the year they'd travelled to Zimbabwe and carried a sweet wicker basket (Clare.V) that had come from America. Actually, Carla never wore those Gucci flats without thinking back to that holiday. As she, Seb and Alfie had made their way to the gate, she'd not only spied the Gucci outlet, but the foot spa right beside it. Impulsively, she'd decided to have a mini pedicure *as* the flight was boarding. It was one of the few times she'd seen Seb visibly agitated. There was no reason to be. Just to be sure, Carla had gone back to Gucci to buy an adorable pair of taupe sandals as well. Now, her carry on contained the Paravel packing cases she'd not sold to be recycled for PPE and the new, delectable Temperley jumpsuit and kimono and the silk dress from the Hambledon. Strictly speaking, the Majors were breaking all the rules by agreeing to have Alfie to stay. Carla would be forever indebted to them but it had been an additional joy to see how happily their son had gone off to his friend's house.

As they drove into the car park, Carla felt the old, welcome shiver of excitement at the prospect of travelling once again. It had been a long time coming.

"Good to be going isn't it?" said Seb swerving into a bay without warning. He pulled on the hand break so abruptly that the car came to a shuddering halt. "Sorry," grinned Seb. "Guess I'm excited too."

Can a Leopard?

Carla grimaced, bending down to spoon the cosmetics that had spilled onto the floor back into her bag. Seb plonked his Akubra on his head and reached over her for his bag. She could smell his clean linen smell - the one that never failed to arouse her.

"We're off!" He kissed her cheek swiftly.

Carla was about to turn away but remembering he hadn't said anything as yet about her new dress, trailed his cheek, in a slightly cinematic (but generally effective) move, waiting for him to compliment her. It was unlike Seb not to say *anything* about her appearance. Normally, he noticed everything. But not this time. She pushed away the uncomfortable thought. After all, they were going to Italy, to sunshine, on a plane for the first time in …? She did a mental check. Well, it felt like a lifetime even if it was only a few months. It had been a lifetime in terms of what they'd all experienced recently. Yes, she thought smugly, they'd all learned so much during lockdown and how lucky they were now, to be escaping! She shook out the creases of her skirt taking care not to touch the mud guard. Hardly waiting for Seb to alight, she skipped out herself, grabbing her bag before he did. It wasn't heavy and she didn't want it scratched. He was a great one for hurling bags onto concrete pavements. Yards ahead of him, she was almost running into the departure area.

"I'll leave my bag with you," she said breathlessly. "And then go for a bit of a wander."

She did a quick scan of the departures area. It wasn't busy at all and she was longing to check out the designer shops on the other side. Not that she was going to buy anything of course - just look.

Seb shook his head. "Um - you're going to have to check your bag," he said.

Can a Leopard?

Carla stared at him. "I *never* check my bag," she replied "That's why I *kept* the Aviator carry-on! You know I hate checking my bag. You can't trust those baggage handlers not to pinch stuff. Besides, it always comes back wet."

Seb scratched his head under his hat.

"Yeah, well this time you're going to have to. We're flying British Airways but Italy has prohibited the use of overhead lockers."

"Well, that's ridiculous," said Carla feeling her cheeks flush.

"Ridiculous or not that's how it is. They don't want the aisles blocked by people standing to retrieve their luggage. Kind of makes sense."

Carla looked at him as if he'd gone mad.

"Well, I'm going to the lounge the minute we've checked in," she sniffed.

"And remember your mask," said Seb fishing his own out from his jeans pocket.

Carla fumbled for hers. She objected to wearing one travelling. It was one thing having to use one at home when it really didn't matter as they weren't doing anything fun but going abroad to a glamorous hotel...She caught sight of her reflection. Except hers sort of matched her lovely dress. The thought cheered her no end.

A crumpled, tired-looking British Airways official moved towards her brandishing a temperature wand. Instinctively Carla tried to duck, before Seb grabbed her by the shoulders orienting her in his direction.

"You're good," said the man. "Just."

Carla made a face. She felt on fire just thinking about her temperature going up. "Where's priority booking?" she asked wanly.

"There isn't any," said the official motioning her to join the queue.

"But it says there is."

Seb gave Carla a stern look - a 'no need to get het up' look.

Within seconds they were back to where they'd started as the official had lost track of whose temperature he'd taken. In the ensuing confusion, a different member of staff waved them through. Carla felt naked carrying only her little basket.

"Right then," she said cheerily. "I'm off. I'm dying for some coffee - let's have breakfast in the lounge."

Carla thought back to the last time they'd flown and her older boy had joined them for dinner in the Concorde Room. They'd sipped champagne and joked that Carla was wearing Chanel seated under a black and white print *of* Chanel. On that occasion, she hadn't needed alcohol to feel giddy with excitement. She wondered if she would ever feel that way again. Did Seb? Her husband seemed absorbed by his phone. He didn't look giddy with anything.

"Think that's going to be hard," he said glancing up.

Carla followed his gaze as they rolled past steel-shuttered concession shops. The escalators to the Concorde Room had yellow tape across them as in a TV crime scene. It would be exactly like one soon if she couldn't get to the Airline lounges. What use was a gold card if you couldn't make use of its privileges? Her stomach began to growl with mid-morning coffee cravings.

Can a Leopard?

Seb steered her to a row of metal airline chairs in the waiting area.

"Cheer up!" he said pointing to the scrawny cables feeding off the various charging stations. "At least you can charge your Kindle."

"Oh, this is too bad," she wailed. "The whole *point* of travel is the Concorde Room."

"Not the whole point, surely?" said Seb amused, briefly distracted from his phone.

"Well, obviously not," said Carla uncertainly. *It kind of was ...*

A short time later they'd boarded; Seb and Carla with precisely... eight others. They were still seated with an empty seat between them, *'I'm self-isolating today,'* scrawled across it.

"I can completely see how you wouldn't want people crowding the aisles," observed Carla grumpily. She cast a glance down the length of the plane. You still had to signal the flight attendant if you wanted the loo - just like being at school - but the staff were making up for the inconvenience by being exceedingly charming and offering snacks of crisps and a chocolate bar. A glass of champagne and smoked salmon would have been more her thing.

Almost immediately, Seb pulled out his laptop and began to work. Carla was still waiting for her compliment. She stole surreptitious glances at him from time to time but he merely smiled absent-mindedly, pulled his mask down, put a finger to his lips and kissed it. Only, he forgot to pass it on. After a few moments, he flipped shut the lid of his laptop and closed his eyes mouthing the words 'tired.' He stretched out his legs and fell asleep. He was very quiet when he slept in public - as though subconsciously aware of not being alone. Carla wished that were the case when they were.

Can a Leopard?

She felt chilly in the sudden blast of air conditioning but the cashmere wrap she always took on her travels was in her bag in the hold. Another idiocy. She couldn't *see* the other passengers let alone bump into them. The plane had been fogged for the umpteenth time and for once she was glad of her mask. She pulled out her phone. There were some twenty messages from Les Girls. Lou was worried about her son who had developed swollen tonsils, a cough and sore throat. Yikes thought Carla.

Tell him to gargle with diluted TCP - texted the doctor among them, Madeleine

Want him to have a test but they won't give it him unless his temperature goes up

Push for the test - he works in the public sector - he needs to have it

Will do - you're so right - he's on his way to buy 2C-B

Hb2? Artist Alice had now joined

We're talking pencils, right? Hardness of?

The kindness behind Gemma's interjection was obvious. It made Carla smile. She was the caring one - the one who always replied to every single text with a positive emoji. Everything was always lovely and bright and good in her world.

Wait! I'm confused!

So am I!

So, it's 2C-B, right?

No!!!

No?

Can a Leopard?

TCP! It's completely different!

Is it?

Tell him to gargle - not drink it obviously

Yeah - obviously

Smiling emoji

What's 2C-B?

A psychedelic drug of the 2 C family

Also known as Seventh Heaven

Or 7 Up

Wow! Maybe could have done with some during lockdown

No, you don't want to mess

Only joking, never even tried a cigi

Really?

No

How do you all know about this?

Teenagers!

Carla had never heard of it either.

It comes in white or pink tablets.

Can make you energised

Can a Leopard?

Alert

Like LSD

Sexually aroused

Aren't those pills blue?

OMG that's Viagra!

Oh, Les Girls, replied Madeleine despairingly, *would there were more scientists amongst us ...*

Carla must also have closed her eyes because it seemed that moments later, they had landed at Leonardo da Vinci-Fiumicino airport which given it was supposed to be the busiest airport in Italy (the sixth busiest in Europe) was deadly quiet. The Italians were as slickly organized as the Brits at Heathrow had been chaotic. Here their temperature was taken by thermal controlled zapping devices, their luggage was waiting (all of the plane's eight pieces) and they were at their car rental within the hour.

Carla felt the tension ease from her body. Lockdown was slowly lifting in England but Italy was ahead and comfortable with its re-awakening. Carla felt nothing but sympathy for a nation that had suffered so terribly but she felt exhilarated to be away from home. Apart from the sight of people wearing masks and hand sanitizing stations, everything else felt normal. The uber chic clerk from the rental wore his mask sticking out of his breast pocket like a smart handkerchief - an upended pale blue triangle. His smile was stellar, his accent a fiction. Seb pressed a button (well after a few attempts) and the roof of the BMW M850i cabriolet collapsed into a neat cavity. He accelerated, a huge grin on his face. Surely now, the compliment would come. Carla leant back holding her hair with one hand - she wasn't going to allow her first blow dry in four months to be undone with a single car journey. Thank you, Lauren, she breathed inwardly. She would never have survived all these months without her wonderful, caring, funny hairdresser who had done more for her mental health than any amount of pill popping could ever have. Beauticians were the unsung heroes! And thanks to Lauren, Carla felt like an actress from *La dolce vita*, maybe the poet Iris Tree not Anita Ekberg. Carla would never have spoiled a beautiful dress by jumping into a fountain. She nestled into the creamy leather of the car's bucket seat. In the side mirror she glimpsed tanned shoulders, the line of cheekbone, Jackie O sunglasses. Surely now?

They were both silent during the 120 km journey that took them along the coast to the Monte Argentario region. Blue sky met even bluer sea, as they rounded craggy cliffs along the final bumpy road. Smiling to herself, Carla rolled down the window. The hotel was a place she'd dreamed of visiting ever since she'd read about its romantic inception - two charismatic lovers: an American socialite and dashing British aviator had fallen in love with the place (and each other) to create a perfect paradise. Over the years, the famous and glamorous had flocked to its secret cove to enjoy moonlight swims and suppers and assignations. It promised to encapsulate everything that Carla loved: literature, history and courtly love. The plus of course was that it was also the anniversary of their marriage. Their wedding… She glanced at Seb who was looking at his phone with one hand, the other lightly touching the steering wheel as they rounded hairpin corners.

"'*Spretzzatura*,'" she read aloud from a pamphlet that she'd found in the glove compartment describing the region and their famous hotel. "'*From Castiglione's Book of the Courtier: A certain nonchalance so as to conceal all art and make whatever one does or say, appear without effort…*'"

6

Which was exactly the kind of wedding - one appearing without effort - Carla envisaged second time around (it was a first for Seb but everyone knew the groom didn't count). Only she'd not known the word then. *Spretzzatura*. A perfect word. First time around, she'd been married at Farm Street in front of four hundred guests -she probably knew thirty personally- the rest were all her mother's friends. She'd worn a beautiful dress from Harrods, with six adorable little children in attendance: three girls and three boys. She'd thought them adorable: a friend of her mother's had told her afterwards that she'd never seen such ugly children. Her darling Spanish father had been gracious and statesmanlike getting everyone confused but doing it with *duende* - charm. He'd paid particular attention to a young man, newly arrived in London, not recognising him as his own son. He'd mistaken one of the waiters for a guest from the Middle East and he'd asked a woman when her baby was due, only to be told that she'd already given birth. Carla had had her own confusion to deal with. Her wedding night had been spent alone or she might as well have been. Mungo was drunk and although they'd then travelled to Venice, she didn't recall him making love to her once. This time it was going to be different.

To begin with, Carla and Seb were married at Chelsea Registry Office with only her best friend Gemma and Xavier (Seb's) as witnesses. *'But don't you want the twins to be there?'* Seb had asked, surprised that she didn't want any member of her family present at the actual ceremony. But Carla didn't. She thought it would be too weird for her children to see their mother marry someone else. Mungo might be many things but he was still the twins' father. Seb had made it clear he did not intend to take Mungo's place. No, this time the wedding was between Seb and herself and no one else.

On the day itself, Carla had been elated in cream Chanel. The signature gold buttons sported tiny sheaves of wheat which Carla thought delightfully auspicious. She carried a darling bouquet chosen by Gemma of tiny roses and forget-me-nots. In the evening, they'd dined at the Chelsea Arts Club with a handful of close friends and Carla's brothers and their wives and Natasha and Xavier (the birth of whose baby Xenia had brought Seb and Carla together in the first place). Their first night as a married couple was spent at the Savoy where... where suffice it to say, Seb did not get drunk or go to sleep. At least, not straight away.

In the morning, Carla had whisked out another Chanel tweed jacket (red and navy and cream) which she paired with jeans and darling Manolo ballerina flats and they'd flown to Avignon for a blessing and celebration. For the actual church service, Carla had worn another Chanel frock: a cashmere shift in pink and white and black stripes. Every alternate stripe was edged in lace. It was simple and super chic and original. Above all, it displayed *spretzzatura*.

Carla had Raoul to thank for the French part of their wedding. Gemma and Carla had known Raoul at Oxford. He was a glamorous, flirtatious, elegant Portuguese whose lifestyle had little in common with theirs. He travelled on private jets all over the world. Carla always marvelled that he managed to finish his degree with all the partying he'd done. But they'd lost touch until a few months before the wedding when Carla and Seb had been at Covent Garden and Carla had found herself three or four seats away from him. At least she'd thought it was him.

"Ask the man on your left if his name's Raoul," Carla had whispered in Seb's ear.

Can a Leopard?

Seb had and it was, and in the intermission, Raoul had introduced them to Carlitos Mi Vida, (Charlie My Life) Raoul's new partner. The last one had left him, he'd said eyes moist.

"I just don't believe he's gay!" Seb had hissed loudly when they were waiting for the third act of *Carmen* to begin.

Raoul looked up catching Carla's eye.

"He wasn't at university," said Carla smiling back but feeling awful talking about him virtually in front of him.

Seb was unconvinced and spent the rest of the opera shooting Raoul disparaging looks.

That was until Raoul learned they were getting married.

"*Chelsea!*" he almost spat. "In the days of the one Beatle maybe, but not now! No, no, no! You have to be married at my house in Baume de Venise. I insist! You must. I won't take no for an answer. Bring your friend Gemma - you are still friends, aren't you? I liked her the best of all Les Girls. She used to wear dresses from Mexicana, long to the floor, with lots of lace."

"OK," said Seb. "Maybe he is."

Carla had felt instant affection towards Raoul, not for his generous offer (which obviously they'd taken him up on) but for the fact that he remembered Les Girls at all. And in talking about their university days, she was pulled into that seductive ring of a shared past.

So that was how they had found themselves arriving in sleepy Avignon, collecting a car rental and heading for Baume.

Can a Leopard?

'My housekeeper will meet you,' Raoul had texted. *'I can't be there until the evening but she'll let you in. Make yourselves at home and we'll catch up with Gemma and Carlitos later. Mi casa es su casa.'*

It was colder than they'd expected and Carla was glad she'd chosen the Chanel cashmere. Still too early to meet the housekeeper, they'd driven around the village, familiarising themselves with the area.

"Oh, my God!" cried Carla excitedly craning her neck to look behind her. "I bet that's it!" They'd passed an exquisite 'domaine' - a square stone petit château set in acres of vineyards. It had the wrought iron gates, grey slate roof tops, neat hedges and gardenia that Carla found inherently romantic. Simple, elegant and utterly sublime. "Oh, how I *wish* now that we'd invited all our friends!" wailed Carla.

"We have," said Seb calmly circling the town square for the fourth time.

"No, I mean *everyone*!" She twisted around in her seat. "But look, Seb, just look!"

"I am, I am."

"It's too perfect, it's divine. Oh, I knew it! Raoul was always so super stylish."

"So why didn't you ever date?" There was the slightest edge to his tone but Carla was too excited by the house to notice.

"That's a very good question," she murmured noting the immaculate olive trees in just the right shade of 'skimming stone,' alternating with full waxy gardenia bushes. "Oh, now I'm wishing I'd brought something else to wear too for the evening! We could have had a dance! A ball!"

"This is perfectly good," said Seb.

Can a Leopard?

"Yes, but the house!" Carla felt her stomach knot with what ifs. What if she'd asked her family and friends? What if she'd asked the twins, after all?

Seb pulled over by the fountain in the middle of the market square.

"It's all fine," he said. "This is how we wanted it, remember? Look, I think that's your lady."

A slim, attractive middle-aged woman approached the car.

"You should follow me," she said in excellent English. "It may be difficult to find."

"Oh, I think we know where to go," said Carla chirpily. "You could always just give us the keys,"

The woman smiled pleasantly.

"I prefer…"

"We-"

Seb leant across Carla placing a restraining hand on hers. "My wife -" and Carla momentarily melted at being called 'my wife' for the first time. "My wife, and I are happy to follow you. Lead the way."

"What could she have meant?" said Carla rolling up the window as they sped behind the woman's deux chevaux (she would be driving one of those) and endless fields and vineyards. "'By difficult to find?' It's the only proper house in the area!"

Fifteen minutes later they were still driving.

Can a Leopard?

"I don't understand," said Carla alarmed as the beautiful petit château flashed past. "There must be another entrance. One with a long drive. And gates."

"Um…" said Seb. "I'm thinking that wasn't Raoul's house."

"What do you mean?" said Carla wide-eyed. "It has to be!"

"Er, *non*," said Seb.

They'd stopped in front of another square house but that is where the similarity with the petit domaine ended. Where one was 17th century mellow stone, the other was firmly entrenched in 20th century … breeze block.

"God," said Carla in horror. "It can't be."

"Welcome," said the housekeeper when she'd parked and come over to their car. Carla was in too much shock to do anything other than sit perfectly still. "On behalf of Monsieur Raoul."

*

Carla soon felt she was part of some *Cage Aux Folles* staging. If the outside of the modern catastrophe wasn't what she'd anticipated, the inside was even less so.

"Yup, definitely gay," said Seb looking around the entrance hall.

The housekeeper had unlocked the front door but refrained from entering herself. Carla soon saw why. Eight-foot murals of naked men cavorting with chains and all manner of sex toys were displayed on the concrete walls.

Can a Leopard?

Now, she was thanking providence that she *hadn't* invited the twins. *Oh, thank God!* she breathed taking in the outrageous artwork. *Thank God, thank God, thank God.*

The tepid sun that had greeted them on arrival in France also seemed to have slunk away in embarrassment. It felt cold and damp; the boîte (decidedly a box not a château) better suited to hot summer days. It was all gleaming chrome, white marble and red vinyl. Carla didn't dare meet Seb's eye. But he had gravitated to a series of what appeared, at first sight, to be surprisingly tasteful charcoal drawings. On closer examination, Carla realised that was only because the drawings were still in their original frames.

"Calderón de la Barca," he said reading the tiny brass plaque underneath. "From *La Vida es Sueño.*"

"Yes, I know it," said Carla breathing a sigh of relief. "I know it. Raoul and I had some Spanish tutorials together."

She peered over Seb's shoulder.

"Good heavens!" This was de la Barca as she'd never known him. Had she missed something as an undergraduate? Had she been that naïve? From a distance, the line drawings were innocuous, unprepossessing even, but up close they showed disfigured, naked men in bondage. She looked away.

"'Golden Age of Poetry,' huh?" said Seb.

"Yes, well. History was my main subject."

"Ah, you like them?"

Carla spun around on hearing Raoul's voice.

"You're here!"

"Ah, yes. *Comme tu vois.*" '*Tu*' (singular) not '*vous*' (plural).

60

Can a Leopard?

They'd not heard Raoul arrive but then he always moved silently, silkily on the softest suede driving shoes, each step a balletic move. He stood behind them studying the pictures, a glint of appreciation in his eye. Carla could smell the musky, scent of sandalwood, taking in the luxurious swathe of silk to his shirt, the starch of pristine linen. He exuded expensive and arguably, slightly effete, masculinity.

"I bought them at auction some years ago," he purred in his perfect English. Only the slightest intonation hinted at something more exotic. "In fact, just after I left Oxford. I think they were my first important acquisition. You remember Professor Pring-Mill?" Raoul had taken Carla by the arm moving her away from the pictures and from Seb, drawing her into an exclusive embrace of reminiscence. Carla shot Seb an uncertain smile which was meant to convey, *'he's our host after all…'* "An expert on Golden Age."

"Oh, God," said Carla. "Of course, I remember. He also liked science fiction."

Seb raised an eyebrow, the bascule wavering about to clamp down abruptly.

"Which you don't," he said but looking at Raoul. With a *'Top that - I know my wife better than you do…'*

"Exactly. But I pretended I did. During my entrance interview, I remembered that Pring-Mill also liked Wyndham so when he asked me what I enjoyed reading, I of course, said sci-fi. Which novelist did I admire? Well, it had to be Wyndham and then which of Wyndhams's novels did I like best? And that's when my mind went completely blank. I hadn't read *any* but I had at least scanned the titles. I said something vague about the novel where the protagonists have the potential to become something else."

"Did you mean *The Day of the Triffids*?"

Can a Leopard?

"That's the one."

"Which is exactly when inside information isn't an advantage," said Seb frowning.

"Luckily, Pring-Mill didn't hold it against you," said Raoul ignoring Seb.

"Seb was also at Oxford," blurted Carla. "He was a Rhodes scholar."

Seb drew himself up to his full height towering over Raoul. Neither Seb nor Carla ever talked about their time at university. Three or four years in the course of a lifetime seemed hardly to matter very much, but somehow it seemed important for Seb to establish his credentials here. He hadn't always just played polo. Raoul's nostril's twitched uncomfortably.

"Obviously not at the same time as us," stammered Carla which resulted in a glare from Seb. The 'us' irritated him more than reference to the difference in their ages.

Raoul straightened the drawing on the wall behind Seb's head with a tanned, manicured hand and turning on his heel he touched his heart, his lips in a gesture Carla remembered from the Middle East.

"You are welcome to my home," he said his chocolate, almond-shaped eyes sweeping over Carla as he straightened, the 'you' again decidedly singular.

*

"He's not gay!" said Seb which would soon become a mantra over the next forty-eight days. "Or he's bi at the very least.

He's after you, I know it. I can always tell." Seb plopped three sugar cubes into his espresso. "I need it," he said defiantly in response to her look. "To deal with this lot."

It would take more than sugar thought Carla shooting Seb a sideways glance but she wasn't going to let the less than conventional circumstances disrupt their wedding week. She was cheered by the feel of her beautiful Chanel cashmere shift across her waist that is; luckily her legs were tanned enough to disguise her goose bumps.

"He *so* is!" she countered. "He was never interested in me! Besides, you saw his place."

"Pure show," said Seb dismissively. "Pure drama. What does he do again? I mean apart from all that theatre?"

They were huddled over a tiny table in the square having coffee and waiting for Raoul who had gone to collect the priest who would say mass. Gemma, her boyfriend Titus and Carlitos Mi Vida, were all coming directly from the airport. Gemma had reassured Carla that there would still be plenty of time to collect the bouquet she had ordered for her.

"And Raoul *has* a boyfriend-"

"*Boyfriend,*" scoffed Seb. "I just don't believe it."

In retrospect, Carla was very glad they'd been married with decorum and elegance at the Chelsea registry office because the blessing in France was nothing short of a circus. The exquisite photos taken by Carlitos Mi Vida could never hope to convey the farce that had gone on behind the scenes.

Seb and Carla waited beneath the porch of the beautiful Romanesque church. For a moment they stood just the two of them, wiped clean of all that was past, with only a future together to look forward to. Carla closed her eyes briefly, feeling the thin sun's rays on her face, Seb's lips on her cheek. But they flew open at Gemma's squeal of excitement.

"Here!" she said thrusting another exquisite bouquet in her hands. Gemma had chosen the perfect flowers for the London registry office and yet again she'd succeeded without even knowing the colours of Carla's Chanel. Carla felt tears in her eyes, overcome with love for her friend.

But that was where any semblance of tradition ended. Carlitos Mi Vida, who had been moderately restrained up until then, went all out camp with the arrival of an audience.

"I don't believe he's a Cultural Attaché either," observed Seb as Carlitos flirted with the priest. "I think Raoul picked him up in some club."

"Could be..." said Carla doubtfully.

Carlitos Mi Vida wore a striped navy and white sailor top and in between trying to hold hands with Raoul, began circling Seb. But Seb was distracted by the priest, a charming giant of a man from the Ivory Coast, prophetically named Père Legros. Seb was convinced he wasn't celibate at all.

"He has the hots for you too!" Seb grunted, which in the priest's case Carla couldn't completely deny. In fact, Carla had spotted Père Legros earlier, having a coffee on the terrasse, but without his dog collar, she'd not instantly identified him as a man of God. '*Ah oui,*' the priest had said to her later in his ponderous, melodious, deep-barrelled voice. '*Je vous ai remarqué - et votre amie, qui courrait après.*'

"He's no man of God," whispered Seb throughout the brief ceremony, "just another hot-blooded man. I can tell. I knew priests like him at school." Carla was distracted in turn, by Carlitos Mi Vida and Raoul practically making out in the vestry and by a maudlin Gemma who'd decided to dump the boyfriend when she got back to England.

"*Et maîtenant,*" said Père Legros. "*Madame Cave deposera son bouquet devant la vierge.*"

Carla stared. She'd had to throw away one bouquet (at the Chelsea Arts Club - Gemma had rugby tackled the other guests trying to catch it) but she sure as hell wasn't giving up this one. She'd only had it for an hour. Seb place a strong warm hand over hers. But she knew what he was doing. Carla gripped her flowers even more tightly. She shook her head. Seb tugged gently, Carla pulled back. There was silence. Even Carlitos Mi Vida stopped pawing Raoul.

"It's the tradition here," said Raoul, stepping forward, chocolate eyes becoming fondant as they bored into in hers.

"Well, it's not where I come from!" she said through gritted teeth.

"Did you *see* the way he looked at you?" hissed Seb. Carla could feel his temperature rising through his hand. His fingers began to pinch.

"*Et maîtenant,*" repeated the priest. "*Madame Cave deposera son bouquet devant la vierge.*"

"It's only a bouquet," whispered Gemma. "I'll get you another!"

"What's he saying?" asked Seb.

"It's traditional here in France," said Raoul translating, "for the bride to leave her flowers in front of the Statue of the Virgin. You should do it."

"*Et maîtenant, Madame Cave...*"

Carla glowered at them both.

Can a Leopard?

"Love affair over," said Seb happily as they left the church.

7

They descended slowly. Seb had the sense to have two hands on the steering wheel and they were advancing so carefully, Carla could release her hair. Nestling within the Tuscan archipelago and hugging the mountain, the hotel appeared to consist of a series of different red stucco-tiled buildings. She shut her eyes, partly because she wanted the full impact of the place she'd held in her heart as long as she could remember, and partly out of sheer terror as Seb spun the car away from the cliff's edge and in again. There was a rich aroma of myrtle, rosemary and juniper, the air thick with the heat and the sound of chirping crickets. Seb came to a stop and Carla slowly opened her eyes. Cyprus trees framed the unprepossessing entrance. Above it, the hotel's name was scrawled in kitsch neon lights - the kind of she'd seen on postcards of Havana in the 1960s. Her 'oh,' of disappointment was subsumed by the bustle of arriving.

Their bags were whisked from the car, in the kind of service Carla had come to expect from lovely hotels. And service was something for which this particular hotel was renowned - the guests' wishes anticipated before they knew what they desired themselves. Except that Carla did know. She was starving. She entered the lobby in high spirits approving of the receptionist's Armani elegance. She was less sure of the accompanying catwalk *froideur* as her own warm greeting faded on her lips. Seb had started perspiring profusely and when he removed his Akubra so that the hotel staff could zap his forehead, his hair was wet. Carla started to fan herself frantically with a hotel brochure fearful of a high temperature reading.

Can a Leopard?

Their rooms weren't ready so they were invited to stroll around the hotel.

"Let's have something by the pool," said Carla taking Seb's arm and dismissing the initial hiccup as minor inconvenience. She could change and freshen up later. There was plenty of time.

"Might have a work call," muttered Seb into his hat as he plopped it back on.

"OK," said Carla. "But you can have something first, no?"

He followed her onto the terrace, to where they'd be taking all their meals. The hotel was half full - deliberately booking out only twenty-five rooms. Its staff wore masks but the guests didn't have to - only if they wanted to visit the boutique shop. *Wanted! What kind of question was that?*

Carla paused. Wide stone steps led to the pool. A few couples lay on sun loungers covered in the hotel's signature yellow and white towelling. On the right, was another dining area - tables arranged under large umbrellas overlooking the sea.

Carla could never see a pool without thinking of the swim they'd all enjoyed later on in the day, after the blessing. Actually, 'enjoyed' wasn't quite the right word. The weather had suddenly improved and Raoul had suggested a swim after cake and a dance back at his place. When Gemma and her boyfriend Titus and Seb and Carla arrived back (minus the bouquet) a light aperitif was waiting - champagne and cake, and the kind of canapés Continentals did best, small delectable *amuse bouches* on miniature doilies. The sun had come out and they'd danced on the terrace, their moods rising and falling as rapidly as the sun's intermittent appearance between clouds. 'He's *not* gay!' hissed Seb virtually ripping her out of Raoul's arms every time their host tried to dance with her. 'Besides, where's Carlitos Mi Vida?'

Can a Leopard?

'I've no idea!' Carla snapped back. 'Look, he just wants to dance!' 'So, let him dance with Gemma!' 'But Gemma wants to dance with Titus.' 'And *I* want to dance with you! Is that too much to ask of my bride?'

The argument was settled by Raoul's abrupt decision to swim. 'Is it warm enough?' Gemma had asked doubtfully. Titus clearly had no intention of swimming or even staying. A short time later, they had broken up and Gemma had left to go back to England. Meanwhile, on the journey back from the centre of town, Carlitos Mi Vida had manged to pick up a carload of stray men. Soon the swimming pool was full of cavorting strangers which made Carla uncomfortable but it was the first time she'd seen Seb genuinely nervous. 'My turn to feel threatened,' he'd said uncertainly. Carlitos Mi Vida, who had not hidden his attraction to Seb, now began accidentally bumping into him. 'That's it!' Seb barked, hauling Carla out of the water by her wrists. 'I'm not staying in this mad house a second longer!' 'But we can't leave!' said Carla aghast, following him into the house. She hunkered down to mop up the trail of wet footprints they'd left on the pristine marble floor. '*Can* we?' But Seb was determined, throwing their belongings into their bags and while Raoul was changing for the fifth time, they'd stolen away into the night and to the gorgeous La Mirande in Avignon.

"Isn't this heaven!" exclaimed Carla now, so many years later, with the memory of that other hotel still in her mind's eye. In the distance, the hotel's pontoon jutted into azure water. Feeling the sun on her face, she willed away the last vestiges of lockdown anxiety. She imagined sipping an Aperol Spritz and eating lobster linguini.

"I'm not really hungry," said Seb scraping a lounger towards him. "Let's have a meal later."

Carla's stomach growled loudly. She thought of her new red swimsuit.

Can a Leopard?

"Oh, OK." *Linguini later then…* "But could I have some coffee now, some fruit?" *Anything…*

A couple lounging on garden chairs, looked up as they approached. Both were tanned a deep mahogany and were whippet thin. He wore the ubiquitous uniform of the Euro-moneyed: Tods, a jewel-coloured linen shirt, and a thin cashair turquoise jumper tied nonchalantly around his neck even though it was too hot for clothes, let alone layers. All Carla noticed about the woman was the green crocodile Hermès slide dangling from her foot. Even her toes looked expensive. Instinctively, Carla hid her own; this woman clearly hailed from a country where beauty salons had re-opened. Carla again ventured a smile but was ignored. What was it with people here? Back in England, there had been moments of tension but by and large folk had smiled more readily than before Covid-19, and she had witnessed countless acts of kindness. In fact, a reminder to be kind seemed to be as mandatory as staying vigilant.

She felt her own good mood deflate. Still- she glanced around her - here they were at last. In this lovely place. The pool looked inviting; the reflection of ornamental orange trees casting zig zag lines across the water. Carla perched awkwardly on the lounger beside Seb's. He'd removed his hat and shaken out his hair which now hung rather fetchingly around his face. He may not have the effete polish of a European, but his Zimbabwean ruggedness was a lot sexier. He also looked much younger than his fifty-eight years. Ah, yes, an Aperol would be just the ticket.

"Two coffees," said Seb when the waiter - also whippet thin- finally approached. His mask was fastened around his upper arm in the way of old-fashioned mourning bands.

"And some fruit?" Carla said hesitantly.

Can a Leopard?

Had she asked the man to strip naked and swim to the Grotta Azzura, he couldn't have appeared more put out. He stared blankly.

"Kitchen. *Chiuso*."

He made a karate chop gesture, which was pretty definitive.

"Oh, that's all right," said Carla too hungry and weak and hot to be anything but compliant. "I'll just wait... till dinner." She eyed the orange trees longingly. *Or I could just help myself...*

Seb smiled, pleased; less so, when the bill came for the two tepid coffees.

"Twenty-seven euros a coffee. We're definitely 'eating out to help out'. Just in the wrong country."

As the sun went down on the Tyrrhenian sea, casting a purple light across the horizon, and Carla imagined the sapphire underwater meadows that awaited their discovery, they were informed that their room was ready. At last. Carla leapt up. *Now* their holiday could begin. Now she could bathe and change into her Missoni, in deference to their hosts (she'd keep the Alice Temperley for their second night) and they would drink their Aperol or champagne or Mojito and Seb would say something lovely about their anniversary, and they would laugh remembering how chaotic the blessing had been and how their honeymoon had really only begun when they'd arrived at the delectable La Mirande. How they'd dined romantically, in the gorgeous setting - all Pierre Frey wall hangings, and exquisite French country furniture. Anything, in fact to bring him back in line and under the familiar umbrella of reassurance.

But when they got to it, by contrast with the gorgeous Avignon hotel, their room in Italy was underwhelming to say the least. Boxy, and carelessly decorated, it was nothing like the setting against which she'd imagined Slim Aarons photographing movie star regulars such as Britt Ekland or Yul Bryner. She'd stayed at more lavish Holiday Inns in Monaco. It wouldn't matter ordinarily, except that this one billed itself as one of the most iconic hotels in the world. And it was their first romantic get-away since the pandemic began. Carla frowned. Seb wasn't being particularly romantic. She brushed away the thought. She was being paranoid, unsettled by the gap between anticipation and reality. She'd get ready for their evening and all would be well, just as it should be when it was just the two of them.

The air was heavy with the scent of expensive perfume when they went down to dinner. Carla wore her multicoloured, patchwork Missoni dress with the swirls that Seb said looked like waves, Jimmy Choo sparkly sandals and carried a Kotor Clutch. She wore the jewel earrings Seb had bought her the year before when they'd sailed from Capri to Syracuse. Syracus- *a* - she corrected herself inwardly. She felt good but still no murmur of appreciation from Seb. She paused, self-consciously on the top step, but no one glanced up, not even momentarily and, in that moment, she understood that she had ceased to be the picture. There was still admiration for the well-preserved but the true adulation would always be for the young. The really young: the toned, beautiful bodies encased in skimpy, designer frocks. Actually, scrap the clothes, youth in any form was what mattered.

Was it Covid that had changed things? She wasn't sure - all she knew was that nothing was ever going to be the same again. She glanced at Seb, he seemed unphazed by any of it. Nor was he picking up on her unease. Perhaps she was trying to re-capture something that had been slipping away for a while now. Only she'd not noticed. Covid had accelerated it all. She wanted to feel the way she used to - with all the magic and excitement that accompanied travel, the sensation of feeling invincible for the duration of a holiday. If nothing else, the notion that one could stay time. And what she needed more than ever, was the circle of his love and attention, to make her feel that she was not alone.

Can a Leopard?

They'd been given a table at the very edge of the terrace by a jasmine hedge. Carla smiled her thanks. It was hard to tell behind his mask and designer suit, whether the waiter had even noticed. He hunched; skinny hip thrust forward, bored by the whole procedure of taking their order. Which actually was pretty straightforward. They never had starters and if he could, Seb would have skipped the main completely and gone straight to dessert.

At last, Seb held out his hands. Even in the heat of the night, she could feel their enveloping warmth. She anticipated the sweet nothings which were rapidly becoming her everything.

"I have a work thing - a call with lawyers in Oz," was what he said. "Really sorry but I'm going to have to set the alarm for 2.30 a.m."

"Right." She pulled her hands away. So far, not one thing during this trip was turning out the way she'd hoped.

"Now, darkling," he said teasingly. "Don't be like that."

"I'm not."

"It's work. We have to sign some documents with a lawyer and that's the time we can all do it."

"Remotely?"

"What?"

The waiter splashed a Bellini in front of her almost knocking it over in his haste to see the woman who had entered the restaurant. *That used to be me*, thought Carla wistfully. It was the woman from the mahogany couple. She wore a skin-tight lace body, a full skirt swishing around killer heels and clung to her husband's arm. A moment's inattention on his part, and she'd end up tetraplegic. Other diners wafted into the restaurant: an older bronzed blonde couple, who Carla later learned was Danish, regulars who'd been coming to the hotel for thirty years, valuing and lauding the place's supposed discretion. Carla attributed the so-called 'discretion' to mere laziness. Much easier just to ignore the clientele completely. There was also a smiling, pleasant American couple. She seemed long accustomed to no longer being the picture and happy in her skin. Carla could learn a thing or two from her. And then the look-at-me Russian - an older, still beautiful woman who attracted glances if only because her transparent lace dress left little to the imagination. Her heavy breasts and thong were clearly visible. But her bottom was enviably firm. Seb did a double take.

"I said," said Carla enunciating carefully. "How come remotely?"

Seb whipped out his glasses. A bar code enabled them to download the menu. He glanced down, looked up and began chewing the arm of his glasses. Both were a new, intensely annoying habit.

"I'll have the lobster," she said without looking.

She saw him frown. "After all," she added sweetly. "I didn't have any lunch."

By the time dessert arrived, they were arguing gently. Carla wasn't sure how they'd got onto the topic of Covid (for a change) given, she thought they were done with all that. They both discounted the reality of a vaccine any time soon. Or at any rate an efficacious one. Seb said he thought he'd start wearing a mask when they returned home, even when they were in the street. Carla blinked.

"Why?"

"Dom says it absolutely lowers the risk of re-infection." Dom was Seb's only sibling, his guru, intellectual idol and twin.

Can a Leopard?

They were virtually joined at the hip and spoke to each other most days. Funny, she'd never thought about it before but she had twins (from a previous marriage) and had married one. "Look at what's happening in Europe."

"Yeah, Spaniards wear masks in the street then take them off to go inside. Completely bonkers."

"Unlike here," they both looked in the direction of the catwalk staff sashaying around the terrace, both sexes somehow managing to still look sexy and stylish.

"Probably why cases are going up," said Seb sanguinely.

And then they'd got on to the science - so-called. Seb still seemed to think she didn't understand it or was ignorant or wilful. But it was none of those things. She simply questioned the way data was collected. An Oxford professor observed that anyone who had tested positive for the virus, but later died of another cause, was included in the Public Health England figures. It was only what she'd been saying all along.

The bascule of Seb's eyebrows stayed raised. His chocolate ice cream had arrived and he wolfed it in one. Seb was generous in all things except desserts. These he kept to himself guarding his plate with the armour of his cutlery. It was fortunate Carla didn't have a sweet tooth. She'd begun to feel hot and itchy. The Russian beauty at a neighbouring table had moved complaining of mosquitoes.

Carla contemplated doing the same but her coffee had arrived so she decided to have that first. They were almost finished dinner anyway.

"You can be as sceptical as you like," she said blowing on the liquid. So far, she'd had two coffees differing wildly in temperature. "But I'm with the wonderful John Lee."

"Who he?" said Seb suddenly alert to the possibility of a rival.

Can a Leopard?

Carla kept her gaze lowered. The coffee had clearly been microwaved as the cup itself was scalding to the touch.

"Only someone I respect more than anyone I've met recently."

Seb's bascule firmly collapsed.

"Who?" his tone was pistol sharp and he moved his head in the owl-like fashion he only did when properly riled.

Ah, ha! Now I have your attention…

Carla sat back in her chair, re-arranging the folds of her dress, running her hands through her long hair, tossing it back even, tilting her head and dangling her pretty Choos as she'd seen Mahogany woman do. At last, she was garnering attention from around the restaurant. At last, she had Seb's.

"Doctor John Lee," she said.

"Yes?" Seb sat bolt upright and motioned to the waiter to bring him another scoop. Ordered her another cocktail. She wanted to say no, that her skin was beginning to prickle that she felt better, more herself again, that she was just testing his level of interest. Instead, she said yes, how lovely and hoped that the next Bellini would be a lot colder than the last. It had tasted like peach-flavoured shampoo. Was this really, what it had taken? There were shrieks coming from a neighbouring table where a veritable United Nations had gathered, a First Nations youth in flame suede loafers, an older, white-haired, tanned man in a crisp blue shirt, the happy hippy American woman in Tory Birch (catwalk not Bicester Village) and a young, breathtakingly beautiful couple Carla couldn't take her eyes off - both dark, and tanned and young the very essence of *spretzzatura*.

Can a Leopard?

Carla was so bedazzled by them she almost forgot her little game. Seb had not.

"Who is he?" he said in a darkly menacing tone.

"Who?" The beautiful brunette wore a simple silk shift, her tanned feet encased in Grecian sandals, minimal jewellery. *That's who I want to look like in another lifetime*, thought Carla.

"The Doctor."

The waiter placed a glass in front of her. Carla could tell it wasn't cold. She'd had enough of taking whatever she was given. This time she didn't smile.

"*Prego*," she snapped in fluent Italian. "Make sure it's *ice* cold." She fixed him with a Melania Trump glare.

"Right away," he stammered. *Wow*, thought Carla. *While in Rome…*

"John Lee writes for *The Spectator*," she said carefully. "He's the only person I bother with and he says that if you look at deaths in the winter/spring seasons for the past twenty-seven years, this year's comes only eighth."

"So?" said Seb rudely.

"So," said Carla pleasantly. "All I'm saying, is that we should keep things in perspective."

She held out her hand. He took hers reluctantly.

"Come on, let's have a photo."

"Well, I'm not asking that dim-wit," said Seb grouchily.

Carla giggled feeling better by the minute. She still had it, Seb still minded enough to feel jealous and even a warm Bellini was beginning to take effect.

"Then let's take a selfie."

She grabbed his phone which lay face down on the table.

"I'll take it," he said quickly.

"Of course, you will," said Carla making a moue with her mouth. "Your arms are *so* much longer."

She scraped her chair over to his, moving into the crook of his arm. She chided herself for feeling maudlin. She had nothing to complain about. As a family, they'd got off very lightly. Maybe it was just Covid, the strangeness of being away, the weirdness of the past few months. Maybe she'd not had enough to drink. Or too much.

"Go on," she said. "Ready!"

Except that the camera wasn't. It took a few moments to focus and in the meantime, a message had popped up, flashing across the screen, illuminating the dark space around them and fluorescent green in the half light.

Carla sprang back as if electrocuted. "Who's Karen?"

8

"Sixty-nine, seventy, seventy-one-"

Carla was awake twice in the night. Once, driven by a terrible thirst from too many warm Bellinis, the second as one hideous, heart-stopping name, 'Karen', seared her subconscious. As she tumbled into sleep, she wrestled with the green-eyed monster, reminding herself that if she was 'expectant of good' then good would surely come her way, that she shouldn't expect too much of others, that the only person who could 'take offense' was herself, bla bla bla. She anthropomorphized the green-eyed monster, then reversed it all and imagined obliterating it completely. When that failed, she ran through slogan after slogan from every self-help group she'd ever attended but it didn't do any good. Her dreams were a confused hotchpotch of guilty purchases (the Alice Temperley kimono which was too hot to wear here anyway), Naked Man (Oman) and the PTSD of lockdown.

It seemed that she'd only just fallen asleep when she was jolted awake by the scraping sound of window shutters. She was supposed to wake up refreshed, on a bed of heavenly softness, stretching sleekly in her new La Perla cobalt blue camisole (blue for the Med) as she and Seb reached for each other. Seb was reaching for her all right, but more in the way a medical student might examine a body. She wanted to feel sexy, relaxed, the memory of lockdown washed away by the sensation of being on holiday again, of being with Seb again, of feeling young again. But she felt none of those things. Her lovely silk cami was stuck to her skin even though she'd thrown off the sheets in the night and her head thudded with a dull ache and the sound of Seb counting.

She squinted, shielding her eyes as a beam of sunlight struck her face.

"Just needed more light. Sorry!" said Seb turning her leg this way and that. "Seventy-four, no five," he corrected. "I've counted seventy-five mosquito bites on your knees alone!" He sounded pleased.

Carla was instantly awake, her eyes wide open. She sprang from the bed to look in the mirror. And froze in horror. Her face was swollen with large red welts entrenched across her forehead. But that was nothing to the rest of her body. She was covered in hundreds of bites but not just pin prick-sized bites either, but large unsightly lumps. She sat down abruptly on the edge of the bed, too stunned to speak.

"Looks painful," volunteered Seb helpfully. "A swim in the sea should sort you out."

Carla nodded bemused. Her head was still foggy and now her arms had begun to itch too, exacerbating her general discomfort. Were these bites really all from last night? She stood up again, twisting this way and that. How was it possible to have been stung in so many places? She wouldn't have minded her body being stung so much but her face… Seb was right. Perhaps a swim in the sea would help. Her mother always said the sea was a cure for everything. Carla felt giddy disappointment shift. Yes, sea salt was known to be good for wounds and the like. She unpacked her new swimsuit and went into the loo to change. She wanted to examine her body without Seb looking. Naked, leaning over the side of the sink she took a deep breath. Even in the dimmer light, the bites looked repulsive and when she donned her poppy red bikini, Carla winced.

"Are you OK?" said Seb after ten minutes when Carla still hadn't come out of the bathroom.

Can a Leopard?

Right - you can do this. It's only vanity, hugely disappointment, of course, but you're an adult. Not a child who stamps her foot when things don't go her way. Yeah, right. It *served* her right for wasting time feeling jealous. Now she really did have a reason to feel sorry for herself.

When she emerged, a striped Missoni wrap over her swimsuit, she noted that Seb took care not to show his true feelings before offering a clichéd platitude. "These things are sent to try us," he said popping on a linen shirt over his Vilebrequin swimmers.

"More *Purgatorio* than *Divinia Comedia*, that's for sure," she said keeping her tone light though her heart felt leaden.

It turned out to be both. Carla hugged the cool walls as they went down to breakfast. Their table wasn't ready - neither was the Mahogany Couple's - and they were invited to sit opposite them on a small outdoor sofa in the shade. Today, the woman wore Hermès orange crocodile slides, knee-length tobacco-coloured linen shorts and a high-collared Victorian-styled lace blouse. Her sunhat matched the shorts. It was the kind of getup Carla would never have considered for herself but the woman looked expensive and chic and managed to make Carla in her too-colourful wrap, feel a bit bling in comparison. The woman was making a fuss over her newspaper which she wanted disinfected. Seb who normally couldn't function until he'd downed a couple of cafetière's worth of coffee, seemed preternaturally calm. Carla eyed him suspiciously. Was it because of this Karen?

So much for the best service in Europe; they waited forty minutes for a table although the time passed pleasantly enough. They were on holiday after all. Besides, if Carla sat perfectly still, her bites didn't itch so much. She studied the other guests as they drifted away from breakfast making their way to the pool or to settle on the various terraced hideaways tucked into the cliff's edge. American woman sported enormous black-rimmed heart-shaped sunglasses and a one-piece bathing suit with so many bits cut out, it would surely have been more flattering (and presumably cheaper) to wear a bikini. Tattered linen canopies fluttered in the breeze. The place was definitely tired but had its devoted clientele. Mahogany Couple being among them. They came from Belgium - the same sea-side town as Alfie's godmother, but they didn't know each other. Along with the Hermès slides, an enormous Hermès beach bag settled at Hortense's feet, while husband Hector (spelled with a 'K') wore a Hermès belt. Even their towel was Hermès (they eschewed the Hotel's yellow-striped variant) but it was rather beautiful - an enormous leopard on a taupe background, edged in navy blue. Had they chosen the fashion brand because they shared the same initials?

Periodically, Hortense swooped down like a heron on a goldfish to pluck an expensive sun cream out of her bag. The supply seemed endless and varied and Carla would have dearly loved to have tried a few dollops. H and H appeared to consume more cigarettes than food. Carla soon understood why. They'd have derived more sustenance from nicotine (at least it would have taken the edge off their hunger) than the hotel food. When they finally got to their table, Carla ordered soft boiled eggs, fruit and toast. The eggs (virtually raw) arrived with the fruit and the toast - despite pitiful pleas - came one whole hour later. So now she was itchy *and* hungry.

"Come on!" said Seb when they'd finished, or if not finished exactly, it looked as if no amount of waiting was going to result in their order ever being fulfilled. He rose and pulled back her chair.

"We'll go for a quick swim and then we can tootle around the coast. Does that sound good?"

Carla perked up at this. "It absolutely does! Let's go into Porto Ercole! We pass San Stefano along the way, home to Michelangelo Merisi."

Can a Leopard?

"Never heard of him," said Seb as they picked their away along a gravel path down to the sea. There were splodgy overblown clumps of alder hedges clipped to appear as a continuous undulating wave. Probably to distract from the fact there was no beach to speak of, just the pontoon and a section of the cove cordoned off for swimming. Seb immediately stripped to his Vilebrequins and hat, flinging his shirt on a sunbed. Carla carefully stepped out of her wrap, draping it carefully alongside. She felt pitifully pale in the glare of the Tuscan light. There wasn't a pool attendant in sight. Gingerly, Carla made her way to the water's edge, to settle on a rock and dip her toes in the sea. Her nostrils twitched. There was the faintest smell of sewage.

Seb sank into the water holding his nose with one hand, his hat high above his head so as not to get it wet, with the other.

"And you *have* heard Michelangelo Merisi," she insisted when he came up for air. "He's better known as Caravaggio."

"Oh, him."

"Yes him. He died in Porto Ercole tyring to retrieve his paintings - well that and hoping to obtain a pardon from the Pope. He was on the run for murder."

"Now that *is* interesting."

But not nearly as interesting as grabbing her ankles and pulling her into the water. Carla squealed, not having wanted to get her hair wet before the evening. She wanted to look her best for their romantic dinner à deux although the state of her skin was fast diminishing any pleasure she might have had in dolling herself up. "Let's go darkling," said Seb after they'd swum around the bay a couple of times, using the term of endearment he knew would make her smile.

Can a Leopard?

Later, nestling into the soothing leather of their car, her face hidden by a broad-rimmed sunhat, Carla's spirits rose even further. The saltwater had eased her bites and she felt refreshed. Soon they were tearing around the Argentario coastal road towards Porto Ercole and the Spanish Fortress.

"It means Hercules."

"What does?"

"Ercole," said Carla her hand pushing against the hot air as though stopping it from enveloping her any further. There was a dense aroma of myrtle and pine and bergamot. "And they still haven't found his body."

"Whose? Hercules's?"

"Caravaggio's!"

"Sorry, you'd lost me there for a moment. The painter - I'm with you now."

"Or they hadn't until a few years ago when bits and pieces said to be his were discovered and subsequently re-buried."

They hurtled around another hairpin bend.

"Elaborate on 'bits and pieces'," said Seb as Carla feared that's all that would be left of them if he didn't slow down.

"Part of his skull, a bit of femur and spine - not much - not much in death if you consider what he was in life. What he added to painting. And I really value mine," she added under her breath.

"And that was?"

Can a Leopard?

"Well, the chiaroscuro style; the contrast of light and dark to achieve three-dimensional volume. I took the twins to an exhibition of his once in London when they were little."

"Did they enjoy it?"

Carla shook her head. "Not really. I think they were a bit too young at the time." Which was an understatement. Poor little mites had been absolutely terrified by the dark, menacing portraits on enormous eight-foot canvasses. But they'd not forgotten the painter in a hurry. "You have to decide for yourself whether he was damned artist or creative genius."

"You're quite fascinated by the man, aren't you?"

"By his painting yes. There was one I remember in particular, *The Taking of Christ* - you could count the wrinkles on the men's foreheads, their frowns. Their skin was luminous, you actually *felt* their scratchy, bristly moustaches, the red tips of their noses, the soft tendrils of Christ's hair, the brutal metal of the soldiers' armour. An extraordinary feat. But I've always been struck by Caravaggio's end. He was thirty-eight years old, ill and pursued by numerous enemies. He'd also been ex-communicated by the Pope - a kind of death in itself at the time. It would have meant living in isolation, unwelcome, shunned by everyone."

"Like lockdown you mean," teased Seb.

"Except I hope ours has a happy ending!"

They'd reached the port. Rows of dinghies and small sailing ships were moored along the pontoon. Sailing was permitted once again but hotels like theirs wasn't allowing visitors by sea to alight and dine (if they weren't also staying) as they had done before the pandemic.

The heat was a physical assault as they wandered the narrow cobble streets following the signs to the various places

Caravaggio had visited. They climbed steadily higher from the stony pier, through arched passageways and watch towers. From every corner there was a view of the sea, a blaze of brilliant cerulean blue and a heady scent of figs. Ficus Religiosa, thought Carla recalling her pharma background. The fruit was everywhere, hanging pendulant from branches, crushed underfoot, lodged between cement grouting and stone walls. Perhaps Caravaggio ought to have eaten more of it - figs along with containing phenols, had antibacterial properties. It was also the tree under which the Buddha had divined the 'Truths.' The smell was nothing like the artificial candles you got at home but rich and velvety.

"I'll take a picture," offered Seb. They had reached the Piazza Santa Barbara which was located almost at the top of the promontory. At the far end was the simple 4th century church of Sant Erasmo.

"Patron Saint of Seafarers," said Carla in awe, craning her neck at the bell tower shaded in palm fronds. "Later a Jesuit church," she added knowing that Seb had gone to a Catholic school in Harare. "Named for a Bishop who calmed a storm."

"Right," said Seb pleasantly but not really interested and framing her in his lens.

"Your cornflower blue will look good against the ochre plaster."

"No!' cried Carla turning her back to him.

"You don't want one for Insta?" he said puzzled.

"I do, yes, but I don't want Olivia to see me in this dress!"

"You think she won't recognise it from behind?"

"No."

86

Can a Leopard?

Seb adjusted his Akubra. "You could *not* post it, of course."

"Just take it quickly. Then I'll decide."

"Whatever you say," said Seb amused.

They left the square and walked down the steps shaded on either side by the city walls, overhanging olive branches and the ubiquitous fig. Ahead lay the port, the sea, a triangle of white sail.

"I'd also like to see Santa Caterina where Caravaggio was taken. It was a hospital then. He was found in a terrible state, hallucinating and half-dead with sun stroke."

"And no one knows how he died?"

Carla shook her head. "No, well yes, maybe. Forensic testing found abnormally high levels of lead in his bones. He was known to be really messy with his paints. Lead in itself wouldn't be such an issue but coupled with infected wounds and sunstroke…"

Seb nodded. "He was done for." He held out his hand. "To the hospital."

Some time later, when they were coming back from the Spanish Fortress, Seb offered to take another photo. He'd wanted to know why the fortress was Spanish not Italian. Carla had explained that it was because at the time, Porto Ercole along with four other towns along the Tuscan coast, formed part of the 'Presidio' which roughly translated as 'state of the garrisons.' Between the 16th and 18th century it had belonged to Spain.

They emerged under the cool portcullis to stupefying heat. Carla's dress stuck to the bites on her back.

"No!" she exclaimed grabbing his phone. "Selfie time!"

Can a Leopard?

He wasn't fast enough: The name Karen again flashed across the screen.

9

With the discomfort of being bitten by two hundred mosquitoes and counting (management explained that due to Covid-19 the company that usually came to spray the hotel hadn't been able to), Carla had completely forgotten about the 2 a.m. call. So had Seb. He'd confused the days anyway and it was this night/morning that the call was due to take place. They'd driven back to their hotel in silence - harmonious in Seb's view, tortuous in Carla's - her churning, stomach-clenching, prickly heat discomfort upending the contentment of retracing Caravaggio's footsteps.

Who was Karen? Every partner in a relationship has a duty not to cause jealousy in the other, Seb had told her once. And yet, he'd been no stranger to sucking in his cheekbones and fixing an attractive woman with his admiring gaze. Now that she was indulging these destructive reflections (and she would a bit longer because she felt increasingly awful and looked such a mess - no amount of foundation could disguise the crusts forming on her face), she remembered one occasion when she'd wrestled back the upper hand with humour.

She'd been heavily pregnant with Alfie and they'd taken polo friends of Seb's from Palm Beach to dinner at Le Caprice. The couple had their own polo teams. Hank's was *Los Diablos*, Candy's (sporting candy pink team shirts and bandages) was *Going Concern*. The perma-tanned Candy had loved the fact that the place had been a favourite of the late Princess Diana's. Carla was sad to learn that Covid had also killed off the iconic restaurant and it had closed forever.

Can a Leopard?

The night being young (Americans ate dinner early) they'd gone on to Annabel's which at the time was still owned by Mark Birley. In those days, it was decorated to resemble a cosy English country house with chintzes and oil paintings of dogs. It felt like home, Carla had confessed to Seb on one of their early dates - it and Harrods. Which was no exaggeration. When Carla was at school and her mother visited London for Carla's half-terms, they practically lived in the department store. Her mother bought all her clothes, food and theatre tickets there. Eugenia, who had never in her life, washed her own hair, also visited the beauty salon every other day. Carla and her brothers were soon as familiar with Harrods as they were with their own Swiss home. And because they were so often in the shop after hours, waiting for Eugenia to finish her latest treatment or dress fitting, this included fire exits and staff basement passages as well.

Carla loved Annabel's at any stage of life and despite being heavily pregnant on this occasion, felt quite fetching in a navy Chanel cocktail dress over which she'd worn a beautiful brocade Diane von Furstenberg coat. It had oversized jewel buttons to compliment her oversized belly. Seb and Carla and the Palm Beach couple had all been in high spirits as they descended into the bowels of the night club.

The attendant in the lady's cloakroom was the very same woman who'd been there all those years before when Carla visited the club for the first time. Carla was just sixteen and her mother had bought her a dress from Way In (at Harrods), speedily on their way out. Too speedily. Eugenia claimed not to have noticed that the dropped waist, tartan taffeta and huge sash made Carla appear even younger. Protesting and terrified, Carla was dispatched to have dinner at Annabel's with a Spanish duke. The man had been spine-tinglingly dull, only really coming to life in the taxi home when he'd tried to kiss her. Carla had spent a lot of time on that occasion with the kind lady in the ladies' cloakroom. She'd dropped her pound coin in the pretty china dish as she went out, catching the older woman's eye as the usual melee of beautiful girls in skimpy sequin frocks made up their faces. 'Where Middle East meets middle age' used to be its catch phrase.

So many years later now, Seb was chatting animatedly to their guests - suspiciously so. She followed his gaze and sure enough, by the bar was an exotic, dark-haired beauty. Seb made a big show of fetching Carla a drink positioning her carefully just behind one of the two pillars that divided the bar area from the dining room. She realised immediately that while Seb could be viewed in all his exuberant post polo match vitality, a blazer thrown over white jeans, a tie borrowed from the men's cloak room, and laughing that deep chest rumble that always attracted strangers, she was camouflaged completely. From time to time, Seb would look up in the direction of the bar. Not in hers.

"Are you excited?" Candy was saying. Seb had told her that after her divorce, Candy had had her breasts enlarged and that at a dinner party in New York, she'd passed around before and after pictures. Carla couldn't really look the tanned, fifty-something blonde straight in the eye without thinking this. Apparently, Candy was also a very successful, very driven realtor. Which was probably why she was more than a little perplexed by Carla's part-time work interpreting at the law courts.

"What?" Carla watched Seb's spirited face as he squared his shoulders, as he flung amused looks in the direction of … Carla followed his gaze… the woman at the bar. "I'm sorry, I mean, I beg your pardon."

Candy gestured to Carla's belly. She'd already asked if she could have 'a feel.' Something Carla abhorred when she was pregnant. The way you were somehow up for grabs - anybody's territory for a grope. She drew a line at men asking to touch her.

"Oh, yes."

Can a Leopard?

"You have twins already, right?"

"Yes, a girl and a boy."

"How lucky."

"Sure," Carla had inadvertently copied the woman's intonation. Saying 'sure' was almost always passive - on the point of rudeness, Seb had once told her. It really means 'I don't want to but I will' or 'if you say so.'

"But Seb has no children from before? I mean he's only been married the once?"

"Yes," replied Carla curtly. "To me."

"Right. A regular *beoy*."

Ain't that the truth... "Indeed."

The woman had got that right. There was a time when they were living in London that they couldn't walk two blocks, go to the theatre, a dinner party or drinks, that some ex didn't appear to salivate over the fact that Seb had finally got married. Except that Seb rarely introduced Carla as his 'wife.' He'd say something like 'oh, come and meet Carla' leaving the ex with the faintest hope that he was somehow still available. They'd once shared the dance floor at Annabel's with only one other couple and Seb had dated her too. They'd not said a word to each other, as if the other didn't exist. But this present situation required action. Carla had had enough of skulking behind the pillar. She emerged much to the beauty's surprise, shaking out her own long tresses, pouting her own rouged lips.

"Phew, it's hot isn't it?"

Seb had had the grace to look alarmed. He'd mouthed an 'are you ok?' But only mouthed it, a half-hearted mouthing if ever there was one, clearly expecting Carla to be reassuringly self-effacing and slink back salamander-like to the coolness of the marble wall. Carla had enjoyed herself then. She'd extravagantly thrown off her beautiful coat.

"Darling," she'd said loudly, languidly. "*Ay, mi amor*, would you hang this up for me?"

Seb had taken the coat doing a sort of second position plié so as not to have to lose his spot or even move at all.

"*Ay, no!*" Carla had pouted. "*Porfi,*" (she used the Spanish slang for 'please') hang it up nicely."

And then she'd moved away from *behind* the pillar to lean *in front* of the pillar, managing to look, without the coat's clever draping, at least fourteen months pregnant. In any event ready to give birth *pero ya*.

Carla hugged the memory to herself. Yes, that had been a wonderful moment. Seeing the bar beauty do her own slinking as fast as she was sexily able, towards a table of investment bankers who were drinking champagne out of a Louboutin shoe. Presumably hers. Now that Carla thought about it, the woman's gait had been decidedly uneven.

But today on holiday, Carla had no other weapons in her arsenal. Certainly not her looks. She caught sight of her reflection. Her hair which ought to have retained its sleek blow dry, was frizzy from their earlier swim and not even her shoulders looked invitingly tanned anymore, pocked as they were with red mosquito bites. During the day she'd got over her disappointment and was now resigned to this being a different kind of holiday from the one she'd imagined - a different anniversary.

A snapshot of their wedding night came back to her briefly: the delectable La Mirande in Avignon, tucked behind the Popes' Palace, each room more gorgeously decorated than the last in French Provincial style, each room scented with the aroma of roses and local lavender, cut glass, mirrors and elegant gilt furniture. And the whole made even more delicious given that they'd managed to escape the mad house in Baume. At last, Carla had begun to have the wedding she'd dreamed of, had woken in a room bathed in honey light. That is, until a call from reception alerted them to the fact that 'a Monsieur Raoul' was waiting for them in reception.

Carla, waiting for Seb now on the terrace, would have been quite happy to be told Raoul was anywhere in the hotel. At least *he'd* pay her some attention. At least he'd have a sense of duty as a host. Raoul had been mortified that the newlyweds had felt compelled to flee his place. (*'Yeah, hello,'* Seb had muttered, *'doesn't he get it? The clue is in 'newlyweds.''*) But not wanting to offend Raoul, Carla had quite understood his sentiment which she put down to old-world Continental charm. Newlyweds or not - they were still Raoul's guests. After all, he'd organised the priest and booked the church and there'd been cake. ('*Cake?*' scoffed Seb. '*You don't even like cake!*') All right, but it was obvious that he felt he'd failed them. It was also clear that he wouldn't take no for an answer. Raoul would show them around the city himself - did they know that La Mirande was the setting for the scandalous film *La Religieuse*? No, she did not. 'Here we go...' grumbled a livid Seb. '*Did you hear that?*' He hissed. '*Do you know the film? It was condemned by the Catholic Church, banned by the Minister of Information no less and this is France we're talking about where anything goes. I knew it! He's not gay!*'

Well, would that Seb felt so honour bound now or rally even an ounce of the passion he was capable of displaying then. Carla watched the other guests drift up from the pool for drinks and dinner. Some of the waiters had dispensed with wearing masks around their faces. They hung either from an ear by the elastic loop or under the chin like a bib. One or two sported them on their foreheads like sunglasses but it made Carla think of the masks you're given on airplanes to shut out the light when you want to sleep. She sipped a watery Mojito feeling more miserable by the minute. The setting was perfection: the sea was bright and glistening, an orange sun was setting along the horizon and pink bougainvillea framed the stone walls of the patio. Bird cages, cleverly converted into hurricane lamps were dotted among the olive trees. Under them, at elegant cast iron tables, beautiful people sat together conversing … well beautifully.

Carla was being ridiculous. This 'Karen' could be anyone. There was a ping on her phone from the WhatsApp Leavers' parents in Alfie's class. For all Carla knew, Karen could well be someone who'd slipped under the radar. That was it. Right. She must dismiss this negative, destructive thinking. One of her favourite quotes from self-help reading was from Lewis Carroll's *Through the Looking Glass*. '*The horror of that moment*' *the King said,* '*I shall never, never forget.*' '*You will though,*' *said the Queen,* '*if you don't make a memorandum of it.*' Mostly, Carla didn't remember, didn't take out her grudges to nurture and polish but there were moments…

She glanced at the chain of messages. The conversation concentrated on plans for the final days of term. Ever. Carla felt a fresh pang of nostalgia. The twins were thirteen when Alfie was born. Tom was thirteen when he had left his prep school, as Alfie was about to, no longer a child but a youth. Winding the clock on, here was Alfie at exactly the same stage. Where had the intervening years gone?

During lockdown, they'd all been consumed with keeping themselves busy, not giving into depression or too much reflection. Now that they were supposedly coming out of it, Carla pondered the six months that had been sucked out of them. Six months on hold or six months constructively spent, she hadn't yet decided. And, although they were well used to the situation, used to no longer being able to make long term plans, she mourned the summer that might have been. All the lovely events for the boys had been cancelled, and with it one final opportunity to bond as youths, to spend time together post exams. And for the parents: the summer ball, drinks, parties and picnics.

For that very reason, the reduced events on offer were taking on greater significance than they might ordinarily have done. As a result, tempers were running high. Some of the parents were still wary of large gatherings. Carla hadn't been there to take Alfie for his first on site visit since the school re-opened but messages had been pinging backwards and forwards ever since. Too many mothers were hanging out apparently, ostensibly to see that their children 'passed' the temperature readings taken every morning but mainly to catch up with each other. And who could blame them? People needed people.

"Ah, there she is," said Seb jolting Carla to the present. "Drink?"

Seb whipped out his glasses - he'd started wearing them for reading and now he chewed the end as once he'd sawn off the caps off countless pens. "What's on the menu?"

As with most restaurants the paper variety was replaced by downloading an App.

"Oh, to hell with it, I can't see my phone with my glasses. I'll have what you're having."

"It's not great."

"I know, just expensive." Seb continued to chew his glasses and when it came, the ice from his drink.

She watched him slowly suck out the liquid with the end of the straw and deposit it in his mouth rather in the way she used to feed Alfie Calpol when he couldn't swallow a tablet. Why was it, that now that the big issues between them were resolved, the little ones grated?

Can a Leopard?

Seb sighed happily.

"We are lucky to be here," he said another chunk of ice muffling his pronunciation. "In your neck of the woods," (he meant Catalonia; her father was Spanish) "there's been another lockdown."

Carla took a large sip of her drink, desperately seeking any kind of hit from the alcohol. All she was getting was a syrupy, warm furriness.

"And in ours," she said a little more sharply that she intended, "another would be a disaster financially. £188.7 billion has been spent on the Corona crisis. Payments to employers in the UK up to the end of January 2021 will cost up to £9.4 billion. It's insane! I'm sure the government will also find out by the end of it, that the whole furlough thing will have been grossly abused."

"There wasn't a choice," said Seb coolly. "We could so easily have ended up like …"

"Like?"

Seb made a movement with his hands. She knew exactly what he meant but his ice chewing bothered her sufficiently so as not to want to make things easy.

"Here!" whispered Seb loudly.

"Oh, you mean as in Italy?"

"Yes, as in Italy."

"No!" said Carla emphatically. "We never would have. I'm so sick of that comparison. Morbid TV isn't science. There were so many variables - the way data was collated; the way deaths were recorded and now the fact that everyone is so hysterical about the number of cases. Covid is here to stay -

we need to get used to the fact. I don't think there's going to be a vaccine, not soon anyway and I don't think we're ever going to cure it. So, we should just get on with it."

Seb took a slurp.

"You OK, darkling?"

Carla felt hot all over. The sun might be setting but it wasn't any cooler. Most of the couples had left the terrace and they were alone. To celebrate their anniversary.

"I'm fine," she snapped.

"Great," said Seb setting down his drink. "In that case let's tuck in. I have to be up at two."

10

There were precisely eight passengers on the flight home and theirs was the only flight arriving at Heathrow Terminal 5 that evening. Seb took a picture of the arrivals board. Neither one of them had ever seen anything like it. When they'd arrived home from South America back in March, just as a partial lockdown was being announced, the atmosphere then had been eerie. But it was an eeriness tinged with the excitement of the unprecedented, the unexpected. Now it was just boring. Carla had had enough of the roller coaster ride of emotions she was still experiencing despite restrictions being lifted. If anything, Carla felt things were more difficult coming out of lockdown. There was still uncertainty coupled with the hardened battle-weary feel of the knowing, of having lived through it, of having experienced how challenging it had all been. Of what it would be like to go through it all again.

From time to time, she'd glanced at Seb's sleeping profile. He was exhausted from an interrupted night's sleep. She'd told him she didn't mind if he took the call in their room. She'd wanted him to but he'd desisted saying he didn't want to disturb her. She was disturbed anyway, aware of him getting up, looking for his clothes, bumping into the wall on his way to the loo, unplugging his phone. So, a romantic break that was supposed to draw a line under their Corona isolation had been anything but. For someone who'd been preoccupied with having enough sex on their holiday, Seb showed a distinct lack of appetite for any once they'd got there. He was preoccupied all right but not with sex. At least not with her. The scene in *Gigi* where Gaston takes his mistress to dine chez Maxim and although she is scintillating and gorgeous

Can a Leopard?

'she is not thinking of me' kept playing in Carla's mind. Carla stretched over the empty seat between them and ran her fingers in front of Seb's face to test that he was really asleep. No, he was not thinking of her…

Carla brewed on the past few days: no sex, no sleep, lukewarm food when it was meant to be hot, warmish when it was meant to be cold, and hundreds of complimentary mozzie bites. The haughty froideur of the hotel owner as she stomped about the place with her high oriental style ponytail swishing angrily behind her, was the final seal of disapproval. They wouldn't be returning any time soon.

Perhaps, it had been too soon to come away; they weren't ready after lockdown. Everything still felt too strange and too uncertain. Travelling abroad had felt the guiltiest of pleasures. Carla felt guilty that is, at not having enjoyed it more. That was the worst bit. Who wouldn't have given their eye teeth to escape the dreariness of recent months? Who wouldn't have enjoyed the warmth and light that was Italy? Carla couldn't stop thinking about Caravaggio strangled by that very light and heat and sun. His whole life was testament to conflict; a dark psyche at odds with its environment. Post pandemic, they were all struggling to find purpose and direction in an irrevocably altered landscape.

"I feel guilty," said Carla when Seb woke just as the plane was landing.

"Don't," said Seb sleepily, gruffly, his mask catching in his mouth.

"I wish -"

"No, to that too."

Carla couldn't help smiling. Seb (nearly) always made her smile.

Can a Leopard?

She swung her Clare.V basket away from her dress so that it wouldn't catch on the material. The mere act of arriving home again, seemed to have caused her bites to shrink.

"It's just that, well, do you think we won't ever be able to enjoy things properly again? I mean in a purely hedonistic, indulgent kind of way? Do you think we're doomed to repeat the same cycle? Only a few months ago, we weren't allowed to drive anywhere that didn't involve essential travel. We got used to that. Then the rule changed to being allowed to drive up to twenty minutes away and we adapted to that too."

"So, what's your point?" said Seb perplexed.

Carla shrugged. "I'm not sure - I guess what I'm *trying* to say is that we humans adapt to pretty much anything eventually, but quickly forget how much we appreciated the small liberties to begin with. Just getting into a car for example. I had so many good resolutions and now…"

Within minutes, they had disembarked, yards from immigration. There was virtually no walking involved. It was just like the old days when they'd grabbed a Lear to fly to a polo game. Carla had forgotten what it was like not to trudge miles through an airport.

"*'The good I would I do not, the evil that I would not, that I do'*," quoted Seb. He was many things, if not well educated.

"Steady," said Carla in alarm. "Evil's a *bit* strong… But if for 'evil' read 'intention', then yes, that probably applies. I *do* wish I hadn't sold my blue suede Manolos though," she added, suddenly remembering how perfectly they would have gone with her Temperley dress, *especially* if this was going to be the new norm in airports and they weren't going to have to walk very far.

Can a Leopard?

"From Nietzsche to Gucci," commented Seb cupping her face suddenly in his hands and kissing the tip of her nose. "It's what I love about you."

*

But did he? mused Carla as she strode down College Street later that afternoon. For the first time in months, it felt almost normal to be collecting Alfie from the school gates - well the gates to the playing fields to be precise - on Wolvesey. It was a beautiful summer's day - as hot as Italy had been. Several mothers she'd not seen since lockdown began, called out to her. One who knew she'd been away mouthed 'how was it?' and Carla re-writing the script, was quick to answer: 'Oh, you know, really lovely, thanks, (small, apologetic laugh in recognition of the fact that many hadn't been away in years let alone months) just gorgeous.'

Excitement mounting at seeing Alfie (after all, it was the first time they'd been apart since March), Carla quickened her pace to a slow jog. Her heart was actually thudding in her ears, in anticipation. She couldn't wait to hug her boy. Vicenzo's ice cream van was parked at the entrance to the playing fields. A queue of boys, snaking halfway down to the College opposite, ensured that social distancing rules were maintained. Carla waved certain she'd be buying Alfie an ice cream on their way back.

She slipped into the gap between the Bishop's Palace and the entrance to Wolvesey where a newly erected fence kept parents away from the site. Peering through the wire, Carla spied Alfie at the far end of the field. She could often tell by the way her son moved whether or not it was him. But he wasn't exactly racing towards her. In fact, Alfie cast a shifty glance in her direction before turning away. Her hand raised in greeting, sidled down the wire fencing as he disappeared behind the cricket pavilion. For a moment she clung to the fence, swallowing her disappointment.

Can a Leopard?

Elsewhere, boys not in Alfie's 'bubble,' circled the field, standing on the pedals of their bikes, coming close to where she stood but then shooting off in the opposite direction. She also failed to attract their attention. It would seem that most of the boys from Alfie's own pod had already left. Carla signalled again pathetically, feeling irritation and frustration mounting at being so blatantly ignored. And hurt. She'd been so excited at the thought of seeing him. Ordinarily, she would have crossed the field, but the gates were padlocked from her side to ensure parents kept their distance. Her son didn't have a phone, so she couldn't communicate with him that way either. She was about to give up and leave, when Alfie finally appeared from the pavilion on a bicycle.

"Yeah, Hal leant it to me," he said sulkily. He dismounted on the other side of the gate and pushed the bike towards her. He was wearing the same clothes he'd been wearing when Carla and Seb left for Italy. His hair was parted down the middle like a pair of dirty curtains. It was a particularly unflattering look. She did her best to control her displeasure.

"And hello to you too!"

He was silent, his eyes sliding away from her. "See you at home," he said manoeuvring his bike through the narrow gate.

So, going back to school had been more traumatic for him than she thought it would... She caught the handlebars, stalling him.

"Oh, no you won't! Come on, walk with me. Darling, I haven't seen you! I want to talk to you; hear how you've been. What's with the hair?" She hadn't meant to start with that but it slipped out. It looked ridiculous. She tried to touch his head but he shied away from her.

"What."

Can a Leopard?

Carla's eyebrows shot up. "What do you mean 'what'?"

Shrug.

"You look like Uriah Heep."

Blank.

Carla sighed. It was always a bit lonely referencing literature that no one in the family had read, let alone heard of.

"OK, Wednesday Adams then." His vacant expression elicited another futile prompt. "From *The Addams Family*?"

Which resonated even less than the Dickens. She took a deep breath. Things were definitely not right. She glanced down. Alfie was gripping the handlebars and he'd started biting his nails again. She felt a pang. He was still only a child, not yet the youth he aspired to be and if she had considered lockdown challenging and weird and lonely, Alfie had felt it a hundred-fold.

"Cobain," muttered Alfie at length.

Carla halted astonished. "You mean as in *Kurt*? You mean *his* hair is the latest trend? But that's my era!"

Alfie nodded. "Also, di Caprio."

"I see," said Carla. "So, it's really a thing."

They had reached the ice cream van. Under the shade of a plane tree, a couple of mothers defied the social distancing rule and sat chatting happily while their children waited in line. Beside them was an ever-growing pile of school bags and coats as pupils dropped them on the dusty pavement beside them. From time to time, the children threw a *'can we just go home?'* to be categorically ignored. Older boys ambled down the middle of the road on skateboards. Little girls,

Can a Leopard?

waiting for their older brothers, frantically pedalled their scooters, weaving in and out of the other students. Carla nodded in Vicenzo's direction.

"Would you like one? Or a drink maybe?"

Alfie shook his head, doing up the strap on his helmet, his hair hanging in ribbons on either side of his face. She wanted to tuck it back under his helmet, away from his face. He had 'bascule' eyebrows like Seb's and beautiful eyes. Alfie forced a smile. "I just want to go home. I'm tired."

"OK, love," said Carla. "You go on then. I'll catch you up. By the way, I like the bike."

Alfie half turned. "Hal says I can borrow this one a bit longer. See how I get on."

She felt a whisper of encouragement. Things were already improving. It always took a bit of time to get used to one another when they'd been away. Didn't she remember what it was like with the twins? She must try and be patient.

"Sounds sensible," Carla agreed enthusiastically. "And if you do, why don't we get you one of your own? That way you can cycle around the city, learn your way around."

Alfie nodded happily. Any moment she expected him to hop on his bike and peddle on home but he seemed happy to walk beside her.

"Oh, can I get a drone?" he added as an afterthought.

Give them an inch…

"What kind of drone?" she asked slowly. *I've just offered you a bike! but she was so happy just to have him walk beside her, that she'd have promised anything.* "Don't you have one already?" Then seeing his face fall, added quickly, "maybe." Caught on

105

the hoof, she hated saying 'no' but knew it was wrong to agree too readily. She was equally completely at sea with this newly depressed pre-teen boy.

"I can show you on Dad's phone."

"Show me on mine."

"Dad's is better."

"OK, then, show me when we get back."

"I'll give up gaming for a month."

Now we're talking...

"No, you won't."

"I will." Alfie stopped and straddling his bike, grabbed her hand linking their small fingers together. "Pinkie promise."

"Pinkie promise." She unhooked her little finger to measure her hand against his. "Catching up," she added wistfully as she used to say to the twins when they were little until the day had come when they had.

"I need to go," he said pulling away.

"All right but be careful! We'll talk when I get back. Wait!"

She snuck in a hug which Alfie tolerated but within seconds, was a blur ahead of her riding on the wrong side of the road. She always felt a shiver of fear every time a child of hers ventured out alone. She followed at a more sedate pace. College Street was drenched in yellow sunlight and even with sunglasses she struggled to see where she was going. She seemed to know every other person and greeted them joyfully. There was a palpable feel of relief and release of tension. The weather and the easing of lockdown had improved everyone's wellbeing. She passed the book shop which hadn't yet re-opened to customers physically but like many small businesses had managed to survive by offering an online service. Parcels piled high on a chair, were ready for collection. She covered the remaining distance in long, happy strides. It felt so good to be out, to have Alfie back at school, to catch a glance of familiar faces. They could now put the wretched Covid behind them.

The front door was ajar when she got back and she could see through to the garden where Seb was sitting with a friend of theirs, a father of one of Alfie's classmates.

"You've just missed him," said Seb.

"Hi Jack," said Carla sinking into a chair beside them.

"It's the bicycle," Seb was saying to Jack. "He clearly loves it, makes him feel independent," He flicked a gaze in Carla's direction. "Maybe we should get him one."

"It's what I was thinking. It certainly is about time!" She sat still waiting for the familiar itching to begin but ever since they'd got back to England, the mosquito bites seemed to have miraculously dried up. They were still there just not as visible, sinking to mere pimples as opposed to raised bumps.

Jack nodded in agreement. "They've all been coming in with them," he said. "As far as I can make out, all they do is ride around Wolvesey all day. They've had a session on bike management too. Should help."

"Great, the little bugger won't have to come to me when he has a puncture," said Seb.

"Anything's better than Zoom," said Carla.

"Yeah," agreed Seb addressing Jack. "Alfie didn't do too well with that. He was really low. He said the teacher never noticed if he raised his hand in 'class'. He became disillusioned pretty quickly."

"Well, they're at the end of it all now," said Jack. Jack was immaculate in pressed chinos, a button-down collar, short hair.

"You've been to the barber's."

Jack patted his tight curls. "Claudia cuts our hair."

Carla nodded. "Lucky you."

"You've not let Delilah near yours?" Jack said to Seb nodding in Carla's direction.

Seb touched his long locks protectively.

"Not bloody likely."

Seb was probably right not to trust her hairdressing skills. Or lack of. Carla had once trimmed Sophie's fringe when she was little. To this day, Carla remembered the horror of snipping away, sweat gathering on her own forehead as the fringe became shorter and shorter until it was a mere inch off the hairline. Carla changed the subject.

"It'll be strange having to watch the prize-giving remotely when the boys are able to gather together on Wolvesey. You'd have thought we could all safely distance there given how vast the field is! Why, Seb could even play polo."

"Almost," said Seb unhelpfully.

"I mean," said Carla ignoring him, "would it make such a difference us being there too?"

Jack looked cagey. "The school has to be careful. One wrong move and the government will shut it down. No one wants that, do they? They can't risk it."

"No, I suppose not."

He looked increasingly uncomfortable.

"People," he began.

"Yes?"

"Cup of tea?" said Seb getting up and heading for the kitchen.

"Earl Grey, thanks. No," Jack shook his head. "Actually, no. I won't have anything. And I have to go. Richard will be waiting for me on Wolvesey."

Although Richard, Jack's son and Alfie were in the same class, they weren't in the same pod which meant pick-up times were different to ensure pupils (and their parents) stayed in their corresponding bubbles. The fact that Jack was visiting Carla and Seb at all, was breaking the rules.

"Er - OK, awkward moment. But here it is."

"What's awkward?" said Carla smiling. She was used to Jack's candidness. It sometimes got people wondering if he wasn't a tiny bit on the spectrum but it never bothered her. He was one of the kindest men she knew. Or he was, until that point.

"So, the thing is, Jules thinks it would be better if you didn't go to the after party."

"Sugar?" said Seb who'd been busying making tea and hadn't heard the last bit.

Can a Leopard?

"No, no tea thanks. Changed my mind."

"What are you talking about?" said Carla her stomach plummeting, her mouth dry - the fight or flight instinct kicking in.

Jack appraised her coolly. "Well, you've been to Italy, haven't you?"

Carla felt every bite begin to tingle. Fight it was.

"And?" she said bluntly.

"Well, some of the parents are worried that you might be contagious. That you might have picked up the virus on your travels and be asymptomatic. They don't think you should have gone."

"It was perfectly legal," said Seb quietly. "Italy's in an air corridor - no quarantine required."

"Did you *see* our plane?" said Carla indignantly. She fished out her phone. "Here! Take a look! There were exactly eight people on our flight! It was safer travelling and being in Italy than it is being here. Safer than walking down College Street!" *Than you being here!*

Jack looked away. "No doubt, no doubt. But parents are worried all the same. They're worried about the fact that you were in airports."

"I just said, the place was empty."

Seb's turn to pull out his phone.

"It's true Jack. You saw this right?" Seb showed him the photo he'd taken of Heathrow when theirs was the only flight arriving into T5.

Jack groaned. "And you posted it all on Facebook!"

"I'm not on Facebook," said Carla coldly.

"Insta then,"

"Ah… I get it," said Carla stung. "These so-called 'people' love to see what we're doing. What a bunch of hypocrites! And chippy to boot. We chose to go, any one of them could have done the same thing. Clearly, they could all do with a few days off themselves. Nosy bastards. Trolls the lot of them!"

She glared. Seb did his familiar pushing down air gesture with her - the one that was meant to alert her, the one that said: '*Steady now, Jack's a friend.*' All it did was enrage her all the more.

"You took a risk."

"No, we didn't," snapped Carla. "There was zero risk. Any one of you could have done the same. I think now is the *safest* time to travel because everything is so empty! And the flights are dead cheap."

"Yeah, well the hotel wasn't," said Seb under his breath.

"Well, well," said Jack getting up to leave.

"I'm guessing that's a definite no to tea." Seb's tone was conciliatory. He didn't seem in the least put out.

Carla followed Jack to the door, Seb hot on her heels. He stood close behind her, so close that his jeans' belt dug into her back. She tried nudging him out of the way, but he wouldn't move holding her firmly, a hand on either forearm. Carla knew it had nothing to do with affection. Seb was fearful she would say something he might regret.

Can a Leopard?

Jack had one (unsanitized) hand on the doorhandle. Carla opened her mouth to comment on the irony of it, the fact that the three of them had been in closer contact with each other than she and Seb had been with anyone on their travels, that they'd spent longer with Jack than with anyone else recently, that for someone spouting messages about Covid, here he was happy to touch all manner of surfaces without washing his hands. Reading her mind, Seb's fingers dug into her.

But Jack turned before she had a chance to speak.

"Oh, and don't be surprised if the school gets an email." He threw over his shoulder as left.

Carla looked at him incredulous.

"An email? What on earth about?"

"Alfie. About Alfie. Everyone knows he was staying with Hal while you were away."

Carla jerked away from Seb. "Oh, for god's sake!" said Carla her voice a decibel off a shout. "What interfering snitches!"

"Steady!" said Seb restraining her as she tried to slam the door in Jack's face. "Nice to see you as -"

"Fine!" shouted Carla. "We won't got to the bloody after party! I'm not bothered either way. But Alfie's going! He'll be at the prize-giving, the picnic *and* the after party at Jules's. Alfie has been at that school for nine years. Jules's family have been with him from the start. When did you join incidentally?"

Seb's bascule bridge eyebrows had shut tight in warning as Carla glared at them both.

"That's irrelevant," said Jack calmly. "What you want to ask yourself is, who will take him if you don't go?"

11

"They're Nikes," the low hum of Seb's baritone, rose through the floorboards from the kitchen below. Alfie's falsetto was equally insistent.

It amused both Carla and Seb that most mornings their son came down to breakfast to announce that his voice had broken when it had done nothing of the sort. It was the morning of the prize-giving for which Seb had ordered Alfie a pair of trainers online. He'd grown out of his leather lace-ups but with a long summer ahead of them during which time his feet would surely have grown, Seb wasn't prepared to buy new ones just for the one day.

Carla was working out to Jessica Smith dot TV (and her dog Peanut) in Alfie's attic lair. It was the only place where Carla could guarantee to be alone. When she had tried exercising in the kitchen, Seb or Alfie invariably trailed after her and even though it might be obvious (mat on the floor, dumbbells at the ready) that she might be in the throes of some routine or other, they would think of a million questions to ask her or step over her, with a *'no don't move I'll just'* or a *'Mu-uu-m! Darkling, where is…Can't find…?'* But escaping to Alfie's sitting room they often forgot that she was in the house at all. Despite Jessica Smith dot TV advocating the use of one set of weights, Carla had improvised on heavier dumbbells by holding two lighter ones together. Exercise equipment had virtually sold out by the second month of lockdown but she was always fearful she was going to drop one of the weights on her toe or even worse, knock out her teeth when she lifted them above her head.

Can a Leopard?

"No, they're not." Alfie was adamant if a little weary. The banter had clearly gone on for a while.

Carla carefully set down her weights with a groan. She couldn't honestly say that her body shape had changed one iota since she first started Jessica's programme. If anything, her arms felt even flabbier if that were possible. She was used to swimming daily but someone had said that at her age (lol) she had to increase her core strength and the only way to do that was by pumping iron - or in her case (very) gently caressing it.

It was another beautiful, cloudless summer's day. She could feel the hot air pushing through the French doors as she went downstairs. The kitchen windows were also wide open and every bird in Hampshire seemed to have converged on their small garden. Italy already seemed a long time ago and with it any residual *spretzzatura*. Jack's comments with regard to their trip had certainly wiped off the last vestiges of holiday glow but Carla was trying very hard to pretend that they'd had a languid, effortless time away. If she tried hard enough, she could convince herself that they really had. With that in mind and a smile in place, she went downstairs.

Seb and Alfie were huddled over the kitchen counter examining the pair of new shoes. Even Carla could see that 'NB' did not equate to 'Nike' and there was absolutely no tic visible.

"What are you talking about? There's an 'N' isn't there?"

Alfie didn't have to state the obvious. There was also a 'B'.

"They're not Nikes."

"Yes, they are."

"No, they're not."

"Boys, boys," said Carla pleasantly, relieved that it was Seb on the receiving end.

"Dad says they're Nikes," said Alfie pleadingly. For once he was dressed, his hair in its signature curtain. Carla ruffled it into a fringe but Alfie pulled it straight back.

"Mmmn…" said Carla.

"What's wrong with them?" said Seb. He had boiled the kettle for her tea and the table was set outside. She did love the way he always had breakfast waiting although Alfie spent increasingly less of it sitting with them, waking up minutes before online classes commenced. Her eyes drifted to the round table. Should she replace the rather tired outdoor cushions with brighter ones?

"Nothing's wrong with them."

"'NB' stands for 'New Balance'," said Carla under her breath.

"What?"

"It's fine," said Alfie quickly but only because Carla had intervened. She could see he was torn between wanted he really wanted and displeasing his hero father. She didn't come into the equation.

"Well then," said Seb pleased.

Alfie could see his advantage slipping away from him. "But they're too big," he said desperately.

Seb wasn't having a bar of it.

"You'll grow into them." He threw away the box dropping the offensive trainers on the floor.

"Right, breakfast anyone?"

Carla smiled. Alfie grunted and then remembering, turned to his mother.

"Have you thought about the drone?"

"No, not yet."

"What's this?" Seb took his phone out of Alfie's hands.

"I just want to show you something," said Alfie taking it back. "Or Mum," he added realising that he'd probably have more luck with her.

"OK, big guy but make it quick."

"Alfie says he'll give up gaming if he can have a drone," said Carla taking the bowls from Seb and setting them on the table.

"I could have it for my birthday?" said Alfie brightly. "I mean I've been such a good boy, haven't I? And I didn't have a party last year."

"Didn't you?" Carla did a mental check, alarmed that he might be right. Having a birthday towards the end of the summer was problematic as friends were often away. Some years he'd probably not had a party at all. "Wait, yes you did. You went ..." *What* had they done? She racked her brains. He was too big for Frankie's Fun Factory. So, it must have been... "Diving!" she said triumphantly.

"Oh, yeah..."

"Exactly." But he looked so despondent Carla softened. "Let's see," she said leaning over him, one hand on his shoulder more to be close than to steady herself. Instagram 'stories' flashed across the screen followed by the jumping jack of TikTok - something she'd not quite got a handle on. Alfie's

116

thumbs flew over the keyboard, tapping messages. Was he interested in some girl? She peered sideways but no, there were just the usual ads for dreadful computer games and messages from friends. 'Tom likes your post' popped up followed by 'Karen is-' *Karen?* Carla sprang back as though she'd stumbled on a porn site.

"Why wait?"

"What?"

Seb looked at her oddly. 'Anything to get the boy off computers…' he mouthed.

"Really?" Carla was only half aware of Alfie's face lighting up. Karen…The name pooled rock solid in the pit of her stomach. *Who the hell was this Karen?*

"Yes," said Seb. "We'll choose one in the next few days. Today you have prize-giving, then a picnic, then the party at Jules's so you'll be busy."

"I love you Dad!" said Alfie grinning then barrelling into Seb. Seb threw Carla a gleeful look over his head.

"And what about me?" she said automatically, her tone dead.

Alfie jumped from Seb to Carla, his arms going around her so tightly that she laughed, in spite of herself. She mustn't think about this Karen woman not now. Alfie's head rested against her all too briefly.

"My beautiful boy," she said a catch in her voice.

"Can I go now? Hal said he'd wait for me at the gates."

"Yes, all right," she said sniffing.

"And what must you do?" said Seb to Alfie's retreating back.

"Stay well and not get Covid."

"Yes, that and?"

Carla made a face.

"What's so funny?"

"It's just that he sounds like Jane Eyre when she's asked what she must do to avoid going to hell. She replies: 'stay well and not die.'"

"Very sensible. Like your mother says," said Seb. "What else?"

"'Hands, face, space,'" recited Alfie. It was the government's latest slogan.

"That's the one. Now off you go."

"I'll meet you in a bit!" Carla called after him wincing as the front door slammed. He'd wheeled his bike through the hall and it had scraped the paint under her newly framed prints. Not just a line of paint either but a great long chunk revealing the plaster underneath.

"What's the matter?" said Seb quietly when Alfie had gone.

"Look at the wall!" she said looking at him instead, his crazily long hair that was still dark although since lockdown there was a tiny sliver of grey at the temples. It only made him more attractive, his eyes a more pronounced blue under those bascule brows. Which were now upturned.

"It didn't work the other day," she said remembering. Anything to avoid the conversation she didn't want to have, the one that shouldn't be so difficult, that they should be able to have. Anything to chase away the instinct that was sending every alarm bell chiming through her entire body.

"What didn't?" Seb said patiently. He was chewing the end of his glasses having followed her to the front door. He ran a finger over the gouge in the paint work. "Easily fixed."

"Tower Bridge," she said. "Except it wasn't. Easily fixed, that is." She brushed past him and went back to the kitchen to begin loading the dishwasher with their breakfast dishes. Her hands were shaking as she dropped cutlery into the tray. Her mouth was dry and every word was forced. Why didn't she just come out with it? Ask him straight who this Karen was? Save herself this agony of speculating. But she knew what he'd do. Deny the woman was anyone and then flounce off.

"Yes, I saw that," said Seb. "The bridge failed to close. It stayed open for over an hour - caused chaos as a result." He took a mug out of her hand. "I'll do this. You get ready."

"Thanks." She avoided his look, shaking her hair in much the way Alfie had done so that her fringe hid her face.

"Everything OK?" he said mildly. "Anything the matter?"

Her phone pinged. It was Alfie's year group going crazy with all the change of plans regarding the morning's pick-up arrangements.

"Fine, everything's fine," she lied. "Just sorting this out -" she motioned to her mobile. "You are coming later, aren't you?"

"Of course."

He blew her a kiss. "Catch you in … he glanced at the small clock by the fridge. "An hour?"

12

A chorus of dysphonic pings accompanied Carla as she changed. The bush wire was working overtime but with information changing by the minute, she didn't dare ignore it. Carla once again missed the early days of total lockdown when they'd not had to contend with other parents for one thing. And that was saying something.

It had been a fraught since Jack had conveyed his message that she and Seb might not be welcome at the final festivities. Carla hadn't minded for herself but she had for Alfie. In fact, Jack hadn't been able to stay away. He'd come over again to apologise for his gaucheness, then again to explain his position vis à vis Covid and then a final time to explain Jules's. By the end, Carla had been so incensed and upset she had confided in Hal's mother who in Valkyrian splendour, and a magnificent display of loyalty and friendship had phoned Jules, relaying to him, that if any more of this nonsense continued, that if the Caves were not welcome, then not one parent from their year group would attend the after party. Carla had been nonplussed and humbled by the woman's courage and willingness to stick her head above the parapet, even though the threat was probably exactly what Jules's current girlfriend would have liked.

Carla contemplated her reduced wardrobe, reduced from before lockdown that is. She had the clothes she'd bought for Italy and the lovely new blue Temperley but she couldn't wear it in case Olivia decided to wear hers. They didn't have boys in the same year but there was every chance she might bump into her, as this was the last day of term. Carla gnawed a thumbnail and flicked through the WhatsApp messages. They were coming in fast and furious.

I don't understand where we're meeting.

Depends on your pod - the pick-up points are different

Picnic and then after party?

But is it one and then the other? Or even either or?

Up to you - everyone is welcome to both. There'll be a socially distanced picnic by the tennis courts so that we have a chance to say goodbye in person if we want. It's meant to be a safe, hassle free plan but of course if there are any concerns then feel free to bail too. Please bring your own picnic and glasses.

Does anyone know what 'collected from Mirabelle' means?

Is this a trick question?

Or a Quiz?

Or PH, deanery out garden, priory or back passage?

Do I have to explain the latter?

He he. Not going there.

Steady.

Now ladies…

It's a Leavers' quiz I knew it!

Ah, ha! 'Mirabelle' is the green outside the front door to the school

Can a Leopard?

Do you think there are other areas of the school with unusual female names unbeknown to us? Changing rooms called Ariadne for example?

The whole thing is certainly becoming a labyrinth…

In more ways than one…

There followed more banter but when it all became too silly, someone else sent through a map of the Cathedral showing the old demarcations, the underpinnings of a beautiful, medieval city. It was incredible to think of what had been, was still: of other plagues the city had witnessed and survived. On the scale of things, Covid-19 probably didn't rate much but it was the first time in history that the Cathedral, which had its roots in the 7th century, had ever been closed.

Carla pulled out a shirt dress she'd bought for Colombia in February - one of the few items of clothing she'd not sold. It had white daisies on an orange background. She glanced at the mirror. All but a few mosquito bites had disappeared - the ones on her face at any rate and as a result she felt much better. She would dress to the nines, she would be charming, she would be there for her boy. She would not think about Karen who ever she was. Nor would she mind about Jack or other parents. Today was about Alfie.

A few hours later, she and Seb went to meet their son at his school. Carla was prickly with emotion. It was thirteen years since her older boy Tom had left the very same place to go on to… the very same place. How quickly those years had flown - all so fast and furious. Only then there'd been a marquee and drinks and lovely music and the Irish prayer bidding them on their onward journey, a fair wind at their back. Now there was a faint drizzle on theirs and parents huddled in socially acceptable pods along the green - Mirabelle - as they'd so recently learned - in front of the school. Carla waved and smiled excited to be seeing so many of the parents. All but two families greeted her back.

"Ignore them," whispered Seb. "They're just ignorant. Fear brings out the worst in people."

"What? They really think we're going to be contagious? That we could possibly pass anything on to them from this distance even if we were?"

Seb raised his eyes. "Yes, and yes. You know how they are."

"I do. It's just disappointing."

Jules's Andorran, sometime girlfriend Pilar, (Pili for short and yes, given that Carla was half Spanish they ought to have had something in common) was huddled under the sprawling chestnut tree tugging furiously on an e-cigarette. Jack and his wife Claudia, were in close consultation with them. Carla nodded in their direction. The return volley was hostile.

"So, how does that figure? They're afraid of us -Jack and Claudia should be afraid of Jules and Pili! Anyone can be a carrier; anyone can be a-symptomatic! Look how close together they're standing! Besides, how many times has Jack been hurtling back and forth from ours?'

"I know that and you know that -"

Carla's phone vibrated. She could feel it through the quilted leather of her Chanel bag. OK, another item she'd not got rid of. But she'd only held on to for a rainy day. And voilà! Rainy day… She glanced down.

"Oh, hello Jules," she said keeping her tone neutral and even so, noting how he had moved away from Pilar, Jack and Claudia.

"I can see you," she said amused.

"I know you can," he said sliding out of sight behind the tree. "Look, I really want you to come afterwards."

We have every intention of...

"Thank you," she said. "But really, if it's going to make people (he knew full well she meant Pili) uncomfortable, then we're happy to stay away (like hell). This is about the boys after all." And the parents. Especially the parents. By which she meant biological parents, not desperate lovers who pretended to be interested so as to endear themselves.

"Look - you know as well as I do it doesn't matter a jot whether you've been to Italy or Timbuktu -"

Oh, boy, not this again...

"Did you see the photos of our plane?" interrupted Carla. She knew he had, that Jack, Claudia, Jules and Pili had spent three mornings, one drinks, two lunches and a dinner examining Carla and Seb's every move. "It was completely empty!"

"I know, I know."

"There are more people gathered here today then we've seen throughout the whole of lockdown!"

And talking of lockdown... there were three people in our home - how many exactly were there at yours?

"I really want you guys to come," said Jules simply "It's important for us all to say goodbye properly. For the boys to say good-bye and for you and me to raise a glass to Elizabeth." At the mention of his dead wife, and her beloved friend, something in Carla crumbled and she felt ashamed of her cattiness. It had been tempting to go all out - to have a proper falling out. Or falling 'off' as her Spanish father used to say. His English was fluent but just occasionally he got an idiom slightly wrong. What did it matter if people had different opinions about Covid-19, which they surely did? They always would. Jules had been a widower for almost five years now and Pilar had somehow crept on the scene. To begin with, everyone, even those closest to Elizabeth had been welcoming. After all, they all wanted the same thing - Jules's happiness and that of his children's. But it hadn't quite worked out that way.

"The boys have been friends for a long time." Thinking of Elizabeth made her voice ragged. She glared in Pilar's direction and all her good intentions went by the by. How dare Pilar dictate what should and shouldn't be done? When none of this, the school, the boys, had anything whatsoever to do with her? Today was, and should be, about the boys and trying to put closure to the end of their time - those formative, wonderful years at an equally wonderful and special school, in as positive a way as possible. "We'll all be there," said Carla firmly. "See you at the picnic first."

She rang off and almost immediately, Jules reappeared from behind the tree. She saw him shove his phone in his back pocket, then, his hand on the nape of her neck, draw Pilar close. Carla watched them a moment longer. Oh, Elizabeth, she thought addressing her dead friend. If you could see him now. How you would squirm and turn and fight to be back on this earth! Then again, who could tell what really went on in a marriage; who was the strength, the glue, who was the pivot, the kindness, the one who loved more?

And then the boys were out - well 'out' - they were kept strictly within the confines of the school yard. From behind the school gates, the headmaster shook hands with the boys individually as they exited. There were no formal farewells for the staff and Carla felt her heart sinking, her stomach clench with nostalgia - a mourning for what had been and a frisson of anxiety for what was still to come. Everywhere were ghosts; not even Mediaeval ones but the spectres of the teachers and pupils who had died, the ones who'd survived, the marriages that had come together and apart, the businesses created and failed, the relationships challenged by the pandemic, the loud characters and the quiet, the fizzing, vibrant, exuberant ones like Elizabeth strong enough to take on the world, but who had left it all too soon.

"Going to miss this are we?" The class rep's arms were full of flowers.

"A bit," Carla conceded.

The boys had ripped off their tweed jackets and were signing each other's shirts - a Leavers' tradition. Alfie looked as if he might burst into tears at any moment. Carla tried to catch the headmaster's eye but he too reacted as if she had the plague staying well behind the gate.

"Mr. Totter!" she called. "I just want to say good-bye!"

"But I see you all the time!" he said scurrying back into the school.

Carla felt deflated, small and irrelevant. And just ever so slightly foolish.

"Do you think he's like that with all the Mums?" said the Class rep.

Carla shrugged. She'd actually thought she meant something, had made a difference. Arrogant of her really.

"Are you coming to the after party? Or did you decide to stay home?"

Carla looked into clear, guileless blue eyes and wondered for a moment...

"Oh, we're coming," she said breezily.

Can a Leopard?

The picnic on the fields by the river went off pleasantly enough. Parents drank bubbles in their 'bubbles' the boys forgot all about theirs behaving like a pack of puppies, jostling with each other, tripping over each other - hanging on to the last precious moments of boyhood when they transitioned from being boys to becoming youths. Some were tall, their voices really had broken, others like Hal and Alfie were still small, affectionate children struggling with their emotions, trying to process six months of lockdown and saying goodbye to nine years of prep school. Carla blinked away tears. They'd all started out with such high hopes, such concrete belief in a future. Pilar smouldered unhappily under one of the trees. Even the kindest of the Mummies ignored her today. The day was about the boys not about making Jules's girlfriend feel less neurotic. Naturally most of her glowering was aimed at Carla.

"It's got nothing whatsoever to do with Covid," said Jaz one of Carla's closest friends.

"I know," said Carla. "But it doesn't make it any less selfish. For once you'd have thought, just for once… it could have been about the boys."

Jaz clinked her glass with Carla's.

"Does a leopard ever change its spots?" she said.

"It's more a question of can it? I don't think it's possible. For all the will in the world. She can't help herself."

"It's so sad. She had so much good will towards her to begin with. Everyone rooted for her and she still isn't happy. I mean what is there to stop her, either of them from being happy?"

Carla shook her head. The subject of Pilar had dominated their lives for the past year now. They all turned over the conundrum that was the woman - examining her from every angle and yet no one could understand from why she always seemed so miserable. And utterly self-absorbed. They all loved Jules; they all loved his children. Some of them like Carla, had been hand-picked by Elizabeth before she died. She called them her 'group of steel.' A steel ring around her family to love and protect and guide and comfort in the dark days that would follow. Each allocated a specific task - some had taken it a little too literally. Carla was pretty certain Elizabeth hadn't meant 'comfort' to mean of the sexual nature - but by and large they'd all tried to honour her memory and do their duty.

Elizabeth had been energetic and efficient in life but her death turned her into something extraordinary; heroic, dignified and beautiful. Carla still had the bauble Elizabeth had left for her, to be opened on Christmas day, after her death. '*For all the playdates and loveliness and fun - bring on 20-*' which was courage of an entirely different calibre when you are writing cards knowing full well you won't live to see Christmas, let alone the New Year…

"She's so insecure. It's all about control. Even on this one day. One small day given over to someone else…"

"Mmmn…?" Carla couldn't manage much more. She felt a crying gag coming on.

"And look, here we are talking about her still!"

"To the boys!" said the Class rep squeezing her arm.

"To the boys!"

There was a piercing scream.

"What the hell?"

Can a Leopard?

"Hal has fallen off the bridge!" shouted Alfie running from the direction of the river. He was as white as his shirt, his curtain hair tangled. "His leg looks really weird."

13

"So, the after party never happened," Carla heard Seb say. "Yeah, I know." He was on his phone sitting in the sun. Was he talking to Karen she wondered?

"I'm going for a walk," whispered Carla.

"I'll come with you!" said Seb jumping up. "Gotta go!" he said into the phone. "Just Brother Dom," he said when they were on the street.

"Oh."

Seb whipped out a mask from his jeans pocket hooking it around his ears. It was difficult to recognise most of her friends behind theirs but Seb's long hair and lithe physique made him identifiable no matter where he was. He looked rather dashing but that wasn't the point.

"I'm not shopping," she said. "I was just going to walk the loop - up St. Catherine's Hill."

Seb nodded. "I know." His voice was muffled. "But Dom says if there's another spike…"

"There's not going to be another," snapped Carla. "Sorry," she said quickly. They didn't agree at all on anything to do with Covid.

"Well, I'm back in the firing line with my age and fragile health."

Carla halted in the hall. "Fragile health!" she echoed. "Since when?"

"Oh, Carla, sweetheart," said Seb holding the mask away from his face. "You know the state of my lungs and then there's the cess pool we were forced to swim in as kinds in Zim."

"Yes, what about it."

"It was vile."

"Yes, and you always said it upped your immunity no end. That's why you haven't got cancer."

"Not yet," he said grimly.

"Where's Alf?"

Carla couldn't see his bike by the front door -the gouge in the paintwork was still plainly visible - or in the garden.

"Oh, he went out earlier."

"I don't mind what he does just as long as he's not on a computer."

"No, he's out. I've just said."

They closed the front door behind them and Seb began striding down the street, head held high.

"Anyway, as I was saying. Dom thinks that given my background, a mask is a good idea."

"Or the healthcare equivalent of trident," muttered Carla.

"I'm sorry?" Seb slowed to a halt, looking at her in amazement.

Carla pursed her lips. Was this the time to say, as an anti-masker, that she really thought that the bits of cloth were government-issued ball and chain? Obviously, she wouldn't slobber over anyone to prove the point and she always complied when required. She stole a glance. Seb was far from amused.

"Have you been asked to shield?"

"What?"

"Well, have you had a letter from your GP confirming that you're one of the vulnerable?"

"I don't need a letter to tell me that," sniffed Seb.

"OK, one simple question."

"Y-yes?"

"Did you or did you not play polo yesterday."

"Chukkas - not a game."

"Technicality. Chukkas."

"Actually, not even. Stick and ball."

"OK, stick and ball. Whatever."

Seb looked shifty.

"I did."

"What was that?"

"I did!"

Can a Leopard?

Carla marched on grumpily ahead. She was aware that she was being unreasonable but she was tired. Tired of the long six months of sameness and bored to death by the lack of variety: the same walks, the same clothes, the same beautiful bloody weather. And if she was honest, she even welcomed the acupuncture sting of jealousy regarding this Karen. Which was probably nothing and because it was probably nothing, Carla didn't really want an answer either way. At least it was a shift in emotion. At least it made her feel something other than completely bloody, boringly content.

The challenge to survive lockdown had been overcome. They were no longer needed to carry out deliveries for their local general store, there was no need to cut up clothing for PPE or masks (that corner of the market had been bagged yet again by the Chinese) and there was no real need to work out to Jessica Smith dot bloody TV, as sports club were offering outdoor exercise classes. Finally, best of all, there was no real need to bake sourdough or cookies or cakes (that Alfie only picked at anyway) as shops were back to pre-pandemic stock levels. What Carla missed was live music and theatre, something no amount of Zoom or live streaming could ever replace. But above all, she missed choice; the freedom to go about unhindered, unfettered by wokeism and nonsensical government mandates.

It was another hot day, in a safe, beautiful city where the number of Covid deaths was on the decline and had been for some weeks now.

"How's Hal's leg?" asked Seb.

"Still broken," said Carla curtly. He knew better than to raise the bascule or anything else for that matter.

They ploughed on in silence along the water meadows to St. Cross. The once muddy fields were dry and parched. Teenage girls in tiny tank-tops sunbathed along the river, topless men jogged on parallel paths, old people almost embarrassed to be out, guiltily clung to the shade. They took the paved road that circled the hill to the steps.

"That's odd," said Seb.

"It is," agreed Carla. They must have passed six or seven policemen on bikes along a route usually frequented only by people walking or mothers pushing strollers. "Oh, my God," she said edging close to him and taking his hand. "You don't think Pilar has said something about us coming back from Italy, do you?"

"Ah, my guilty little Cath-o-lick." said Seb amused by her alarm. "You think the police are here for us?"

"Maybe. Because of quarantine?"

"Don't be ridiculous."

"Didn't think so either," she said dropping his hand. Except she had. The woman was capable of anything...

Carla was self-consciously aware of the police. Uncomfortably aware. They were weaving behind them. Despite Seb's attempt at reassurance, Carla felt anxious. Could Italy have gone back on the amber list reserved for countries going back into lockdown? She didn't think so. She knew that Portugal and Switzerland were hovering. That Greece had come off, but some islands had gone on.

"Excuse me," Seb had turned on his heel forcing one of the police officers to brake abruptly. "Is there any reason for so many of you? We've seen at least seven of you guys during our walk."

Carla held her breath preparing her answer, their defence. Pilar was bitter, everyone knew how she felt in competition with Elizabeth even though Elizabeth was dead. She didn't feel Jules loved her enough, or he did but would he have chosen her over Elizabeth had they met when the latter was still alive? Did the children like her? Love her? Did his friends? She was just unhappy. The ring of steel cut her a lot of slack but sometimes Pilar was her own worst enemy. And their flight had been all but empty - never mind Heathrow. Here look at the photos! (She'd never shown pictures of a plane so many times.) The same went for their hotel. Which had been half full.

Her hand was in her pocket ready to whip out her phone and show him. She'd access Instagram first, it was always easier somehow to find that, rather than trawl through photos. She'd once made some poor, unsuspecting granny at Alfie's school wait a full twenty minutes while she tried to find a photo of the poor woman's grandson.

"There's been an incident," said the policeman. He pulled his bike over to the fence to allow other walkers to pass, indicating that she and Seb should do the same.

Carla swallowed.

"What kind of incident?"

"Involving children. Indecent exposure."

And all at once it came back to her. Now's your chance...

"I don't know if this is relevant," said Carla slowly. "But a few weeks ago, I saw a naked man."

The policeman looked from her face to Seb and then back again.

OK, now I feel really foolish, thought Carla. *Never speaking up again...*

She half turned to go.

Can a Leopard?

It's completely relevant," the policeman said quietly.

Carla could feel the joke rising in Seb but didn't dare look at him. There was a small silence filled after a few moments by children shouting. Was a mother's response the same in every language? *No crideu! Ne crie pas! Don't shout! Keep your voice down!* Carla would always remember other sounds too: a bicycle bell, a dog's bark, the policeman's two-way radio, his two mobiles, his (she had time to count them) seven pens lined up in his neat black vest as they creaked against the hard plastic of his gilet.

"Where was that exactly?" the policeman took out a note pad and began scribbling.

"St. Cross. By the water meadows. Does that fit with what you have?"

He nodded.

"Oh," she let out a whistle of breath.

"Can't say too much at this point but a family was picnicking just about where you say you saw the man. On the field opposite St. Cross. The children - five in total- went off to play hide and seek. All but the youngest came back. A little girl of six."

Carla felt her knees begin to twitch.

"When they eventually found her, she said that a naked man had exposed himself."

"But - but nothing else?" her voice croaked.

"No. The children gave various descriptions. You know what kids are like. And the youngest couldn't remember much. We're being cautious. We want to don't want to alarm the kids too much or ask them too many questions."

Can a Leopard?

Carla nodded her thoughts whirling, her response extreme.

"Could it be 'my' man do you think?"

"We don't know. But the location fits. Your description fits. Would you be willing to give a statement?"

"Yes, of course."

Again, Seb looked at her surprised.

"And your name is?"

Carla ran her tongue over her dry lips.

"It's Cave, Carla Cave." And then she added 'Dr'."

It was the policeman's turn to express surprise. Normally, she loved that moment, relished the moment even, keeping it bright and polished and honed, judiciously in reserve for the most deserving: pompous men at dinner parties, aggressive career women, the arrogant brainless children of the absurdly wealthy, the entire staff of shops on the Avenue des Anglais and a select few among the female flight attendants on Iberia.

Only this time, she'd said it to lend credibility, if only in Seb's eyes, to what she had witnessed. And what was that exactly? What exactly had she seen? A naked man. That was all. He hadn't done anything. She'd not seen his face. They'd not spoken and yet everything about the encounter was wrong. Even in the re-telling, she felt a seismic shift, felt the protective walls of her psyche begin to crumble and other stronger emotions break through the barrier. And here it was, that other memory lifting off the thin scab of a wound she never even knew existed. And here it came again, only in more detail. The same beginning, the same memory only this time complete, seeping pus and venom on to a clean foreground.

Can a Leopard?

*

Time stopping was a cliché and yet the minutes seemed interminable as the policeman and Seb considered her words, her expression, her tense figure. But she was no longer aware of either of them consumed in that moment by a purely visceral reaction, her body folding with the effort of rationalising the experience. Time stopped now as it had so completely then, taking her back through the years to the village hanging in the clouds.

Carla would always recall the eerie silence broken only by the trickle of water descending from higher terraces. Carla remembered that she had even lost the man Khalfan and so had paused by a frankincense tree to take stock of her whereabouts. She remembered the absurdity of being puzzled by geometric shadows expanding beneath palm fronds. The sound of her breathing hammered in her ears. She looked ahead. There was a flash of robe, a barked order. Khalfan was on the move again.

In clear flashes she remembered the slightly ludicrous sight of him, hopping from one slippering stone to the other. Her breathing was increasingly ragged, her sense of panic growing with every step they took further into the hills. Everything in her screamed a warning; her instinct told her it was all wrong. And yet, she reasoned, Mungo knew the Middle East, he knew Oman. He would never have brought her to this place if he hadn't thought it was safe. He must know local custom. Perhaps he was right. She, with her naïve Western ways was quick to judge theirs, insulting them with her suspicions. Supressing further unease, she concentrated on clambering over rock crevices, sometimes having to pull herself up on all fours.

Can a Leopard?

And then it was that moment, when everything stopped, even her breathing as she sucked in air. When he'd turned to her with the knife.

*

"Tell me about him," said Seb reaching for her hand as they retraced their steps. "Your naked man."

Which one?

Seb was still making light of the affair even after hearing that Naked Man had exposed himself to a little girl. 'It could have been a friend's child,' exploded Carla. 'It could have been Alfie!' The children they knew were all so trusting, so polite. It troubled Carla now that although the three of them usually set off on walks together, Alfie nearly always ran back alone, eager to resume whatever ghastly computer game he'd been playing. She would invariably hesitate, and to appease her, Alfie would say he was building something wonderful in Mind Craft (which she didn't mind as much as other games) or that he was playing with a classmate who was desperately ill. There wasn't a mother in his year who could say no to that. But how would Alfie have dealt with seeing a naked man? Would he have been frightened? Pushed the man away or stood frozen as she had once, for that split second? She shuddered. The pressure on her fingers increased, anchoring her to the present.

"He's not *my* naked man," she snapped.

"No, OK."

Seb didn't contradict her or remind her that she had said 'my naked man' earlier. He glanced at her; Carla looked away. She knew that no matter how upset she was or unsettled by memories from the past there was no need to be irritable. She was aware that she was impatient with him and had been for a while. Ever since total lockdown ended. Ever since Italy. Something was splintering between them but she couldn't say what exactly.   She needed to try harder. She took a deep breath.

"I don't know how to describe what was wrong exactly," she said more carefully.

"Apart from being stark naked."

"Well, that, obviously." She could tell Seb hadn't grasped at all how traumatic she'd found the experience. They'd turned back in the direction of the policemen, following their tracks as they weaved in and out of other cyclists who had taken to owning the route although it was meant to be shared with other walkers.   Children on scooters, a group of boys carrying a paddle boat and the usual regular joggers crowded the path.

"I didn't see his face at all and yet there was something odd. He was doing this jigging movement."

"Oh, yes?"

"No, nothing like that," said Carla. She couldn't, wouldn't make light of this. "It was a sort of dance. You know as in some of those Scandi films we've seen were there's a tattooed man rising out of a lake, or-"

"Did he have tattoos?"

"No."

You're missing the point...

"Actually, I meant the other one. The one in Oman."

Carla could see that Naked Man by the river didn't rate with Seb. He'd dismissed him as unthreatening to him but the

Can a Leopard?

Oman story which had occurred when she'd been with Mungo, was a narrative over which Seb had no control. She wasn't sure she did either.

Carla pulled away her hand, flexing her fingers. Had she ever told Seb about what had happened? Not really. She'd never told anyone. But she realised now that her overreaction to Naked Man, had everything to do with the other. She'd relived the experience in her head several times now, and each time the images returned in more detail. But talk about it? Where was the language, the neutral words to somehow trivialise the fear, the terror, the moment she thought she might die? How to craft a story in which Seb might take part and in so doing, not feel threatened or jealous?

And yet and yet… she would dearly love to describe Oman to him, a country that was still 'new' with limited access for Westerners. The arrival of Petroleum Development Oman had put the country on the map a mere twenty years after its Sultan declared, *'the people shall not have what they want but what I think is good for them!'* This was, after all, a country where the state issued postal stamps although there was no postal service and passports valid only for Egypt and Saudi. When Carla arrived, the capital was full of signs that hinted at an Arabian Nights past: Burq al Kabrita, Bait Al Alam (The Palace), Wadi al Uwar, while the dramatic approach from itself to Muttrah, with Fort Jalali on its own little peninsula shaded by mountains, was breath taking. In the distance, jutting out from Muscat Harbour, the fortress built by the Portuguese in the sixteenth century, boasted canons bearing the coat of arms of George III.

The country promised adventure - the combination of all that Carla hoped for, loved best: historical buildings set against azure sea and skies. The only cloud on the horizon was the mandate to find romance wherever she could. Eugenia was clear on that score. Carla was there to find a husband, at least to return with the promise of one. What had not been on the agenda was what happened in Misfah. It was not something she could talk about now, in between throw away comments about Covid, and the end of the furlough scheme.

"Oh, that," she answered Seb airily. "It was a long time ago."

14

The dinner party was in full swing -well Carla wasn't sure you could call it either. Now that they could have members of two other households visit out of doors, Carla had invited two other couples. The problem was that no one had done anything or been anywhere (the subject of their recent trip to Italy was well and truly exhausted) and the conversation was drifting, lacking in both humour and originality.

They'd spoken about mask litterbugs, rigged elections in Belarus and the poisoning of the opposition candidate Alexei Navalny (which naturally President Lukashenko claimed was fake), the ghastly tragedy in Beirut, the blast effects of which had been felt as far away as Cyprus, the return to lockdown in Spain, the closure of Hungary's borders to all foreigners (never mind the rest of the world: Bali, New Zealand and Australia were also pretty much closed to foreigners), the requirement to self-isolate when returning from some Greek islands (and a host of other nations), the need for a unified approach throughout the United Kingdom (which was anything but at the moment) whether Sweden might have got it right after all, the chances of a new vaccine, the varied requests to join vaccine trials, (inhaled steroids seemed popular) whether it was too late to invest in drug trials (especially in Synairgen when its share price rose 540%), and finally the numbers themselves, the fact that Peru had reached first place in terms of deaths per million with 28,000. Carla found it hard to believe it wasn't even a year since they'd visited that glorious country on the equally glorious Belmond Andean Explorer. And then they fell silent. For once, no one had the energy to mention Trump.

The other problem was that they all had such a magpie approach to debating. They were all pretty adept at using social media: they could tweet and text and zoom but that's as far as it went. None of them had any real insight into current affairs. Carla had an online subscription to various dailies but skipped everything to do with Covid-19. She was so fed up with the whole thing. None of them present could claim to be a scientist. Had Gemma been a guest, (founding member of Les Girls) she'd have pointed out that there was a 'hierarchy of evidence' in classifying data quality and as far as Carla understood it there'd been descriptive-only studies, without using controls. Furthermore, that all Covid policy: lockdown, social distancing, face masks, quarantine, R-numbers etc., derived from this premise and wasn't peer-reviewed. This was something she understood, that made sense, that was common sense.

Seb, who did fancy himself a scientist took a different line and made it personal. He was fearful, reminding everyone that because of his age and history of ill health he was the walking dead. Carla's knees twitched with irritation. With every sip of wine, one half of the other couple grew louder as the other male grew quieter. Bored, now that he had made his various pronouncements, Seb's eyes closed and Carla knew that if she didn't act quickly, he'd be snoring in minutes. She was too far away to aim a kick in the shins.

The quieter of the two men had cut up his food into minute baby-size pieces and was eating slowly, setting down his fork between mouthfuls. The female half of the married couple was as cheerful as if Covid had never happened, as though the world was still available to them, still their plaything, as if schools would re-open in September. Carla felt tears prick her eyes. Things were supposed to be so much better, weren't they? Now that pubs, restaurants, hairdressers and shops had reopened. So why did she feel so low? She cast a glance at Seb's drooping eyelids, or this remote from him?

Can a Leopard?

Carla got up from the table to make more coffee. The weight of the cafetière was worthy of working biceps with Jessica Smith dot TV. She balanced the milk jug with her other hand. Tripping on her overlong Alice Temperley jumpsuit (not even having the chance to wear it tonight had cheered her up) she leapt sideways when Alfie shouted, "Duck!" Hugging coffee and milk jug, Carla sank into a side lunge as a sudden buzzing whizzed past her ear. Amazingly, she managed to splash the minimum of milk on the hem of her pants.

"Alfie!" she squealed as the newly acquired drone neatly decapitated her beautiful blush-coloured roses. Surviving wisps of lavender poked through the bald fuzz of foliage. "Oh, Alfie!" she repeated in dismay.

"Sorry Mum!" he said cheerfully chasing after the drone which he steered onto the patio - a move that proved much more successful than any amount of coffee might have done in terms of rousing Seb. Her husband jerked awake, the artist screamed, the quiet singleton bit down on his fork loosening a tooth, and Carla's singleton female friend grabbed her hair or what was left of it. The drone had managed to slice off her ponytail at the crown.

"Oh, it's not mine," she volunteered pluckily as Carla looked on aghast. "I don't mind a bit.

"Alfie, control that thing!" yelled Carla as it continued to hover above their heads, its blades whirring menacingly. Every few seconds, a branch of overhanging honeysuckle or rose or fig fell with a flourish onto their laps

"That's enough!" said Seb patting his own long locks protectively. "Go on, take it inside!"

"Not the drone!" said Carla fearing for her china and soft furnishings. "Bring it in, make it land, whatever you do to make it stop."

Can a Leopard?

After a few aborted attempts Alfie managed to land the drone without further mishap, carefully folding its spider-like legs flush against its body and carefully replacing it in its box. There followed a discussion about the technology and efficacy of drones in general and whether or not a license was required to fly one, which there was. The singleton friend whose tooth had loosened (more apologies - promises to pay for a private dentist etc.,), returned from the bathroom where he'd gone to inspect the damage. None of the other guests had used the loo all evening, but he said that Covid was the least of it given what he'd just experienced at the dinner table. Someone else brought up the subject of privacy laws.

"Any images taken from a drone are subject to them," argued Hugh (half of the married couple), Genevieve his wife was the city's famous artist.

"From what distance?"

"150 feet"

"You think?"

"Something like that."

As long as they didn't get on to the subject of personal injury, Carla didn't mind.

The buzz of the drone had been replaced by the ra-ta-tat of gunfire she could clearly hear coming from Seb's study. In between moments of quiet, Alfie and his friend were happy to blow each other to smithereens. A semblance of calm returned. The night was balmy and thanks to the freshly shorn blossom, sweet and fragrant. Carla felt the evening settle and the apprehension she'd felt earlier dissipate gently. A gauzy spider's web settled above Seb's head and she moved to uncoil it, shaking it off her fingers. She bent over him, hoping that now was the moment when he would look up and catch her eye; that now was the moment when he would catch her hand, in the gesture that let her know everything was all right, that would send her back to her own place reassured and compliant. But he was looking past her.

"Someone's at the door."

"What?"

But even as she straightened, she could see Alfie clearly through the sash windows, the length of the house to the front door which was wide open. He was talking to two police officers. The same men she and Seb had seen on their walk up to St. Catherine's Hill.

"I'll go," she mouthed to Seb who couldn't have moved anyway, wedged in as he was at the foot of the table by the Roman wall on one side and the shoulder-high herbaceous boarder on the other.

"Never a dull moment, eh?" commented Hugh.

Carla left the hum of conversation behind her as it turned to the government's test and track and whether or not they should download the NHS App. Seb's eyelids once again began to droop.

"Alfie," she said orientating her son's shoulders away from the entrance and in the direction of his room. "Go and get ready for bed."

"But it's early!" he protested pulling at his curtain hair and looking apprehensive.

"We just wanted to up-date you," said one of the policemen and catching Alfie's openly curious expression, said cryptically, "on that other matter."

"Mum?" hissed Alife tugging at the tie hanging loose on her halter so that she arched backwards like a horse being reigned in.

"What?" said Carla. "You need to go up to bed."

"So, it's not to do with the drone?" he whispered in her ear.

"No, of course not," she whispered back. "Should it be?"

Alfie shook his head violently.

"Well then, don't worry about it. Go on up. I'll come and say good night in a bit."

When Alfie had thumped his way noisily down the corridor and up the stairs and she could hear him bouncing his way to his attic rooms, she motioned to the policemen to follow her into the living room.

"Can I get you anything?" she asked. "Cup of tea? Water?"

They shook their heads. There was a whirring from their radios and one of them dropped his chin to listen to the barrage of staccato drummed directions.

"Oh, should I be wearing a mask?"

"Not if you don't want to," one of them said.

Carla sank into one of the two sofas in front of the fireplace and motioned to the men to be seated. She could see them visibly relax, happy to be off the streets. She was equally happy to be away from her dinner guests, enjoying albeit briefly, the quiet room, the prettily arranged anemones in their crystal vases.

"This is a nice area, isn't it?" he said looking around him appreciatively. "We don't get called out here."

Can a Leopard?

Well, that's a relief …

"Is it busier now? With Covid?"

Carla kept her tone light. They'd said, 'an update' and if the news had concerned one of the twins, they'd have said surely? She wasn't alarmed - her internal radar wasn't triggered. On the contrary, she sank back against the sludge linen cushions suddenly exhausted by the evening. They'd socialised so little since lockdown that they were out of practice and as much as she craved company, anything to feel pre-lockdown normal, she tired quickly. She was happy to leave her friends with Seb, who no doubt would come looking for her shortly. He liked to sit back and let her do the talking.

"It's picking up," said his partner. "We've got all the homeless off the streets because of Covid and housed them in the Wessex Hotel."

"Lucky them," Carla murmured. The Wessex wasn't luxury but it was a perfectly clean and decent place. She said this. The older of the policemen - a redhead with a kindly smile, shook his head.

"Not any more it's not," he said. "They've trashed the place. Has to be refurbished."

"And with pubs re-opening fights have broken out." He lived near Salisbury, he explained, but worked in Winchester. He'd requested a transfer as he found it increasingly difficult bumping into blokes he might have arrested when he went to the pub. But on his way into work this evening, he'd already broken up several fights.

"It's mad," he said. "And no end in sight."

"No," Carla agreed.

There followed a few moments of silence broken by more fuzzy interference. Carla heard woman's voice from the control centre which the first policeman ignored.

"We thought we'd call in for an update on that man you saw."

Carla grasped her hands. Now her internal radar was picking up.

"Oh, yes?"

The redhead looked away, taking in the heavy, interlined curtains, the candles, the velvet cushions, the external trappings of a certain kind of life.

"There was a rape a few days ago," he said. "Quite a violent rape involving a knife." He let the words sink in but they didn't have to. His voice seemed to fade as through a funnel or tunnel or both.

"Where?" Carla's didn't seem familiar to her, it came out high-pitched, strained.

"Up by the bridge. Whiteshute Lane. On the way to Sainsbury's - it's -"

"Yes," said Carla. "I know where you mean. You don't think...?" Her voice trailed.

He nodded. "Obviously we're not jumping to conclusions but we're trying to find out whether the incident is linked to the indecent exposure. If the man you saw might be our rapist, whether the two are connected."

Carla sucked her teeth. "Did you say 'knife'?"

The policeman's was impassive. "Yes, and in broad daylight. The victim was threatened at knifepoint."

"I see." Carla concentrated on the small details, trying to steady her thumping heart, the way he said, 'broad daylight'. She'd read an amusing article in *The Spectator* recently, that said it was a phrase used by sub editors to deliberately make things sound more depraved. Who sunbathed *except* in broad sunlight, for example? But bad things did happen during the day. The policeman didn't have to exaggerate for Carla. Her hands were clammy with perspiration.

"So, could we run through what you saw again? We'd like to take an official statement. I'll write it down and then you can have a read through and if it's all OK, then you could sign it? That way there's no need to come up to the station, you know with Covid restrictions."

Carla nodded.

"Right then."

And all at once she didn't hear the redhead or his friend or the fact that the sound of a bird calling loudly made him cock an ear and say, 'Is that a Kite?' to which she'd shaken her head. *No idea…* and then the other man while writing notes had commented on the Peregrine Falcons nesting in the Cathedral.

15

"Just going out!" called Seb as she came down to breakfast the following morning. She hadn't heard him dressing as stealthily as he must have done, to slither out of their bedroom undetected. She'd not heard the shower, the buzz of his electric toothbrush, the transferring of change left on his bedside table to his trouser pocket, or any of the panoply of sounds that usually accompanied his ablutions. Generally, when he was awake, he wanted her and Alfie to be up too.

"Oh, OK." That in itself was unusual. Exactly where was her breakfast? Seb always made breakfast. She glanced at the table which was set with the bare minimum. The placemats - bunches of muted pink tulips (a pink Seb called 'elephant's breath') on an ochre background - were upside down. Sugar trailed from the breakfast bar to the floor when she didn't ever have sugar. Neither did Alfie. There was no signature dish porridge simmering on the grange and her tea had been made some time ago. She could feel it wasn't hot. Was it this Karen? Was that why Seb was behaving so oddly, so out of character? Carla reverted to being suspicious. Seb had seemed more distracted again lately. He never went out this early. And where would he go? There was nowhere *to* go. Very occasionally, if they'd run out of milk, he'd shoot out to buy a pint from the High Street if their local food store was closed. But he was always back before she padded downstairs. Besides, they did everything, apart from exercising, together.

Her phone rang the moment the front door slammed. Early too for others it would seem. It was Tom.

Can a Leopard?

"Darling!" she exclaimed. "How wonderful to hear from you!"

It had been a while.

"And you too," said Tom dryly. "Actually, Mum, I'm in a bit of a hurry. I have a telephone hearing in ten."

"Ho, ho. Good luck." Carla liked to envisage her older boy twirling in his gown, the tight curls of his wig fetchingly framing his angular face. The image didn't quite stretch to Zoom or BT Meet Me.

"Thank you," he replied politely enough but Carla could hear the desperation behind the words, to keep to the point. "I was wondering if I might borrow the car on the weekend. I need to run up to Oxford and get some stuff and then -"

"Of course, you can darling!" interrupted Carla quickly. "You don't have to ask. But the deal is you have to have dinner with us when you pick it up."

"Deal," said Tom smiling into the phone. "Will Alfie be home?"

"Of course."

"Then I'll come."

Carla punched the airt. It was months since she'd last seen her older boy. She knew that his chambers had faced all kinds of challenges since the outbreak of the pandemic - not least the dramatic decrease in civil hearings - so she didn't complain. There were no jury hearings and everything was conducted remotely, via video link or telephone. Even so, he seemed to be busier than ever for which she was thankful. He texted from time to time and during their brief chats, meted out stories about clients intended to amuse.

"Any interesting cases?" she asked now hoping to stall him.

Tom hesitated before quickly outlining the barest details. One man had gone into a shop and stabbed its owner.

"Was it because something was 'sold out'?" She felt instant sympathy. *Could* she ever go that far? It was a fair question. She thought of the tan Loewe belt she'd seen on Olivia recently. Which was so utterly adorable and would go so well with the cream Armani palazzo pants she'd had in her cupboard for years. An item that had happily survived her lockdown cull. Except they weren't called that anymore. Her forehead puckered. 'Wide-legged',' airy' and 'flowing' was the description she'd read when she was secretly trawling Net-à-Porter. Sophie called them 'street dusters' and had always fancied a pair in pink.

"What? No!"

"Oh, I thought my stab (he he) at humour was -"

"It's not. It's really not."

"No." Shame … she had a number of puns at the ready. "So, did you send him down?" Cringe. Lame she knew.

"Who?"

"The man who stabbed the shop keeper, of course."

"Ah, well, see…" there was an intake of breath. "That's when things get tricky. He has rights too."

"Rights? That's bonkers! What rights could he possibly have?"

"Well, he's pulled the Race Card for one thing."

"So, you didn't?"

"Well, I didn't obviously."

Of course, he hadn't. Tom wasn't a judge; he wasn't even a QC. There was a hesitation. Carla could hear a voice in the background. Was it Tom's girlfriend?

"Do you ever consider going back?" said Tom

"Back?"

"Yes, back to work."

"What do you mean?" She'd been genuinely perplexed. "The KPO no longer needs help with deliveries." The Kingsgate Post Office was their local general store having lost its 'post' bit a decade or so earlier. Everyone continued to refer to it by its acronym. The shop relied on the College - selling tuck to students and supplies to staff in term time. By contrast, holidays were always a lean time but Covid hadn't helped. Those who continued to frequent the shop did so out of loyalty and sense of community and a desire to see the lovely place - heart of their community - survive. The numbers of older people self-isolating had dropped. Many of them could now get out and about or knew others who could on their behalf. The one-way system in the shop starting from the adjacent house, had ceased, but you still had to wear a mask. 'Hands, Face, Space.'

"I don't mean the KPO!" said Tom dismissively. "I mean your proper work. Interpreting."

"Oh, that."

"Yes, that."

"It seems to be the one area where you can do face-to-face meetings. There are measures in place, of course: screens and hand-sanitizers. But it's only what we've become accustomed to. Should suit you."

"Why is that?" she said through thin lips.

"Well, you don't really believe in Covid, do you?"

Carla could feel her sense of glee evaporating.

"How could I not believe?" she said reaching for her laptop. She flipped it open to do a quick google. "When the total number in the world who have died with coronavirus to date is…" *Come on…!* "…is 728,796." *Phew…*

"Very good," said Tom wryly.

"I think the point to be made is 'with coronavirus.' There's a difference. Viruses have always existed. Which is why 40% of our genome is made up of incorporated viral genetic material."

Tom coughed.

"You didn't come up with that though. That's not you."

Carla sniffed. "Maybe not. But I follow Dr. John Lee. I'm devoted to him. Only person on the planet talking any sense."

Carla could hear clicking on the line. Or was that his legal brain whirring ready to slap a contempt order on her?

"Surely not the *only* person…" There was a pause. "What else does this Doc say?"

"Well, that a virus like Covid-19 isn't anything new but that our response is. That we're watching its progress in real time and that we're gaining an awareness of what viruses do rather than the abnormality of a new bug."

Can a Leopard?

"So, we should do nothing?"

"I didn't say that!" There was an unfortunate edge to her tone. "My doctor," she added more gently, "also takes umbrage with the idea of modelling and how it relates (or doesn't) to science. Any prediction made by any scientist is still just opinion."

"I'd go with that," said Tom mildly. Carla let out a breath. Squabble averted. And just in time by the sounds of it. She didn't realise she'd been so tense. But then conversations with her adult twins invariably left her stressed. She wanted things to go well, not to revert to the dynamics of former times, to be calm with them.

"So, what happened?' she said changing the subject back to the shopkeeper.

"I'll be brief," said Tom. "I really do have to go."

Carla didn't dare make the obvious pun. And he was. In summary, he told her that the police had given chase to the perpetrator who'd almost immediately suffered chest pains. He'd run directly into the nearest hospital, chased by shop keeper, bystanders and police. It reminded her of a story the twins had loved when they were little about a gingerbread man who was chased by various villagers. What was less of a fairy tale was A&E. On that particular day the wards had been overflowing not with Covid cases (of which there'd been none) but with victims of domestic abuse. Apparently, during the first seven weeks of lockdown, a call was made every thirty seconds to the police. Carla had wanted to talk about that. But Tom had been firm. "Not now."

But her elation at chatting to Tom and even sweeter, the prospect of seeing her older boy dissipated with the reality of what his visit might entail. They were a one-car household which worked pretty well most of the time. Certainly, during lockdown there'd be no need for a car at all and even now they were pretty limited as to what they could do. After mourning the loss of a swimming pool when sports clubs closed in March, she hadn't been once now that they'd opened. It was true that you got used to anything. Eventually. She used to swim four times a week, outdoors, no matter the weather. In the interim, she'd become accustomed to the face of Jessica Smith dot TV. She wasn't concerned for herself; she didn't foresee rushing to the pool any time soon but Seb had mentioned polo on the weekend, especially now that he had his new helmet. He'd need a car for that. This was when children from a former marriage (no matter how inadvertently) caused or were the result of conflict. Had Alfie wanted to borrow the car, she was certain Seb wouldn't have hesitated to lend it to him.

Carla thrust away the disquieting thoughts. Seb always said children came first therefore, there was no reason to think he'd not understand Tom's need for a car. So why did she feel this anxiety? This twinge of apprehension. Perhaps it was because she'd not felt particularly close to Seb recently. He seemed distant and because he did, so was she. Carla poured herself a cup of tea. Yep, it was tepid. It wasn't as if Tom was asking to borrow the car long term. He only wanted it for a couple of days. It should be no big deal. She poured away the tea and boiled the kettle. She'd make a fresh pot and she wouldn't think it about it just yet. She'd discuss it when they went on a walk later on, just mention it casually. In the meantime, she had Alfie to get to tennis and then on to sailing. She'd think about it later.

*

'Later,' Carla was still trying to rouse her youngest son. Mornings were becoming predictable. She began by calling up to him gently, her tone becoming ever more insistent the more she was ignored. Then, inwardly irritated, she would venture up to his attic lair reminding herself that he would soon (as in a few weeks) be a teenager, that the years to come (as with the twins) had flashed by all too quickly. *'Not soon enough!'* grumbled Seb as her bickering with Alfie commenced in earnest.

Picking her way through a trail of discarded clothes, books, cans of fizzy drink, books, a WW1 gas mask (not such an outlandish object given the circumstances) and packets and packets of brand new, unused pencils and coloured felt tips, she would then throw open his bedroom door. Despite the open plan nature of his upstairs attic room apartment, Alfie always slept with the door shut. She would invariably wrinkle her nose at the smell of boy and wet towels. "OK, that's it. Now! Tennis is now!" she would say and only then would Alfie open his eyes, sit bolt up-right, looking around disorientated. "Hi Mum, just showering first," he would say reasonably.

Then he would come down (as he was doing now) neither showered, nor dressed in his dressing gown clutching his phone.

"No phones, come on, you know the drill."

Carla plopped his cereal in front of him. Six months of good humour (on her part) was wearing thin. It was time to be going back to school. On site. Not just in a field. Since the end of term and with the prospect of a whole summer still ahead of them (it felt as though they'd already had a lifetime of summers and all of them boring as, behind them) both Carla and Seb had been in agreement that Alfie should be kept as busy as possible and off the computer. With the result that he played tennis every morning and of an afternoon, one or other parent would take him to a local (not so local as it turned out) sailing club.

"Can I fly my drone?" he said now. Carla cast a glance at the cereal, the phone and the drone. "While the Weetabix dissolves?"

"Sure." Absolutely anything was better than hearing the incessant ping of messages and video clips that kept Alfie distracted. They had a 'no phone at the table' rule but somehow, they managed to hear it no matter where it was located in the house. Even when Alfie was out, Carla imagined she heard the sound transmitting through the floorboards.

Within seconds, a whirring had begun as the drone swept through the kitchen. This time when Alfie shouted, "Duck!" she did.

Carla watched the concentration on his face as he stood in his boxer shorts, his trademark blue robe hanging loose. Alfie had rarely taken it off during lockdown, no matter the weather. It had fast become his Linus blanket. He looked so young that her heart jolted.

"Set it down now," she said gently. "Come and have your breakfast."

Alfie grinned. "Did you see that?" he said. "Did you see it hover?"

She nodded. He really was very adept - flower beheadings notwithstanding - and now he landed the device deftly on the paving stone. It looked like a giant spider, slightly menacing but also sleek in its dexterity. With utter care Alfie collapsed its wings holding its central body away from his as though it were a tortoise shell.

As if on a timer, his phone pinged the minute he sat down at the table.

"Mum, do you want to see?" said Alfie.

"No phones, darling," she said robotically.

Alife was still engrossed in his.

Can a Leopard?

"I'm not playing a game."

"Yeah, no videos either." She knew his little ruse.

"It's not," he thrust the phone. "Look, it's taken from St. Catherine's Hill. I've set it to music."

"Ah, yes." Carla glanced down. "Actually, that's incredible!"

She was genuinely impressed. He had a steady hand and wasn't alarmed when the machine disappeared from sight. It felt as though they were both riding on its back swooping low as it grazed grassland dotted with quietly grazing sheep. It soared once more above the Hospital of St. Cross before breaking through wispy cloud to reach blue skies. There was the kak-kak-kak of a falcon on a hunting stoop as the drone followed its barred white underparts before suddenly plummeting to hover just over the Handlebar Café, the wooden log-style curved building at the foot of the steep climb up. It was a perfect place to meet for a drink either before or after a long hike. As its name would suggest, it was especially popular with cycling enthusiasts offering all manner of assistance including a free pump to keep up pressures, cycle accessories and spares. There was even an on-hand bike mechanic. The cakes were good too.

"Very good, darling," said Carla straightening. "Hang on!" she said suddenly. Couples were grouped at the small tables along the balcony side of the Café, others waited beside their bikes. But there was one man in particular who caught her attention. He had shoulder length dark hair and wore a white t-shirt. His hands were in his pockets. He appeared utterly engrossed in his much younger companion.

"Is that *Daddy?*" said Carla.

16

Carla wanted to ask him. She *needed* to ask him. Carla glanced at Seb nervously. But then if she did, was she prepared for what he might say? Carla had waited a few days, hardly sleeping at night self-absorbed and distracted by day. She could feel the tension rising. She needed to sort this before, if they went away. Now that they could travel even further afield, they were supposed to be planning a summer holiday but her mind kept drifting to the Karen woman, *girl* she corrected herself. The girl in the video.

Seb was chewing his glasses in the way that irritated her most but she gritted her teeth. She viewed him dispassionately. Was he having an affair? What did her instinct tell her? She closed her eyes trying to feel an answer, willing her body to tell her one way or another but all she could hear was the rumble of her stomach - she hadn't eaten since breakfast. When she thought about the blonde in the video clip, she felt queasy. Not any blonde either but a stylish beautiful one with the elegant white blouse and jeans look that Seb loved. Actually, he preferred the jeans look to Carla's slightly over dressed one. And now that Carla thought about it, it all made sense.

Of course, Seb had been hiding something! She'd just known, he was. Even before Italy things had cooled between them. Not necessarily in an obvious way but Seb was distant, often out playing polo or now that the ban on 'essential travel,' had been replaced with 'staying alert', going god only knew where. He just wasn't his complimentary (she was still waiting for him to comment on her Temperly jumpsuit) flirtatious, tactile self. She had known it wasn't her imagination playing up or that in these exceptional times, when she had too much time to brood, the whole pandemic thing was making her paranoid.

She was hardly listening. She heard the words 'summer' and 'sailing' and even more than the words themselves, the exasperation in his voice. Seb resented the fact that they were here at all. In England that is. In normal circumstances they'd be heading for the Greek Islands on a yacht, loaded up with fins (for Alfie), mallets (for Seb) because you just never knew when you might stumble across a polo field in the middle of the Med right? and a Kindle for Carla. They still might have gone, of course, but with Alfie due to start his big school in September (the Minister for Education had confirmed that teaching would resume then), Carla didn't want to risk travelling to a country that suddenly and without warning was added to the 'no-go' list. As had happened with virtually all the islands they'd wanted to visit: Crete, Mykonos, Santorini and Zakynthos. It also seemed that every time Carla looked, some desirable destination was removed from the travel corridor with tourists scrabbling to return home before the cut off time of 4 a.m. Why was it always an ungodly hour? The alternative though was staying at home with a bored Alfie and, she shot Seb a mistrustful look, a leopard on the prowl.

"Sod, it," said Seb, talking out of the corner of his mouth and biting down on the arm of his glasses. "Why don't we just go? Take the risk? Too bad if Alfie misses a few days."

Carla blinked brutally transported to the here and now. What had he said? He couldn't be serious? Alfie had been home for six months. Not days, or weeks, but months. Carla felt light-headed at the very idea that schools might not go back in September. It had seemed incredulous back in March that Alfie might be home until Easter. How naïve had they been? Those unsuspecting, trusting months when they'd truly believed the pandemic would be over in three weeks, seemed a lifetime ago. Carla wasn't sure how they would survive another six months of home-schooling.

She fished out her phone from her pocket, frantically searching the gov.uk's website, more importantly, its updates.

"So, let's see," she said brightly. "Looking at countries where no quarantining is required on our return and coming in at number one is … the British Antarctic Territory!"

"For a *summer* holiday?"

"No, you're right." Carla continued to swipe up. "How about the Pitcairns? Or Curaçao? Actually, not Curaçao. It's just come off the travel corridor. I know. What about Cuba?"

"I'll go there!" said Alfie appearing in the kitchen, shoeless, his tennis racket tucked under one arm. "Can I borrow your phone?"

Seb glanced up.

"Aren't you going to be late big guy?" he said handing him his mobile all the same. Although technically, Alfie had his own, he preferred to use Seb's for the unlimited data, the games he was able to run on it and the speed with which those games could be run.

"Five minutes," said Alfie his fingers flicking the screen.

"You hated Havana, remember?" said Seb addressing Carla.

"I didn't *hate* it. I was hungry that's all. It was so hard to find anything to eat, let alone decent food." As if on cue her stomach did a summersault.

"Do they do roast potatoes?" said Alfie raising his head briefly.

Can a Leopard?

"No," said Seb and Carla in unison.

"There's Gibraltar - actually I'd rather eat my toenails," Carla studied the list. "South Georgia, the Vatican State -"

"What's the Vatican State?"

"Tell you later," said Carla, "this is important. I've got it! How about the Faroe Islands? Tom loves them."

Seb was virtually inhaling his glasses whole. He removed an arm briefly before sucking on the other. "Nope. I want sun and sea. I don't want to freeze my butt off."

Alfie giggled. At first Carla thought it was because of what Seb had said but then she realised that he'd slunk over to his father, waddling with his racket between his legs, to show him an image and a TikTok meme.

"Would you settle for just sea then?"

"Mmmn?" Neither were paying her any attention, their heads bent together over whatever it was that was so important.

"I said a nudist colony in Pretoria."

"That would be nice."

"Really?"

Carla closed her laptop abruptly. "OK, I'll book it. At least it will cut down on new clothes."

Seb blinked. "What will?"

"The Isle of Wight," she said grimly. "Our 2020 summer destination."

Can a Leopard?

*

"I think it will be fun," said Carla trying very hard to be upbeat later that afternoon. "To be by the sea. Alfie can take his diving gear. And a friend. We could ask Hal."

"You mean when he's out of a cast."

Oh, yeah…

"Or even with?"

"Really? With all the lifting involved if the boy can't walk properly. Would there be any point in him coming if he can't swim or go on walks?"

Maybe not. Seb was probably right. Carla was going to have to try harder if she was going to get Seb to commit to Project 'Get them to the Isle of Wight.' Get them anywhere frankly. A change being as good as a cure and all. She hovered by his study door. Seb seemed to have forgotten about their earlier discussion and was now engrossed in his writing. During lockdown he'd written a blog entitled *'Oceans Initiative' ('Did you know that fish have a chorus of song just like the dawn chorus of songbirds?'* was one of the posts) reverting to his old love. He'd studied Natural Sciences at university. 'But Zim isn't by the sea?' Carla had asked on one of their early dates. *'Exactly and that's why I was so fascinated. I love the ocean and yet I grew up in a land locked country.'* She glanced over his shoulder now. *'We tend to think of the air-water interface as a barrier to noise,'* he had written. *'Planes fly over the ocean all the time. Most of the time sound bounces off the ocean having little impact on the whales and dolphins but-'*

She took a breath. Now was as good a time as any to ask about Karen, to firm up on their holiday plan and move on. They all needed something to look forward to. She'd do it.

166

Ahora mismso. It was time to rid herself of this uncomfortable splinter in her psyche... But then she also had to mention the car and Tom... Her heart began to hammer painfully. She let out her breath.

"No rush, we can talk about it another time."

"You've just been to Italy," he snapped. "You want to go away *again*?"

Carla swallowed. *Excuse me but wasn't it you who said we should go further afield? What's changed in a couple of hours?* "No, you're right. Staycation." She patted the architrave of the door frame. "Staycation..." She thought of all the lovely holidays she'd organised: the hours spent online, or on the phone, researching, booking, re-booking, talking with tour guides, finding guides, reading up on tourist sites so that she was sometimes as informed as their guide, organizing childcare, organizing insurance, vaccinations, visas, first aid kits, clothing (not to mention footwear) for different climate zones. When they'd travelled to South America they'd gone from the frozen, snow-bound natural parks of Tierra del Fuego to the heat (during the day) of the Atacama Desert. It had all been tremendous fun and she'd enjoyed every minute but it had taken not inconsiderable effort. She scanned Seb's study. There were photos of Machu Pichu, the Great Wall of China, the opera house in Manaus, the exuberant red of shrine gateways in Japan. She'd organized them all. Staycation maybe but she wouldn't stay quiet.

"The Isle of Wight is hardly adventurous," she said trying to keep the rising irritation out of her voice. "I mean Yarmouth is probably closer to Winchester than London or Basingstoke!"

Seb turned owl-like from his desk.

"I'm busy," he said.

Can a Leopard?

There was a frosty silence.

"Fine," she said. "I'm going for a walk."

Carla felt tears prick her eyes as she went into her dressing room to kick off her sandals and grab a pair of sneakers. She called up to Alfie. The familiar tell-tale whirr of his laptop indicated that he was gaming. With the unhappy experience of lockdown, come the summer holidays both Seb and Carla had been determined to keep Alfie as occupied as possible. His free time though was his own although today she didn't have the strength to try and cajole him into coming with her.

Carla had hardly got down College Street when she heard Seb's unmistakeable tread and then his fingers locked onto hers.

"I'm coming with you," he grinned restored to good humour.

"Great," she said less enthusiastically still smarting from his earlier coolness.

The place was crowded with walkers and the queue for ice cream meandered from the van parked in front of New Piece the length of the Bishop's Palace. Children on scooters weaved in amongst dog walkers and young people on bikes all enjoying the lovely weather and the lifting of restrictions. They could all take as much exercise as they wanted now not just once or twice daily. Sports clubs had reopened along with outdoor swimming pools and golf courses. There was exhilaration in the air, relief and pure enjoyment at being with people again. But Carla was tense with the need to ask Seb about Tom borrowing their car, preying on her mind. The lingering scratchiness between them though somehow made it easier. *Right. Here goes.*

"Tom was wondering if he could borrow the car," she said her voice a squeak from holding her breath for too long.

Can a Leopard?

He dropped her hand as though she had Covid. "Why?"

"He needs to move some books." She let out her breath and felt dizzy.

"So why doesn't he rent one?"

Carla shrugged. *Because he doesn't have so much money… it's a hassle with Covid… you know it is. Take your pick! Ten different reasons probably. Besides, the last time we rented a car we had to take a taxi into Southampton to collect it as the Winchester branch had closed. In the end, the cost of two taxis amounted to three times the cost of the initial rental.*

"I don't know. He doesn't ask for much. I like to be able to help and it's really -"

"No," said Seb. "The answer's no."

They'd reached New College. If you forked left, you could walk on past the Kingsgate Tennis Club and then along the paved path to St. Catherine's Hill. If your turned right, you would reach the Alms houses of St. Cross, then the farm (where she'd seen Naked Man) approaching the same hill but from a different direction.

"You know what," she said her head throbbing. "I'd like to walk alone. I'm going this way." And she stomped off to the right, taking the longer route.

She blinked away tears. What was the matter with him? Where had the calm, patient, attentive Seb she knew and loved gone? The Seb she relied on to be consistent and strong? Was it this Karen, whoever she was? It had to be. There was no other explanation. Carla thought back over their married life. Had there been other times when he'd… lapsed? She couldn't think of any and yet what could possibly explain this moodiness, this indifference? She passed St. Cross avoiding the path where she'd encountered Naked

Man, taking the longer way around and then because that was crowded and she might encounter Seb, she opted to go straight up the hill which would wrap around the adjoining ridge before emerging on the far side of the earthworks. If she didn't feel like climbing the last bit, she could avoid that part of the walk altogether.

Although it was late afternoon, it was still warm and she regretted not having changed out of her jeans and long-sleeved silk blouse. But otherwise, she was unencumbered having left her bag and phone at home. She pushed open the wooden gate. Not many walkers chose this route as the climb was steep and overgrown, unsuitable for the disabled, pushchairs or cyclists. But it was a route she knew well often taking the opportunity to chat on her phone and catch up with friends knowing she wouldn't disturb anyone along the way. She was panting as she walked. The sun was hot on her back. Brambles and hawthorn were overgrown and she had to push against rhododendrons to clear the way. As busy as the other side of the hill had been, here it was quiet with only the occasional hum of an insect or Willow Warbler to disturb the quiet.

Wrinkling her nose, Carla could smell the faintest honey scent - well she didn't have Covid that was certain, if loss of smell was a symptom. Hunkering down, the aroma grew stronger and she was rewarded with the sight of a musk orchid. 'Herminium Monorchis', she said aloud almost whooping with excitement both that the Latin name should have stayed with her after all this time (her years as a translator for pharmaceutical companies belonged to another millennium - quite literally), and that she had found one at all. Generally, the orchids were incredibly difficult to spot, their greenish yellow tubular petals unmistakeable yet often perfectly camouflaged within a chalky or limestone habitat. She stroked the waxy, oval-keeled leaves a final time before rising slowly, shading her eyes. She marvelled that the musk orchid could reproduce vegetatively, that these pretty horizontal shoots or 'tubers' were not only beautiful but functional. They would eventually grow into new plants. As she gazed out across the Itchen Valley, she also thought it astonishing that these fairy-size bells could have scattered all over the world from Northern Asia, Mongolia, Japan and Siberia to this grassy knoll in Southern England.

Perhaps the spirit of Cameron Bespolka really did live on, guiding walkers to spot these precious gifts of nature. On the brow of the hill, was a bench erected in his memory. With far-reaching views of the city, walkers were invited to pause and sit and listen out for the Chiffchaffs and Linnets the Winchester schoolboy had so loved. She would do the same and recalibrate. She would forget about Karen. She already had. How foolish she'd been, was being! Had she learned nothing from lockdown? A couple of phrases from one of the many self-help books she was forever reading came back to her: '*Some of your hurts you have cured, and the sharpest you've even survived. But what torments of grief you've endured from evils which never arrived…*' Well, that was her. Fretting and worrying about something she knew nothing about.

As a family, they'd survived the severest months of lockdown; they should be joyful now. She should relish every moment of their new freedom, rejoice in it, not torment herself with petty jealousies - *unfounded* jealousies. Based on? She did a mental search. She'd seen the name Karen across a phone a handful of times. She'd seen an image on a video clip which probably had a perfectly rational explanation. Was that really enough to send herself into such a spiral? And the car business with Tom? She'd not worry about that anymore either. The young were constantly changing their plans. If worse came to worse, she'd simply hire Tom a car herself. Either way, a solution would be found. She thought of that other line: '*everything will be all right in the end, and if it's not all right, it's not the end.*'

Feeling much calmer and quite pleased with her newfound self-awareness, she inhaled the heavy air, thick with crushed, dried leaves and scorched grass. Her thoughts wound back

from summer to the glacial cold of the winter in which
Cameron Bespolka had died. By an unhappy coincidence
Carla and Seb and Alfie had also been skiing in Lech on the
very day the avalanche occurred: the stuff of nightmares, of
films, not the kind of thing to happen to a sixteen-year-old
schoolboy on holiday, the week before Christmas. And what
a stunningly beautiful day it had been! A picture postcard
kind of day, in a picture postcard part of the world - Lech am
Arlberg - with brilliant blue skies white capped mountains
gleaming, seemingly benign in the distance.

At one o'clock they'd been having lunch on a terrace at
Daniela Pfefferkorn's restaurant (Alfie called her 'pepper
pot') gaping at the plates of *kaisershmarnn* (Emperor's
Pancake) coming from the kitchens. The plates were
Emperor-size too, rich, indigestible (Seb always complained
of a belly ache afterwards) ribbons of rum-soaked pancakes
smothered in caramelised plums. They'd laughed and joked
enjoying the picturesque village with its onion-domed
houses, its fur blankets, its cosy pre-Christmas glamour. And
while Carla and Seb and Alfie had all tucked into their
dessert, Cameron buried in an avalanche, had died.

Even now, skiing in Austria was the place in all the world
Alfie and the twins loved best. No matter whatever else was
going on in their lives, the Hospiz, where they had stayed
every year since the twins were little, was a constant, a
second home and Florian its owner, a member of the family.
Carla thought back with a pang to those days. With
neighbouring Ischgl credited with drenching its visitors in
Covid-19 and transmitting the virus to forty-five countries,
Carla wondered if they would ever ski together as a family
again.

Lost in thought, Carla hardly noticed the group: two men,
two women, a pram and two dogs gathered by the bench.
Except that there didn't seem to be a baby and Carla
wondered vaguely how they'd managed to get the pram up
the steep hill when she had struggled, hands free, not even

having to carry her phone. She also felt mildly offended (out of respect for Cameron) that one of the men, with a beer can at his lips, should be drinking there at all. She didn't have long to wonder for the next minute she was flat on her back, her tentative smile wiped off her face as one of the dogs leapt at her knocking her completely off her feet. As her head cracked against stone, she lay prone. Dogs do this… she told herself. Sometimes they just don't know their strength. But then she felt its teeth on her back and the second dog belted forward its mouth clamping onto her left thigh, its incisors sinking easily into flesh. She gasped with the agony of skin being punctured but not released, the teeth gripping ever more determinedly, as they dragged her down the hill.

As Carla lay still, too stunned to move, as no sound came from her mouth even as she wanted more than anything to scream, anticipating what was seconds from occurring, Carla could only think back to the only other moment in her life when she'd been similarly shocked and fearful. Her mind, her body, her speech became a blank of continuous terror taking her to a whole new sphere. And the other event came back to her now almost as a defence mechanism to ward off the horrible event taking place in the present. As if her body had a memory all of its own. There was a Chinese belief that to ward off one pain, you recreated another. Well, here it was - flooding her senses now.

*

Carla didn't know Arabic, couldn't make herself understood and still she was compelled to follow. What else could she do? She had no idea where Mungo had got to either. She'd read somewhere that the Omani 'interior' was still the Wild West and its Bedouin shaiks 'loveable but rascally.' She glanced at the man's dirty feet. There was nothing of the sheik about him nor the loveable. She had no choice but to quicken her pace as they climbed through plantations and date gardens. Water trickled from the falaj system and for a while they followed its course, the snaking channels hugging red sand and stone. Ever higher, he appeared to be leaping in perpendicular ascending stages until at one moment she had had to haul herself up to a ledge, scraping her knee, ripping her skirt. This wasn't right, this couldn't be right.

Stop! Her voice at first a whisper became stronger. If she couldn't understand him, then he couldn't understand her but her speaking at all surprised him.

She was bent double, catching her breath.

"Enough!" she'd said firmly.

And then at last, he did stop, did turn, did meet her eyes. And she immediately wished she'd kept going, hadn't looked at him defiantly. They were on the smallest ledge with dizzying drops behind him and behind her, an even steeper climb vertically up towards the sky. He whipped around suddenly, and that was when she saw the flash of his knife, held limply in his fat fingers. Her gaze travelled from the knife to his face, confused. But as he took a step towards her and she could smell the body sweat odour on him, the stench of goat and sickly dates, she knew. There was no mistaking his intention. And suddenly she felt a blinding rage at the man's arrogance, his assumption that she would comply. And for the first time in her life, after years of being too frightened to say boo to a goose, she found her voice. It was as though all the pent-up silent sounds of a lifetime, were concentrated in that one clear, bloodcurdling cry. It was as if every cistern, clay pot, or jar channelling rainwater echoed with her screams to pierce limestone terraces, and steps and to reverberate through the green mountains. It was as if the sound of her scream protected her.

As he came towards her, Carla ducked. Caught off guard, the man hesitated and, in that moment, Carla seized her advantage lashing out and kicking his slender, shins with all her strength. Hearing him double in pain, she sprinted ahead and ran.

17

She would never know what made the dogs stop. Not the owners who stood watching: the man in the singlet continued drinking, the youngster didn't move at all, as passive as the two women. But for whatever reason, the dogs suddenly released her, dropping her arm, her leg, as they would a toy or smaller prey to turn their attention to something more interesting. Seb had recently told Alfie as he was setting off on his bike on one of his mystery visits into town, that he would only really stop him doing something if he knew it was going to be really dangerous. Other than that, Seb trusted him to be sensible. Alfie had looked his father in the eye and replied in all seriousness, *'But Dad, the prefrontal cortex part of my brain that assesses risk isn't yet fully developed so…'* Carla had smirked and Seb had dealt Alfie a mock punch. But she wasn't smirking now nor had she any concept of the risk involved as she jack-knifed to standing position to run straight down the side of the hill tripping over small bushes, and stones just as she had that other time. Except then, she'd run *up* the side of a mountain not down it.

Carla was too shaken to think logically. It never occurred to her to stop anyone and ask to borrow their phone and so she limped all the way home, crying soundlessly, willing someone, anyone to inquire after her, to offer help. But no one did. Once home, she rang the doorbell. She could hear the sound of Alfie's game coming from Seb's study and her son pounced on the door. He was still in his robe.

"I didn't take my keys," she said.

Can a Leopard?

"The police have just been," said Alfie sprinting up the stairs.

"Oh, my God, when? I need them."

"You just missed them," said Alfie.

"Why were they here?" Carla began stripping in the hall in front of the large mirror. She had a great desire to get rid of the clothes she'd been attacked in. Even her jewellery. In between sobs, she carried on a mundane conversation feeling hysteria creeping into her voice as she unwound her pendant from her neck, removed her earrings, bracelet even her wedding ring dropping them onto the clothing. She suddenly felt overwhelmingly tired and yet she knew she was going to have to go to A&E. If she could only remember when she'd last had a tetanus shot.

"*Mum!*" yelled Alfie in disgust from the top of the stairs.

"Sorry, darling but I was attacked my two dogs," she said grimly. Her hands shook as she peeled off her jeans and blouse and stood in her bra and panties twisting to see her back. "Where's Daddy?"

"Oh, are you OK?" said Alfie averting his eyes. "Don't know. He went out with you, didn't' he?"

Not exactly…

"What did the police want?"

"Dunno." Alfie was already disappearing into Seb's study. "Update!" he called down suddenly remembering. "They said they wanted to update."

But Carla wasn't listening. Her eye was drawn to the areas that throbbed as she twisted to see in the mirror. There was a bite mark on her right hip, just above the kidney area; another on her shoulder blade but the back of her left thigh was the

177

worst. It formed a large circle of deep puncture wounds, the dog's teeth clearly visible. Blood had pooled around the holes in thick scabs and around each of these, a wide black bruise was rapidly spreading to extend to the whole of her leg. It reminded her of a ghoulish ghost mask (with teeth), the kind kids wore for Hallowe'en.

Her phone was where she'd left it on the hall table and she picked it up now to call Seb but he didn't answer. She couldn't bring herself to text what had happened but she didn't need to. Moments later he arrived home. Carla had resolved not to be annoyed with him but the minute he opened the door, she felt irritation sweep over her. Where had he been? Surely not on a walk as she'd have bumped into him somewhere on her run back. She didn't really want to talk to him but she needed him to drive her to A&E.

"I'll take you," he said.

She'd expected a rush of sympathy, to be enfolded in his arms, tenderly told he'd kill the dogs, anyone responsible for inflicting such damage but he did neither and for a moment she stood in her underwear (Schiaparelli pink La Perla) feeling utterly bewildered.

"Put some clothes on," he said. "I'll drive you up."

She nodded stepping over her discarded jeans and blouse and went up to her dressing room. But what on earth to wear? Even now in an emergency, Carla couldn't help seeing this as another sartorial challenge. She'd sold so much of her wardrobe during lockdown - yes, a few expensive articles had crept back in but she had to consider their practicality when exposing her leg to a doctor or triage nurse. She didn't want to bleed onto any of her new Alice Temperley and she couldn't bear the thought of anything figure-hugging or too tight. She flung on the shorts and t-shirt she usually wore to work out in and grabbed a pair Hermès flats. No one in Winchester would (sensibly) conceive of spending so much on a pair of sandals so would assume them to be fake. (At least they weren't croc like H's in Italy.) She didn't take a bag or phone or bother with jewellery - not even bending down to scoop up her wedding band from the pile of clothing. She wasn't thinking straight or at all. She looked awful - a complete mess. Never knowingly overdressed…was not today's motto.

Seb flattened himself against the wall allowing her to pass.

"I've parked in Culver Road," he said.

Thank Goodness! No one will see me…

"Fresh masks," said Seb when they were safely ensconced in the car, leaning over to release the glove compartment.

"Oh, you spoil me," said Carla dryly. How on earth had they got to this? That their conversation boiled down to one about masks.

The run up to the hospital took minutes. Carla found herself waiting outside the rear entrance, sanitizing her hands and having her temperature taken, before being allowed in. A man and his young daughter were in front of her. Seb wasn't allowed to accompany her due to Covid and Carla stood in the sunshine feeling ridiculous and sorry for herself. Apparently, the little girl had also been bitten by a dog but in her case, the family pet was to blame.

"Don't wait," she said breezily over her shoulder as she walked through the heavy PVC doors. "I'll walk back."

"No, you won't," said the triage nurse. "Your husband, right? We'll call him to come and fetch you when you're done."

Which was no mean feat as it transpired. Carla's mind went completely blank when it came to giving her personal details. She stood in her tiny shorts, balancing one Hermès -clad foot behind the other in front of the counter. Two kindly women sat in front of their computer screens, appraising her with all the tenderness and concern as if she'd been a victim of domestic abuse. With every passing moment Carla began to feel like one, increasingly vulnerable in any case. She cast a glance at all the drawings by children thanking the NHS for their 'superb care.' 'Support the NHS' posters, together with all the other recent slogans to do with Covid-19, were plastered on the walls and around their workstation. Carla always felt completely in awe of hospital staff on the few occasions she'd visited friends and family in hospital. And a great need to be cocooned. Too great. Her head felt woolly as she struggled to remember the simplest information. Anyone would think she'd suffered a concussion - perhaps she had- when she'd fallen after the first dog knocked her to the ground.

She couldn't remember Seb's mobile - actually she could never remember it. She had never registered with the local doctor when they moved from the country and she certainly couldn't remember having had any jabs. Or at least non relevant to a dog bite. Their recent visit to stay with Seb's family in Zim, had been so impulsive and hastily arranged, that they'd not had time for rabies shots. She did remember taking malaria tablets when they travelled overland from Harare to Bulawayo on their way to Vic Falls. Or rather she had. Seb, as a native, said he didn't believe in them and binned his. She'd had vaccinations for yellow fever (for South America) and hep A (she'd wanted hep B but Seb said there was absolutely no chance she'd contracted that disease) and typhoid.

"OK," said the receptionist displaying endless patience and superb emotional intelligence. "We'll try this another way."

"Ah!" said Carla triumphantly. "The twins! They were born here."

Can a Leopard?

The receptionist looked up. She was a dead ringer for Jenni Murray, one pair of glasses perched on the end of her nose, the other around her neck on a chain. Her NHS ID card hung on a thick cord. Only her voice was entirely different.

"Yours?"

"Yes."

"Recently?"

"Er… not exactly." *Come on Carla. Come clean.* "Twenty-four years ago," she whispered.

"I'm sorry?"

Carla winced. "Twenty-four years ago," she said a little louder.

Twenty-four? God! How was it possible?

"Well, that's good," said the nurse. "Cave is it?"

"Er… no. Douglas-Elwes."

The receptionist began typing.

"Date of birth?"

Was this a trick question?

The nice woman (Tara said her badge) looked up, fingers poised above the keys.

Summer. Definitely summer. Or maybe Spring but it had felt like summer.

Carla counted on her fingers.

"May!" she said jubilantly. *Phew!*

"Date in May?"

Date? Oh, this was becoming ridiculous.

"25th" said Carla sighing.

Lots of typing. Tara changed glasses, now balancing one pair on top of her head and bringing the other closer to her face. She dived behind her screen coming up for air after a few minutes.

"No, nothing with that date."

"26!" said Carla suddenly. "26! Definitely, 26. Did I say 25?" She emitted a strangled giggle.

"You did. Are you sure?"

"Yes," said Carla.

There followed an interminable silence. One in which Carla began to be afraid Tara might have called someone from the psych ward to examine her. She cast a look down the empty wating room. The water dispenser had sprung a leak and water was spreading over the floor.

"Happens all the time," said Tara catching her eye before going back to her search. "Got it! Tom Cave, right? And Sophie? Twins."

I said that. "Yes."

"Birth weight 3 kgs. Head circumference 32.8."

"Gosh - never knew that."

Tara looked at her. "It would have been in their notes. The little red book? Their Personal Health Record?"

If you say so… absolutely did not ring any bells….

Carla smiled pleasantly. "Amazing the detail…" and let her voice drift.

"Here we are. Most recent vist. Coat hanger in …?" she frowned.

"Yes?"

Carla knew her memory wasn't great but she categorically didn't remember anything to do with a coat hanger. And given it had to do with clothes, she would have.

"Looks like… an … ear lobe. Tom Douglas-Elwes was admitted with a coat hanger hanging from his ear." Tara glanced up. "Unusual but I've seen worse."

Carla smiled weakly. "Must have been when he was at school."

Now can we get back to me?

*

Seb was waiting in the ambulance bay when Carla limped out of A&E an hour later. The lovely triage nurse had given her two giant pink pills which were probably Ibuprofen (whatever they were was making her woozy) and a course of antibiotics. But she was going to have to make an appointment with her GP (she'd not visited one since she'd had mastitis with Alfie) in order to get a tetanus jab.

Carla was happy to see Seb although he still wasn't showing her quite the level of concern (or interest) she expected.

"Poor you," he said and then volunteered that he'd gone back up St. Catherine's Hill while she'd been in A&E to try and find the perpetrators. Which she thought was unbelievably foolish but didn't say so.

"And did you?"

"No. There were beer cans so they'd obviously been there."

Carla sighed. "And the empty pram? What do you think that was about?"

Seb looked uncomfortable. "Not sure."

Except that glancing at his passive face Carla suspected that he was. A few hours later, just as she had got out of her bath and was planning to hop into bed, the doorbell rang.

"It's the police!" called up Alfie who was still in his robe although by now Carla had given up trying to get him to change. Come September, his next school could sort him out. "Two of them!"

"Yes, all right!" All she wanted to do was get into bed and sleep. Stepping out of her bath, a towel wrapped around her she froze, and then for the second time that afternoon, hurtled into her dressing room in a panic. It was ridiculous. Now together with summer and winter Paravel packing bags, she was going to have to assemble a 'hospital visit' one and another for 'unexpected police visits'. She grabbed the same shorts and a t-shirt. Only this time, because Alfie kept hissing, "they're waiting!" and Seb, catching up on his blog (having spent so much time looking after her - not) was firmly ensconced in his study so was unable to deal with any visitors - Carla didn't have time to put on any underwear.

Can a Leopard?

Too late, catching sight of herself in the hall mirror she realised the stretch t-shirt (nude and navy stripes) looked... well nude. Carla made an odd sideways movement to the living room as though there wasn't enough room to pass and then sank into a sofa leaning forwards in an attempt to cover her breasts which without a bra, seemed to have descended to her navel. How was it possible to have aged this quickly? There was no way she was going to offer them tea and coffee and risk having to stand up.

"So, we'd thought we'd update you," said the same redhead policeman, Carla had given her first statement to a few weeks before.

"Surely, it's the other?"

"I'm sorry?" the older of the two looked confused. He pulled out a mask. "Sorry," he repeated. "I forgot."

Redhead pulled out a note pad. So, they really did still use them... and began reading back.

"Looks as if the man you saw on the water meadows, might be connected to the rape. We've arrested him. Thought you might like to know."

Carla sank back for a moment forgetting her t-shirt.

"Oh," she said shocked yet strangely disassociated at the same time. The pink pills were definitely taking effect. "You're here for that."

"Was there something else?"

Carla twisted around.

"Yes, actually," she showed the men her leg. The bruise which had begun coronavirus-like was fast spreading down the back of her knee. "I was attacked by two dogs this afternoon."

There was a pause. "Sorry to hear that. Where did the attack place? You know it's an assault don't you?"

Carla then recounted the episode and the empty pram.

"Why the pram, do you think?"

The police exchanged a look.

"Drugs," said one of them. "Those people use prams to distribute drugs. The dogs - if the attack was unprovoked - would be trained to bring you down. They're guard dogs. I think you were lucky."

Carla went cold in the small silence that followed. "Well, if there's nothing else?"

Crikey wasn't that enough? How often did you encounter a rapist and suffer a dog attack in the space of a month? And in leafy, urbane Winchester? The happiest, best place to live in the UK, or at least it was in 2016. It might have slipped recently.

"No, nothing else."

18

Carla sat in the front room, her leg propped on cushions and her laptop balanced on her stomach. She was tired. She'd slept badly. No sooner had the two policemen left (to do with the alleged rape), than PC Ollie (who looked no older than Alfie) had arrived to take a statement with regard to the dog attack. She'd been getting ready for bed a second time when Alfie once again called up the stairs to tell her there was a policeman on the doorstep. It was becoming comical. This time she'd managed to grab a jumper to wear over the nude and navy t-shirt so had been more relaxed during his visit. She supposed she should have been flattered. Sunday evenings in the city were apparently busy, with only three police officers on duty for the whole area. Over the course of the evening, all three had been with her. Carla had had trouble identifying the dogs though and was still confused as to whether they'd been Rottweilers or Staffies.

"But surely you know the difference?" said Tom now over the phone. Um… She wasn't sure that she did… She frowned trying to remember but was quickly distracted by how pretty her tanned feet looked in crimson suede Manolos. The one good thing about the dog attack was that both Tom and Seb seemed to have completely forgotten about the car. Tom was starting a new case and couldn't get away so he no longer needed it - at least not yet and Seb, although he wasn't necessarily showing it, sounded contrite. "I mean one is a small if ferocious dog, the other is much bigger. Google them. And what exactly are the police doing? It's an assault, you know. They've got to get the bastards. It's shocking."

"Probably drug-related," said Carla quoting the police. Not that they'd said it was definitely.

"Really?"

"They had a pram," she said mysteriously.

"That's your evidence?"

"Well, not all of it obviously but why else would they have had one?"

"Er…for a child?"

"There wasn't one."

"Not one that you saw."

"True," she agreed doubtfully.

"Well, it's still awful. Try and remember more about the owners. They need to be prosecuted. A child could have been killed."

"*I* could have been killed."

She dangled her pretty suede mule. Another item that had thankfully escaped the lockdown cull. She wasn't quite sure if the 'cull' thing had really worked. She had an overwhelming urge to replenish *all* the old with wonderful and entirely new; the Temperley acquisitions didn't count.

"Nah, you're tough," said Tom ringing off which prompted Carla to send him a close-up of her bite.

Bored, she began perusing online fashion sites. I know, she thought… what I really need is a neat little cross-body bag small and light, but big enough to fit a mobile. Nothing more. OK, well maybe she could slide in a credit card and some lippy; one that she could take with her when she went walking so that she was never caught out again. Having said that, she wasn't sure that having had a phone would have made any difference. Not for summoning help although it would have been good to have had a photo of the dogs. She'd been far too shocked to have had the wherewithal to pull out a phone and presumably had she tried to resist, the dogs wouldn't have let her go at all. Or their owners. Especially if drugs really had been involved. Carla shuddered involuntarily.

It's the pack mentality! Les Girls texted helpfully. *Lunging and barking is bad enough. But if dogs get into a pack they'll attack. You did the right thing. Lying still.*

I can't take any credit. It wasn't a choice! I was too stunned to do anything else. And then too terrified to do anything other than run!

Well, that was the right thing to do too - not try and engage with the owners either - you just had to get the hell out of there.

And then to cheer her up, they'd pinged her a new meme. Memes in general had been rather thin on the ground recently. There appeared to be less incentive to keep spirits buoyant now that lockdown was over. Either that or the country had finally lost its sense of humour. This latest was a drawing issued from Nat West. Under 'suitable' there was a face in a protective mask, under 'unsuitable' a man was shown sporting a balaclava. Carla gave it a thumbs up although she wasn't sure how funny she really found it and went back to scouring the internet for a cross-body bag. Russell and Bromley had a quilted camel-coloured, padded leather case very Chanel-ish with its gold chain strap. It wasn't a brand she particularly liked but it would do. Carla placed the item in her virtual shopping bag and went to check out. Seb could collect it as the store was located near the top of the High Street. Except he couldn't, she was informed moments later. They were out of stock and the bag would have to be delivered to the house. Carla hesitated only briefly before hitting 'next day' and 'pay now.' It wasn't as if she intended walking far any time soon but it would be nice to have it in reserve for when she finally did. She touched her thigh gingerly. She could still feel the dog's teeth in her leg - it felt as though there was a canine or two embedded in the muscle.

Do you realise Bush warned of a flu pandemic as long ago as 2005? Les Girls were back at it.

In comparison to our buffoon, he seems positively statesmanlike!

Agree!

There followed a photo Alice had taken when she had travelled by tube recently showing fellow travellers. Only one man was actually wearing a mask correctly. One wore his around his chin (so that he could see to text), another had lowered his exposing his nose and the other was asleep - his covered his eyes.

The final YouTube video was one she'd seen before but still found touching. It consisted of a series of short clips. A baby elephant wallows in a tub, kicks his trainer in the bottom, chases a flock of birds before finally falling over and running back to the protection of its mother. For some reason it brought tears to her eyes. It was the simple things that mattered - that should matter. She glanced at her phone. There'd been several more messages including a whole conversation to do with friendship. She sent a series of emojis: her trademark lips and a smiley face with hearts for eyes.

The last one was the longest: *'Sister, I am with you.' Oh, yes?* Carla scanned the text quickly. There was stuff about girls' weekends (when had she ever been on one of those?), brunches (ditto) beaches in Florida (tick). She was already bored. She opened a tube of arnica cream and began massaging her leg, reading at the same time. There appeared to be another message she'd missed - no it was the same one.

Or maybe she'd misread it? Ah, she had. What it said, was that friendship wasn't about those things at all, it was about being welcomed into a person's 'real.' (Whatever that meant). No need to wonder for long; the author of the text went on (and on) to explain this 'real.' But Carla took on board the final message, the gist being that the real honour of friendship was being invited into someone's 'real': the hard stuff, the nitty gritty, being privy to the vulnerable moments.

OK, reflected Carla, *the cross-body bag isn't enough. As it's only R&B, I may as well have the matching flats.*

*

It was just as well Carla was experienced at spoiling herself as Seb appeared less inclined to. In the days that followed the dog incident, Carla took it uncharacteristically easy. She was on a heady, extra strong course of antibiotics and had been to her GP for tetanus jab. Her waist and shoulder blade still showed the indentation of the dog's teeth but didn't hurt - it was her thigh causing most of the discomfort. It throbbed and still felt as though she had an animal latched to her. The puncture wounds had stayed pretty much the same but a large black bruise had spread the entire length and width of her thigh. It was dramatic and Carla actually enjoyed the shock factor it produced when she flipped up her skirt to show friends. Everyone was kind and attentive - neighbours popped in with bunches of flowers, chocolates and cakes. Even Kevin (DHL) and Ian (DPD) stopped by for a chat. She'd flipped up her skirt for them as well. And she was interviewed for an article: '*Yes, it came out of the blue! No, the owners stood by, doing nothing to help. The worst part? That I couldn't say a word for at least half an hour afterwards…*'

"A feat in itself"' said Seb overhearing. Carla glowered.

 "Nice pic," he said now dropping a couple of copies of the paper in her lap.

Can a Leopard?

"What page?"

"You'll find it."

And she did and it was. A lovely, long article showing a flattering picture - Carla was glad she was wearing the Missoni - and an equally detailed picture of her injury. It looked even more dramatic in black and white.

"'*I thought I was going to be torn apart,*'" Carla read. "Well, they got that right," she cast Seb a sideways look to see if he was listening but he was engrossed in his phone. "'*Those were the words of the woman who suffered puncture wounds to her leg and back following a vicious dog attack. Carla Cave of Canon Street, self-employed, translator, forty-si-i-*'" What? She threw down the paper. "How did they know my age? Seb?"

"Huh?"

"My age? And address?"

Seb shrugged. He lowered himself onto one of the corner chairs - rather than sit on the end of the sofa. She felt a pang. Why this aloofness? Where had the *spretzzatura* gone between them? Where was the tenderness that she knew he was capable of demonstrating when she'd been ill in the past? She remembered lying in bed at the old house, in their wonderful bedroom that overlooked the park and actually enjoying feeling unwell, warm and cosseted as she was by Seb who brought her trays of tea and toast. The room had been bathed in a coral pink light; enhancing the gold patina of the walnut tall boy and the delicate aqua silk fringe of the pelmets under which the ivory curtains billowed gracefully. And there, Seb had been attentive, warm and loving. Which was not the case now. She cast him a thoughtful look. 'Frisky.' Was the word she'd use to describe him. He was decidedly frisky.

"Oh, I told them," said Alfie smiling happily pushing his bike through the hall. "A nice lady called on your phone."

"Did she indeed?" Carla reached over to pick up the paper again. She clocked the journalist's name. She'd have a word with that one. "How come you answered?"

"You were in the bath," said Alfie. "Dad said not to disturb you."

Carla glared at Seb.

"Thanks."

"Just going to town," said Alfie knocking into her Gustavian table. Seb leapt to intercept one of the glass hand-blown glass candlesticks mid-air.

"Be careful, darling!" she said sucking in her breath. "Please!" But this time she meant, 'be careful' on his bicycle. She wasn't sure how clued-up Alfie was on signalling and he tended (as she did when she was out walking) to ride down the centre of the street as though it were pedestrians only.

"I heard some man talking about the dog attack outside the Cathedral," said Alfie.

"Oh?" said Carla brightening. "Did you tell him it was me?"

"No."

She glanced at the article again. It had given out a lot more information than she would have liked.

"There was another message too," said Alfie stopping to do up the strap on his helmet. The curtain of his hair had disappeared and his freckled face was clear and innocent, the almond-shaped eyes, red-brown flecked with yellow. They looked like tiger's eye. "That guy Ollie - the young policeman?"

Can a Leopard?

"Yes?"

"Some news channel wants to interview you. They want to know if you'll show your bite?"

At last, Seb's attention was pricked. He turned owl-like.

"Oh, yes?"

"Yeah, Ollie said there'd been a surprising media response." He rattled the words proud of himself for remembering. "Will you do it? My friends think it would be cool."

Carla eyes widened. So, Alfie had discussed it with them before she even knew about it!

"Do they actually, as you would say?"

"So, will you?"

Carla shrugged. "Not sure. Have to think about it."

"Oh," Alfie looked disappointed.

"Where are you going, darling?" said Carla.

"Town. Friends," replied Alfie.

"I'll come with you," said Seb suddenly leaping to his feet. "Not with, with. I'll walk out with you."

"Anything you want while I'm out?" he added hardly looking at Carla.

So much! You staying put for five minutes for starters. So that we might really talk. So that you might explain this coldness, this distance that is creeping wider and wider and stretching like gooey pastry over the counter sticking in all the wrong areas. The kind that you scrape and try to lift off the base and end up throwing out

*and then you have to start afresh. They'd got through the most
difficult part of lockdown and now things seemed no better.
Everything felt flat and strange.*

She held his gaze saying instead: "A real end to lockdown, a
box at the opera house, a trip to the Med and a new Erès
swimsuit. Emerald green. But not the one with scallop trim."

Seb opened the drawer of the Gustavian desk to fish out a
mask.

He didn't miss a beat. "OK, scallops for dinner sounds like a
great idea."

*

Had NO idea you were that old! Les Girls texted.

Same.

No seriously - we all thought you were younger!

How'd you figure that, if we were in the same class at school?

Well, yeah but a year or two tops.

*OMG! You're so right! Alfie got it wrong! I'm a whole year
younger than I thought! Oh, feeling SO much better now. Gotta
tell that reporter at the paper right away!*

Carla did feel unaccountably cheerful. A whole year
younger! If Seb were being friendlier, she'd have called him
to tell him. But she settled with telling Alfie when he
appeared a few hours later. Kicking off his trainers and
dropping his helmet and bike lock in the entrance he seemed
puzzled that she should mind.

Can a Leopard?

He shrugged. "It's only a year," he said perched on the end of the sofa and pulling out his drone from his rucksack.

"Believe me," said Carla grimly. "A year makes a big difference when you get to my age."

"Whatever," he said adding enthusiastically, "got some amazing videos, Mum." His cheeks were flushed and he was losing some of his lockdown podginess. He was a different boy from the one who'd been depressed only a few months before.

"Show me, my love," she said sitting up re-positioning her leg, the throbbing alternating with a sharp sting.

He took out his phone connecting it to the drone's camera before snuggling beside her.

"And you've set it to music!" Carla pulled away. "That's really impressive."

Alfie had filmed from the top of St. Catherine's hill. At first all Carla could see was white mist and the spire of the Cathedral.

"See the buzzard?" He homed in on the rounded pale wings of the bird.

"The one with yellow legs and a hooked beak?"

Alfie didn't reply but enlarged the footage even more.

"I do!" She pulled back to look at him in admiration. "But where were you when I needed you? Can you imagine if you'd managed to film this last Sunday? We could have nailed those dog owners if you'd been out and about then."

"Sorry Mum," said Alfie sheepishly although it couldn't have possibly been his fault. He leaned in and together they studied the sweeping panorama of the city: The College towers, the hospital and prison ('I wouldn't get too close to that darling,' she'd said recoiling in alarm), even the street where they lived. His filming had improved too. The camera crossed far and wide, high and low so that Carla felt she could touch every individual leaf and flower and… Seb.

She blinked rapidly. Surely it was a man who *looked* like Seb. After all there must be hundreds of jean-clad, middle-aged men with that characteristic long hair (slightly) hippy look.

Steady!" said Carla gripping Alfie's wrist. "Go back!"

She frowned. No, there was no mistaking Seb's long hair and jeans. She looked again. Except he wasn't wearing jeans. Well not blue ones anyway. He was kitted out in polo gear. Her heart started hammering in her chest. She thought back rapidly to the last clip she'd seen on Alfie's phone. Was this part of the same stream or was it another day altogether? The change in his clothes would suggest it was.

"Where was that?" she asked shakily.

Alfie shrugged. "Dunno. I just fly the drone."

"Show me more," commanded Carla sitting bolt upright now, ignoring the twinge in her leg, the feel of a phantom dog yanking her back.

Alfie was silent angling his phone this way and that.

"There's Daddy again!" she said incredulously. "And there. Gosh, you're clever."

Alfie looked less convinced. "I should go Mum," he said. She could tell he'd not anticipated such an enthusiastic reaction. "Can I have Domino's tonight?"

"Anything," said Carla distractedly. "Just a bit more."

"Have to go," said Alfie firmly. She snatched the phone from him as he got up to unplug the drone. The last bit of filming took in Alfie's old school close and 'Mirabelle', as she now knew it was called.

"Oh, look you've even got the water garden!" she exclaimed. The water garden had been created by a former MP and was a gift to the city. It was a delightful semi-walled garden enclosing a small patch of green, two piers and a stream. Shaded by fig trees, the lion's head fountain emitted a constant trickle, lending an almost Arabic feel to the space. It called to mind the Alhambra in Granada. From that corner it also afforded a first glimpse of the Cathedral. But that was not all that could be glimpsed from that sheltered copse. As Alfie's hand covered the screen and the drone sank low, hugging the stone and flint wall, Seb's dark head momentarily came into the fore, as did a pretty blonde's as it rose to greet him.

19

Carla cast a swift glace at the latest text from Les Girls:

Gemma's birthday on the weekend, are you coming?

Well, she hadn't planned on going but she sure as hell intended to, now. Anything to keep her away from Seb before she exploded, before their lives imploded. She kept to her side of the bed at night, rigid with unhappiness, her mind gnawed away with suspicion and doubt, while her leg felt gnawed by a phantom beast. The bruise was not only enormous but had turned yellow and purple - a flower within a flower. Tom said she needed to make sure the bites didn't become infected, to check that they didn't become red or hot to the touch. Red wasn't the problem - her thigh boasted every colour in the rainbow but. '*You need Arnica*!' the girls texted and she'd been applying the stuff religiously. Until someone else said that was the worse thing she could do, that she must stop rubbing the wound and let it be, and so she had.

By day, she watched Seb miserably, stealthily, on the alert for any change in behaviour, but on the face of it he seemed no different. No different that is from the way he'd been ever since they'd returned from Italy. He made breakfast the way he always did, played polo then worked on his science blog. His latest was actually fascinating, detailing the use of TAST (Targeted Acoustic Startle Technology) in keeping harbour seals away from the fish ladder and thus allowing migrating salmon a better chance of survival. The only live thing startled these days, was Carla herself by the speed with which Seb donned his Bose 700 noise cancelling Bluetooth headphones after he'd written his six thousand words. Before she'd even had a chance to comment on young smolts or the use of sound to induce a flight response, Seb's attention was elsewhere. Motioning to his ears, he gabbled, 'Underwater sounds - bit like watching a sci-fi - you won't like it.'

Maybe, maybe not, but Carla had no difficulty whatsoever envisaging seals and sea lions lingering at migration bottlenecks ready to pounce on unsuspecting salmon. She was feeling that predatory instinct herself. And now fired up, not at all pacified, she was heading to Oxford and a reunion with Les Girls. It was the first time they'd met up in person, in what? A year? Was it possible? Lockdown had gobbled up and spewed out six months of their lives, it had seemed interminable at the time, now it felt as though it had passed in a flash.

She turned on the radio which of course was all about their favourite subject. More than 1000 doctors in the UK were set to resign over the government's handling of the virus, total cases within 28 day of testing positive stood at 41,623 - 74 more than a week earlier. Of the 8,996 deaths from any cause registered, 83 mentioned Covid-19 on the death certificate - the lowest since March. Then there was the issue with testing. Many people (including doctors) were finding it difficult to get a test at all. One caller from Birmingham, said that she'd been advised that the closest testing station was County Antrim. Actually, Carla didn't have to listen to the caller for confirmation that the NHS test and trace was a failure. One of Les Girls had been told to isolate after been informed that she'd been exposed to someone with Covid-19 which she had duly done. Two weeks later she was sent a text congratulating her on the fact that her test results had been returned and were negative. Good news indeed, as she'd never had a test to begin with!

Carla was bored out of her skull by the only subject dominating the news, with the flip flopping, shambolic and confusing, often inconsistent government's handling of the pandemic. And if there was a second wave as the media was heavily suggesting there would be, it was unlikely there'd be the rally-round-the flag effect this time, just a growing sense of ennui.

Which led her thoughts neatly back of course, to Seb; from where, truth to tell, they hardly strayed. Was it boredom that had prompted Seb to deviate? Was he having an affair with the blonde she'd seen twice now in video clips and was this blonde woman Karen? And instead of making herself ill over it, what was preventing her from having it out? The problem was that they were never really alone. She needed time to think, to be away from the house. To be... as daughter Sophie was constantly telling her. She thought with a pang that the one person Carla wanted at this moment was Sophie but she was the one person she couldn't confide in. Sophie's response would certainly be, *'well you married him.'* Eugenia had said she knew his 'type' by which she meant 'playboy.' Except that these days Seb was more playfather than playboy which was exactly why it was so ... so unbecoming. They were both too old for these jealous fits and tantrums.

Carla turned onto the A34 towards Newbury. Gemma lived virtually due North of Winchester. The traffic was intense and such a contrast from the early months of lockdown when driving had felt illegal - well it had been - and after her one and only trip out of the city in May, she'd slunk off the motorway terrified of being apprehended. She thought back to the early days of lockdown, the goodwill towards Boris when he became ill, the very bad will towards Trump when he suggested ingesting bleach, the jokes about loo paper, the music shared from balconies and empty stages. Then it had been uplifting to read about or see the creativity with which other nations met these challenges. For a live performance, the Liceo Opera House in Barcelona had filled the empty boxes and seats with 2,292 palms, Ficus trees and Swiss Cheese plants. She thought of their own challenges as a family when school was suspended and Alfie had come home. And then her own dip into depression followed by a sort of epiphany. She'd re-evaluated her life (at any rate, she'd *intended* to) sold many of her clothes to garner funds for PPE, tried as much as possible to help out locally, enrolled Alfie in all manner of summer activities, felt an overall unbridled, capricious joy as lockdown restrictions were lifted.

But almost just as quickly Carla's sense of elation began to wear off to be replaced with one of dissatisfaction, of wanting more. They had a kind of freedom but the world was reduced; there was only so much they could do. They certainly couldn't hop on a plane and fly anywhere they wanted, the way they were accustomed. Yes, they'd all adapted to a different way of life. They'd learned to queue patently outside shops, maintain the 2-metre distancing rule and wear masks. They had all done it because an end was in sight and by and large the Brits were an obedient race. And as promised, the end had come but it wasn't the definitive end end. It was an end tinged with uncertainty. Uncertainty as to whether there'd be a second wave, and if so, how severe it might be. Uncertainty, as to whether schools would go back in a few weeks' time, uncertainty as to job security, as to whether house prices would fall. Above all, at this moment, there was uncertainty in an area of her life under which Carla believed she'd drawn a line forever. One of trust. Of Seb.

*

Carla passed the exit to Wendlebury, home to Gemma's octogenarian parents. It was curious to think that Gemma and her family had started off in Oxfordshire, had lived abroad for many years and then had returned to live within a five-mile radius of their original point of departure. By contrast, Carla's family and Seb's were cast far and wide, the world over. Carla also passed signs for Bicester Village, a moan of desire escaping her lips. Was there time to make a stop? She glanced at the dial on the dashboard. Given social distancing and the need to book specific time slots, the days of popping in anywhere were over, at least for the foreseeable future. Besides, what was the point? She really didn't need clothes for a special event. They weren't travelling abroad; they weren't going to parties - not with the 'Rule of Six' in place and there certainly wasn't a ball in the offing. Balls in particular seemed a thing of the past and the beautiful frocks to wear to them. Carla felt an acute stab of nostalgia; thinking back to those heady days of her youth, when the future was an endless, vast expanse - middle age so far into it as to be laughable. And balls were intrinsically part of that time, although now, especially during the pandemic, that kind of event seemed to belong to another lifetime, another history entirely. Carla smiled to herself remembering the excitement generated by an invitation to a ball or dance.

As if on cue, Classic FM began playing the *Kuss Walz*. Carla thought it deeply romantic that Strauss should have written the '*Kiss*' for his second wife and that the series of so-called *Acceleration Waltzes* were composed on the back of a napkin. Oh, that inspiration would strike her in such a fashion! As the music gathered momentum, and Carla with it - she was transported to each and every ball she'd ever gone to with Gemma, steering the car as though she were doing huge sweeping twirls on a dance floor.

The motorway faded as she saw herself and Gemma in various stages of girlhood. She made a mental inventory, sifting through the clothes rail memory of past gowns. The Madonna years were probably their least successful. Carla cringed at the memory of their matching tartan taffeta, tartan bows in their frizzy hair, ropes of plastic pearls that popped together (and invariably apart) around their necks.

Too terrified to talk, let alone dance with anyone other than each other, they huddled together drinking warm peach-flavoured champagne and imagining themselves to be a good deal drunker than they actually were. Later, at university, they'd worn toned down versions of the same, only with the hemlines lopped, alternating those with glitzy, sequin, columns that might have looked better on the six-foot models they were designed for. Carla had thought herself all shimmery seductive until Gemma said she looked aquatic all right, but more in line with a goldfish than mermaid.

There had been weird Catholic Society balls (to which in an experimental moment they'd worn Empire line gowns they'd run up themselves on Gemma's battered sewing machine) where the boys understandably expressed more interest in each other. Carla remembered the balls one summer, shivering in May drizzle, Gemma's Mexicana fetish causing fake tan to streak down her legs while for some reason Carla wore sunflower yellow, a colour she had always hated. Winter balls in College were more fun. You just knew the weather was going to be freezing and so were prepared. Plus, they coincided with the release of *The French Lieutenant's Woman* which meant that every other girl (and a few boys) wore a hood. Carla had loved her aqua velvet frock and matching cloak and fancied herself much more than she'd fancied her date.

Then there were countless charity balls and privately held balls to celebrate birthdays in grand but arctic conditions. There were dances in cold castles to which they'd worn white only because Gemma had dragged Carla to an obscure sample sale of wedding dresses in Shepherd's Bush. The overall bridal effect was enhanced by the loan of a tiara by Carla's granny. But there was only one, so Gemma and Carla had shared it. Not a completely satisfactory arrangement with one of them having to keep an eye on the tiara the whole time in case it was stolen.

The Anglo-Spanish balls should have been lively enough but the Spanish girls were threatened collectively by anyone female and the boys were snobbish to the point of caricature. Gemma had been effortlessly seductive in slinky blue crepe, Carla markedly less so, in a little-bo-peep inspired number which only needed a staff to complete the picture.

Can a Leopard?

There were balls they'd simply written off on arrival, where one or other had spent the evening in the cloakroom crying over some boy or some dress. There were hunt balls to which they went out of duty sporting Alice Bands (before Kate Middleton made them popular again) and countless, countless New Year's Eve balls where they'd given up on wearing dresses altogether and thinking they were absolutely the *dernier cri* - wore mis-matched pyjamas instead. But then Gemma and Carla had always considered themselves to be ahead of their time. Apparently, nightwear sales during lockdown were up 1000%.

The Kiss had seamlessly segued into the *Kaiser Walz* and with that final exuberant outburst, Carla reflected that the 'King' of balls really had to be the Viennese ball and that nothing could ever compare. The sweeping music made her want to fly and leap and dive and dance until she dropped with exhaustion. It made her feel all the more frustrated and desperate to be a million miles away from Covid-19 and lockdown and boredom.

Carla kept time to the music, tapping the steering wheel as she edged the car into the quicksand of gravel that was Gemma's drive. She switched off the engine but not the radio and closed her eyes listening to the hypnotic final bars. *'Balance, balance, on one spot!'* their dance teacher used to say, *'Et alors!'* Carla giggled every time she thought of Jean-Pierre and the way she and Seb would teeter on the balls of their feet, 'balancing' all right, often for a whole dance sequence before plucking up the courage to take that first step into the throng.

In her mind's eye she saw the Hofburg Palace once again, a mirrored fairy land of lights and crystal, white plaster walls edged in gold and beautiful women in gorgeous gowns and men upright pivots in white tie as they twirled their partners, the man leaning in first and then the woman, then the man, then the woman- a neat rhythmical slalom. That is, when it was done correctly, when you were Viennese, when waltzing was second nature. Carla's problem was that she always wanted to lead, so excited was she by the beat of the music beating in her blood.

But you didn't have to be Viennese to be excited by an invitation to a ball. And that last one Gemma and Carla had gone to, really was the ball to end all balls. They had finally got their look just right too. 'Only had thirty years to get there!' Gemma joked punch drunk with excitement in a way she'd never felt when young, smoothing the skirt of her peacock-blue gown, adjusting her mask and gloves.

Carla was just excited to have straight hair. For no obvious reason, she also found her friend hilarious giggling until she hiccupped much to Seb's disgust. It was testament to Gemma's generous and loving nature that she'd never held it against Carla, never blamed her for the Vienna fiasco. Carla let the afterglow of the waltz wash over her, moved her feet in time, moved her arms touching the car ceiling and allowed herself to be transported…

*

"Ho, ho, ho!" Carla had said animatedly one evening the Christmas before last. "Have I got news for you! Or more specifically *'ein mann'*."

"What's with the German? Not interested in dating, if that's what you're getting at - oh, so not subtly." Gemma's voice on the other end of the phone was curt. Carla could hear the whirr of machinery in the background. "I'm not."

"You will be when I tell you why. We're going to Vienna. To a ball. And not just any ball but a masked ball!"

"What are you talking about?"

Can a Leopard?

"Where are you?"

"Potting," said Gemma. Carla could hear the inhalation of a cigarette. She always wondered that Gemma chose to smoke in her shed at all. She could imagine the cigarette burning on the edge of an ashtray while Gemma turned the wheel, only ever taking the occasional puff. Sometimes she would forget about it completely, the red tip gobbling up the white paper until only ash remained.

"I know where you are," said Carla. "But isn't it a bit late? The light and all that."

Gemma's potting shed had electricity but the electric light was poor and she preferred to work in the morning.

"It wasn't dark when I started. I'm in with my babies. But they're all a dismal failure. I think I've jinxed them."

Carla rolled her eyes knowing Gemma couldn't see her.

"You can't have done," said Carla reasonably.

The whirring started up again.

"I just shouldn't have answered," said Gemma sulkily.

Then why did you?

Except Carla knew why; they were always there for one another.

Carla was contrite. "Oh, sorry. Do you want me to call you later? When you're in the house?"

"No. I've already messed this up."

Carla could hear the machine being switched off and another sharp intake of tobacco. When Gemma spoke again, she was notably more relaxed. She was probably leaning back now, feet propped up on the edge of a wheel blowing smoke out of the corner of her mouth, lights turned off, the glow of her cigarette weaving like a glow worm.

"You might as well tell me."

Carla was rapid in conveying the news. Seb and she were off to China but stopping off in Vienna on the way. They'd been invited to a ball by an acquaintance of theirs, a certain Johannes, an Austrian they met up with once a year, the week before Christmas when they all stayed together at the Hospiz in St. Christoph.

"Is he ill?" Gemma's tone had developed an edge.

"Come again?"

"Hospice? You said Hospice? Is the man dying? Is this a joke? I'm not up for being a nurse maid. Not good with ill people. I only have a fixed quota of 'nice' hormones in me and those are on the decline."

Carla frowned.

"Oh? I see! No, no, no! The Hospiz in St. Christoph is…" her voice faded. "Is…"

"Is?"

Gemma was becoming impatient but Carla paused. How to describe a place that the children and she held close to their hearts, a place they returned to year after year. No matter what else had been going on in their lives, they'd always been happy in the pink turreted hotel, nestling in the Arlberg region. A winter wonderland, a hideaway located at 1800 feet, traditionally a place of refuge for travellers attempting the pass, St. Christoph was a tiny access village on one of the access roads to St. Anton.

"The Hospiz is one of the most iconic hotels in the region. It couldn't be further from a hospice if it tried. Unless dying and going to heaven is a daily occurrence, then maybe you could describe it as one. Quite frankly I'd be very happy to end my days there. But no, think roaring fires, wooden beams, hot chocolate waiting after that final exhilarating sometimes frightening last run of the day. And snow! Lots of snow!"

"Only North Americans or Scandinavians eulogise about the cold," said Gemma.

"Yes," said Carla. *As do I*...Carla felt the snug memory of white winters envelop her now, the complete silence on waking, that only ever really comes after a heavy snowfall. And something else. "Did you ever read *Miss Smilla's Feeling for Snow?* I think the Eskimos have about fifty words to describe -"

"Back to the point, kid," said Gemma. Another sharp intake. "What about this hospice/hospiz?"

"Well...we go every year the week before Christmas, as do most of the other guests. It's where we first met Johannes. Only he's an awesome skier. As you would expect being Austrian. Much better than Seb or me. He likes to ski with Tom. They can take skins and disappear all day - it's not what-."

"*Skins?*"

Carla could hear Gemma's panic over the ether.

"Climbing skins - they're strips that attach to skis - bit like winter tyres- so you don't slip backwards. The first skins

were made from sealskin which is how they got their name.
They're for climbing high when you go off piste they-"

"Stop!" said Gemma. Carla knew she was probably picking
off bits of tobacco from her lip. "Stop right there! I have to tell
you right now I don't ski, I have no more than German
O'level and I absolutely don't waltz. Why on earth should I
be interested?"

Carla sighed. She hadn't thought it would be this difficult
selling a ball (opera thrown in) and a date. How many balls
had they gone to when they'd only had each other to dance
with?

"Look, Johannes is charming. He's single, he wants a family,
he's generous and well off. You're charming (sometimes)
single (mostly) and want a family (possibly) and (not so) well
off. It's perfect. In fact, you're not saying no! You've got two
months to learn to waltz. You'll be fine. Only don't be like
me. The man has to lead. Johannes is Austrian, dancing is like
breathing to the Viennese."

So, it was settled. Gemma was taking dance lessons and had
investigated local dry-ski slopes. Carla had been a little
nervous about recommending she go down that route. At
least, Gemma could honestly say she'd been skiing. She
didn't have to be too specific as to where. Johannes was
passionate about his winter sports, so if they got on, perhaps
Gemma would take it up too. Carla and Seb had also signed
up for another course of waltz lessons with 'the boys' who
held dance sessions in the nearby Methodist church hall of a
Friday evening. *'Come, dance with me,'* Jean-Pierre would say
in his seductive French accent, enveloping Seb in his
muscular arms while Jean Pierre's softly spoken Lancastrian
husband, Luke, beckoned Carla. With a toss of his toupé,
Jean-Pierre was off twirling Seb around the dance floor.
'Help!' mouthed Seb every time but no matter how quick Seb
was to advance on Carla, Jean-Pierre was even faster,
pirouetting Seb away from her.

Can a Leopard?

By the time they boarded their early morning flight to Vienna, Gemma and Carla were giddy with excitement. They were off to a ball in Vienna - it didn't get much more romantic than that! Gemma had spent the night before their departure at theirs, so that there was absolutely no chance of missing the flight - or if they did, they would do it together.

The past few weeks had passed in a flurry of activity. Carla not only had the ball to plan for but a month in China. Clothes for that trip were easy enough - heavy duty walking shoes and layering. She'd found the most ingenious Max Mara two-in-one coat which had an outer cashmere shell that could be worn separately for smarter, urbane occasions but worn over the waterproof, fox-lined parka it made for an extremely warm garment. Mornings in Beijing could start at minus three degrees but by mid-day have gone up to plus twelve. The parka could also be worn separately for wet weather hikes around the Panda Sanctuary in Chengdu for example or on the boat when they sailed down the Yangtse to the Three Gorges Dam.

The gown for the ball promised to be more difficult. Lipstick pink, with a full skirt and ballerina neckline, it had finally arrived from New York. Earlier it had sold out on the Net-à-Porter website. But those two little words were enough to strike mortal terror in Carla's heart and set the research skills she'd honed in academia to proper use. The dress had arrived just in time as had the masks. Neither were very original: Seb's monochrome *Phantom of the Opera* the go-to for countless fancy dress events and Carla's was diamanté. But what was more recherché was the Roland Mouret wine velvet dress with matching velvet shoes and a cropped black mink bolero she would don for the opera on their second night in Vienna. Their party clothes would then be packed and left at the hotel, to be collected by Mybaggage.com and returned to England when Seb and Carla flew on to Shanghai. It was perfect.

Can a Leopard?

What was less than, was their very early start (they'd had to wake up at four a.m.) so that by the time they arrived in Vienna, Carla felt light-headed and faintly sick. The three of them had headed immediately for the glorious hotel Sacher and then the tea-room. Seb dispensed with a main course choosing the famous torte straight off while Gemma and Carla giggled like school- girls, stopping short of designing wedding dresses for the wedding Carla was certain would be the outcome of their two days in Vienna.

Even when Seb chided them for being ridiculous, reminding them both that Gemma hadn't even met the man Carla proposed she marry, the subject lay between them, like the evening ahead, unspoken, crackling with promise and intrigue. As did the city, with its snowy cobbled streets, muffled sound of horse's hooves as tourists rode in horse-drawn carriages and warming smells of cinnamon and chocolate coming from the many coffee houses. The carnival air was accentuated by the sale of fantasy masks on sale at every street corner.

"Come here," Seb had said when they'd gone up to their room at last to change and get ready for the ball. "Don't worry, I won't mess up your hair," he added rapidly seeing her imperceptible pucker of annoyance. He kissed the nape of her neck and her back and her hair… which in the end of course, was completely messed up.

An hour or so later they'd met Gemma in the foyer, the panelled room awash in crimson and golden hues. The grand yet cosy effect was created by thick-piled Oriental rugs, ornate ormolu side tables, over-stuffed sofas in red brocade, red silk pleated lampshades and huge gilt mirrors. Carla could hardly breathe with excitement. Seb looked devastatingly handsome in his white tie. The stiff waistcoat made all men stand ramrod straight but Seb was taller and broader than average, so that the effect was even more commanding. His eyes were starling blue and the white of his collar accentuated his perennially tanned face. Even in winter, when Carla compared their skin colour, his was always the darker. 'Och,' he'd say exaggerating his South African accent which years living abroad had mellowed. 'Too many years in the sun yah,' which made her giggle.

Tonight, everything was pleasant. Carla glanced at him. He was every bit the dashing, debonair godfather he'd been when she first met him. And Gemma was beautiful too in a turquoise Thai silk gown that had belonged to her mother. It brought out the blue of her eyes which contrasted with the inky black of her shoulder length hair. Carla beamed. These two people were her best beloved. Gemma winked, fidgeting. They could hardly stand still with the headiness of the place.

Seb handed them their tickets.

"This is really for you," he said winking at Gemma. "Just in case you decide to ditch us."

"Fingers crossed," she said, a hysterical catch in her throat. "I have every intention of doing just that!"

"And we're meeting Johannes for dinner first," volunteered Seb.

"Reminds me of the White Knights Ball or the Feathers," said Gemma, "Remember Carla, when we could only afford after-dinner tickets."

Carla didn't need reminding of any of it.

"Yes, it's a bit like that," agreed Seb. "Johannes assures me we have a table in prime position, in one of the best rooms in the palace. There are nine and each one will be themed. Rock'n'roll in some, jazz in others but of course the main ballroom is for waltzing which is why we're here."

"Well, one of the reasons…" giggled Carla.

Can a Leopard?

"And you really think I'll like him?" said Gemma overcome by last minute nerves. "I mean this is no ordinary blind date."

Seb smiled assuredly. "A hundred percent as Alfie would say."

"Actually, where is your fine boy? I never asked," said Gemma.

"School," answered Carla and Seb in unison. "He weekly boards now."

Gemma fluffed out her dress and hooked her mask behind her ears. Her eyes were large mysterious and bewitching.

"You'll like him," said Seb reassuringly. "Johannes is a gentleman. We've known him for years, as Carla says. And you speak German. His English is fluent but I always think humour is something best captured in one's original tongue, don't you think?"

"Exactly," agreed Carla joyfully. "It's going to be a wonderful evening!" She hugged her friend. "We're all grown up now, Gemma darling. No more skulking in loos, no more wall flowers for us! I mean the four of us at a ball in Vienna - and no ordinary ball but the Rodarte students ball at the Hofburg! What could possibly go wrong?"

Which was something Carla would repeat over the next forty-eight hours. What could possibly go wrong? Why had it? Seb wrapped Carla in her pink mink which matched her pink dress exactly and she leant into him for a few seconds, gathering strength from him as she always did, reassured by him, loved by him. Gemma beamed and the three of them set off for the restaurant, which was walking distance from both the Sacher and the Hofburg. They could see its vast outline ahead of them alight with thousands and thousands of candles, golden and dazzling against a star-studded sky. It had begun to snow, fat swirling snowflakes settling on her fur and hair. Twirling between her husband and best friend, Carla felt she was dancing on air as they saw other revellers in beautiful gowns making their way to dine.

Just off Heidenplatz, Seb stopped in front of a tiny unassuming eatery. He frowned looking at his phone.

"This is it," he said puzzled.

"You think?" Carla had somehow expected something grander given Seb was dressed in white tie and they were in ball gowns.

"Definitely. Look," his finger highlighted the address.

It was the kind of restaurant that had curtains half-way up the window so that peering in you could see the top half of the diners. Seb straightened slowly and his face which only Carla would have noticed, had paled. A muscle twitched in his cheek.

Gemma, in a rush of confidence entered ahead of them. After all there couldn't be too many other men also in white tie waiting for them, could there?

"Jo--oh-hannes," yelped Carla. His name coming out strangled, somewhere between a cry of surprise and a distress signal.

Even now, Carla didn't recall Johannes actually standing up to greet them. He of the impeccable manners in St. Christoph, was something or someone else entirely, in Vienna. He was at a table set for four and half-way through eating a main course although, Carla glanced at the elegant little Cartier dress watch, Seb had given her when they got married, it was only 6.45 p.m. That was bad enough. Perhaps there were a million reasons why he would have started a meal ahead of them. Maybe he was a diabetic, maybe he'd had half his stomach removed - who knew?

But he *had* known that Gemma was coming. Johannes had bought their tickets for the ball and for the opera the following day. Now he looked up, cool as a cucumber, not so much predatory as stealthy. He wasn't eating alone. A young girl - twenty-years old at most, in an emerald silk dress (hired Carla later told Gemma as if that was going to make her feel any better) was seated with her back to them. All Carla could see was bony elbows, as she too scraped the last of a mushroom risotto from her plate.

"Hi," said the girl turning, sensing people watching her. She spoke with an American accent. "I'm Geena."

"And I'm Gemma," said Gemma.

Was that it? wondered Carla. Had there been a misunderstanding? A mix up with names?

"Johannes," said Seb with a curt bow of the head.

"Oh hello," boomed Johannes as though they had stumbled upon each other by chance, still not rising from his seat. On the contrary, he remained bolt upright, an array of dishes in front of him and he held a small plate in front of him now, giving it his whole attention. He sampled *calamares* and strips of *weiner shnitzl* his tongue darting in and out like a salamander's. His eyes flickered with concentration.

"Taste this," he said, ignoring Seb, Carla and Gemma but turning to Geena and spoon feeding her as though she were a child.

Carla didn't dare meet Gemma's eye but sank into the first available chair. She would leave the problem of there being one short to their host. Not bothering to remove her mink shrug, she grabbed a bottle of the wine Johannes and Geena were so clearly enjoying and poured herself a tumbler full. Even after several more, the evening continued to stretch

216

before them as a hideous, agonizing desert of disappointment, a ribbon of film on the cutting floor, burnt and destroyed.

20

" And that was only the beginning!" Carla and Gemma had told the rest of Les Girls later.

Carla had been so tipsy by the time they'd reached the Hofburg, she'd walked straight into a mirror mistaking it for a door.

'Seriously?' The infant Geena had commented with such disdain Carla had wanted to slap her. It also made Carla feel that she and Gemma were playing Lumley and Saunders in a scene from *Absolutely Fabulous* although in their case it was more *Absolutely Furious*. Carla certainly was, barely noticing the *Seitengalerie's* sweeping red carpeted staircase which led up to the *Fetsaal*. Huge chandeliers cast a lunar glow shimmering and gleaming and bathing the entire ballroom in milky-way magic. Only the debutantes wore white and now they arrived in single file to the opening bars of Strauss. And soon the pool of disappointment Carla felt on Gemma's behalf, dissipated as Seb took her in his arms. With the soaring beat of the music, Gemma forgot everything but the desire to skip and float and leap. The music coursed through her veins and her heart as she sought the one spot ahead on which to concentrate, to stop her from feeling dizzy. Seb guided her across the vast ballroom, through the weaving dancers, their feet barely touching the parquet flooring.

"Should I offer to dance with them?" he whispered at one point. Carla knew he meant the infant or her friend.

"*Don't you dare!*" Maybe it was unkind but Carla hadn't waited all these years to come to a ball in Vienna, with someone she actually wanted to be with, to sit it out. She'd done enough of that with Gemma, when they were young. But it did mean that it was an exhausting evening. Carla was so terrified of Gemma's reaction as her friend sat like Scarlett O'Hara (in the scene where she drums her feet at the Charity Bazaar unable to dance without breaching decorum), that every time Seb showed signs of flagging she dragged him off for yet another waltz.

When Carla finally danced with Johannes, who had sat immobile until midnight not dancing with anyone, she'd mouthed the words *'but why ever not?'* He hadn't answered immediately, preferring to clamp her by the forearm and whip her around the dance floor in ever faster, shortening, quickening steps until she felt like a tornado violently rotating on one spot. Any moment Carla was convinced she was going to end up like the tigers in the story book, whizzed into a circle until she blended into ghee. It was at that moment that Carla realised that Johannes might actually be mad, that the mild, generous, exquisitely mannered man they knew - correction *thought* they knew, was actually a stark raving lunatic. Either that or he had a twin brother who had taken his place for the evening.

The faster Johannes spun her; the dizzier Carla became. He was moving so fast there was no chance to pick a spot, let alone focus on it. Carla thought of their dance teacher with a giggle, the way, nose in air, he would head off on the diagonal. In those dance routines, there had been plenty of space for her gown to sway bell-like between them. Now, her head was pressed in an arm lock, against the studs of Johannes's evening shirt and her own beautiful faille silk was so tightly furled that she felt as though she'd been entered in a sack race. And then, without warning Johannes came to a halt so abruptly that she'd spun across the shiny dance floor careering into one or two couples in her wake. He stood waiting for her too, not rushing to her side. Gasping for breath and a little shaken, Carla dodged the waltzing couples to make her way back to him. He still hadn't moved but stood statue-like in the path of oncoming dancers, completely oblivious of the mayhem he was causing.

"They're unmarried," he said in his accented, correct English pushing his mask briefly away from his face. "In answer to your question."

"Who's unmarried? Gemma? Geena?" said Carla through dry lips. She'd forgotten what she'd asked him. She felt parched and shaky and wanted to go back to Seb.

"Only unmarried women can ask a man to dance at this ball," he said in all seriousness. "Until midnight and then the man can ask whomever he likes."

So… my friend Gemma has come all the way from England, spent a fortune on dance classes, not to mention her flight, hotel and ball ticket and you didn't think to tell her this? And not that I much care for her but Geena is also sitting in hired dress. All three of you have spent the entire evening sitting! This is after all 2019, not 1862! I mean Scarlett O'Hara's era I get but now…?

But then Carla was equally irritated by Gemma's blushing virgin act. Gemma was normally a feisty, independent, strong character, what the hell had gotten into her? Why wasn't *she* asking Johannes to dance? What was she waiting for? Perhaps, she didn't want to leave the infant on her own but that was sort of too bad. They hadn't invited Geena and by all accounts she was pretty grown up. Certainly, grown up enough to accept an invitation to a ball with a man old enough to be her father. Besides, it didn't take both Johannes and Gemma to babysit her all evening.

"*Ja voll toll*," she said at a loss as to what else she could say. "So now, that it's after mid-night, will you be dancing with the in- with Geena?"

Johannes sniffed. "Of course." He began escorting Carla back to the central hall where Geena and Gemma were seated at their tiny little table and had struck up a conversation of sorts. Seb was pacing impatiently.

Carla no longer felt responsible - they could all get on with it and dance or not. But there was one more thing. Carla put a hand on Johannes's sleeve restraining him.

"Johannes, who exactly is Geena?"

"So?" asked Seb when they'd left the main ballroom at a polka gallop. His eyes crinkled with mischief. "Who is she then?" He paused briefly to cast a look over his shoulder. "Look at him! Caught between his two G... spots!"

"Think I prefer the analogy of a thorn between two roses."

They wandered hand in hand, through the salons of the vast palace. The strains of *Por Una Cabeza* evoked a Pavlovian response as looking at each other, they bolted into one of the smaller darkened rooms decorated to resemble a bar in La Boca district of Buenos Aires. Carla gasped when Seb grabbed her by the waist, his knee prising hers apart to begin the slow, seductive walk, the hardest part of the dance. Without that walk, both backwards and forwards, both stealthy and assured, you couldn't learn the tango and it had taken Seb the better part of eight years to master. When he was playing professional polo, before he became a patron and living in Palermo in Argentina, Seb had danced most weeks. For Carla it was a difficult dance for a different reason. In the tango, the woman has to learn to wait for a signal, a non-verbal dialogue and she can never lead.

"He says," said Carla as she moved around him in a figure of four, pretending she was circling a chair as she had been taught, only for him to pull her to him abruptly. She would then step over his feet delicately, as though she were picking her way along a line of stones, before moving off again in that slow, balletic walk. "That she's a friend of the family. That last winter, he spent most of the skiing season at her family's place in Vermont. That she was coming to Europe and that he promised her family he would look after her."

"Yeah, right. Horny dog."

"Seb!"

"The man's bullshitting. To be honest, I don't care what Johannes does and the kid may be young but no one forced her onto that plane to come here. She knew what she was doing. What I want to know is, did he invite her to this ball knowing Gemma was coming too?"

Carla's head was turned away but not in the theatrical way people danced tango in films.

"Yup," she said. "I asked him that too. He says that she turned up unexpectedly, she's touring Europe, that she's leaving tomorrow and that he didn't want to leave her on her own on her last night."

"In her hotel?"

The strains of *Por Una Cabeza* took up again; Carlos Gardel's achingly poignant music pooling desire in the pit of her stomach. It made her think of Jessica Biel dancing with Colin Firth in the film *Easy Virtue*. She thought that it wasn't just the seduction of the piece that was so affecting in that scene, but the nostalgia of the older women as they looked on, the pain of lost youth and beauty clearly etched on their faces, the envy at someone else being the most desired woman in the room.

Carla kicked her leg behind her, then Seb's as they set off once again, gliding across the room.

"Ah, but she's not staying in a hotel, is she?"

Some hours later, as pale morning light eked its way through the Renaissance windows, Seb led Carla by the hand to the winter garden. Carla could only guess at the loneliness of the beautiful yet ultimately tragic Empress Sisi whose ghost seemed to permeate the glacial formality of the palace. She'd hated life at court and been obsessively dedicated to preserving her youth and beauty. Carla had read with a fascination more akin to horror, how every night the princess slept with a face mask made of raw veal and crushed strawberries.

"At least if she got peckish, she could just give her face a lick," said Seb wryly.

"She slept with cloths soaked in vinegar," said Carla reading a blurb on one of the plaques under a portrait of Sisi. It depicted a pretty young woman with coils and coils of hair. It looked as if she were hugging an Irish wolfhound but peering closely, Carla could see she was holding an armful of more hair. "It took three hours to comb and pin."

"She should have cut it."

After the ball ended and the women were presented with silver bracelets ('*Oh, look Geena,' said Gemma to the American infant. 'Party bags!'*), Johannes at last saw sense and put the child in a taxi and sent her home.

Thank God, for that! breathed Carla hoping that at long last, Johannes might redeem himself. He had a long way to go but it might just be possible. He now proposed breakfast. He knew of a place - a lovely coffee shop dating back to 1824, located in a street where Beethoven and Mozart used to perform. It was popular with students.

"Great. Any age group quite frankly at this point," said Gemma. They walked huddled together in their little mink

shrugs. "Do you think now he'll take off his mask?" she
hissed.

Which of course, in this time of Covid, thought Carla, where
wearing masks had become the new normal, it didn't sound
odd at all. Except that unlike everyone else, Johannes
continued to wear his mask into the early hours, removing it
only to sip coffee.

"Will you?" asked Gemma when they were seated at a
wooden table in a dark, slightly gloomy coffee shop. They
were all just grateful for the warmth. "Won't you please
remove your mask?"

"Should I?" Johannes replied. Probably the longest sentence
he'd addressed to Gemma all evening. "Why?"

Gemma shot Carla a look that said, *'Is this guy for real?'*

"Well," Gemma replied a great deal more carefully than Carla
would have. "It makes you more … approachable."

Johannes nodded, seemed to consider this but in the end,
decided that it wasn't enough to persuade him. He drained
his coffee and promptly placed the full mask covering over
his face.

One more day… thought Carla. There's still time to salvage
this train crash of a blind date. Johannes had said Geena
really was leaving later that day and wouldn't be joining
them at the opera. Hallelujah! Carla inwardly thanked
providence. He'd then gone on to change his plans several
times. He'd meet them for brunch, then lunch, then tea, then
neither, nicht. What he would, could do, was meet them for
cocktails at a little bar he knew close to the opera. 6. p.m.
sharp. *'Don't be late!'* he'd warned them. *'Unlike last night.'*
He'd been so hungry he'd had to start without them. *'Really it
was too bad!'*

"No apology either!" fumed Seb, finally riled. "And what was that about being late? At 6.45? It was a fucking ball! We didn't go to bed until 6.45 the next morning!"

"I know," soothed Carla. "I know."

Gemma had been angelic and Carla had gone into overdrive to try and compensate for the horror of the night before.

"Oh, it wasn't so bad," said Gemma graciously. "A non-event but not horrible. Christ we've known worse, haven't we? I mean remember the Snow Ball where some twerp asked you where you came from and you replied with your usual convoluted life history and he said, *'Bit of a mixed bag, aren't we?'* Only he pronounced it 'beg.' And the party in the house that's now a school in Hampshire? My date was wearing trews and someone called him Rupert Bear and he punched him."

"God, yes. I remember. I mean I'd forgotten…"

"And I'd never have seen the Hofburg like that," she added gallantly. "As it should be seen, all decked out for a ball."

Early afternoon, they'd taken a taxi to the Belvedere Palace hoping to see Klimt's famous portrait of Adele Bloch-Bauer. Gemma had loved the film *Woman in Gold* starring Helen Mirren but it turned out the picture wasn't there.

"You'll have to go further afield if you want to see it," said Seb consulting his phone.

"Why?" said Gemma pausing before Kimt's *The Kiss* and supressing an urge to finger the protruding bits of silver and gold leaf.

"That's coz it ain't here." He whistled. "Apparently Oprah Winfrey recently sold it for $150 million. It's now in a private collection."

Can a Leopard?

When they were tired of seeing pictures, they strolled out to the park. From their vantage point, it was clear that two baroque palaces had been merged together. It was a glorious, bitterly cold, bright blue-skied day. A romantic day for those with a partner, mockingly cruel for those without. The three of them sauntered by tiered fountains, an orangery and stables.

"Amazing to think this was a summer residence," said Carla. "The scale on which buildings were built is mind blowing." She squeezed her friend's arm. "Now that the infant has gone, I'm sure Johannes will be quite different."

"He did have nice eyes," said Gemma. "I can only imagine the rest."

"That's the spirit," said Seb although his own widened in amazement that they were still flogging what he would have definitely said was a dead, dead horse.

Back in their suite at the Hotel Sacher, Carl laid out the beautiful clothes she'd chosen for the evening. As Seb zipped her up (after mock attempts to *un*zip her) Carla twisted in the mirror.

"I don't know what that was about last night," she said, "but now that Geena has gone and it's just the four of us, I'm sure it'll be all right."

"The man's a dog," said Seb violently.

"Was it even legal?"

"She was older than she looked."

"Really?"

Seb shrugged. "Let's put it this way. Closer to the twins in age rather than Alfie."

"How reassuring."

Carla tightened the back on her diamond earrings and spun around. Her Roland Mouret dress consisted of velvet on the front and stretchy black material on the back with the designer's trademark zip the length of the garment. It was sexy and demure at the same time. Her Gianvito Rossi pumps were the exact same colour velvet.

"How'd I look?" she asked her eyes shining.

"Gorgeous," said Seb huskily. "Just gorgeous." He lunged towards her. "I promise I won't mess up your hair-"

"Uh uh, I've heard that before. We don't want to be late."

"So, this time," said Seb as they approached the square. "The place we're meeting is famous for its tapas."

"Excellent," said Carla. "Exactly the worst kind." Although Carla was half Spanish, she loathed all Spanish food. She pulled her mink around her chin as she and Gemma weaved their way through tables set on the pavement. It was a bohemian part of the city and Carla felt ridiculous in her high heels and slinky dress. And freezing cold.

"And it's 6 p.m. on the dot."

"There it is," said Gemma pointing to a wine bar where everyone was smoking. "I didn't think you could. That it was against the law."

"Not in Austria it isn't," said Seb. "Not until May."

Can a Leopard?

"Well, I'm not going in," said Gemma suddenly and uncharacteristically pulling a prima donna stunt. "I get asthma, it's way too smokey."

Seb gave her a penetrating look but something refrained him from saying, 'but you're a smoker, aren't you?'

"I agree," said Carla before Seb said something, she'd regret, in solidarity. It was the least she could do.

"Right," said Seb. "I'll go in and find Johannes and bring him out. Tell him that we want to go somewhere else."

As if on cue, Seb's phone pinged.

"Well, he's already there - it being one-minute past six, naturally. So, I'll just pop in and see him."

Carla and Gemma stood shivering on the pavement. It was a crisp, cold night, already dark -the stars pin pricks of hope (or anxiety).

Seb emerged a few moments later.

"Nope, can't see hm."

"But he texted?"

Seb nodded.

"I'll go in." Carla dropped Gemma's arm. They'd been standing huddled close.

"I couldn't see him," insisted Seb.

Carla made a face and went into the smoke-filled tapas bar. Customers stood at tables eating *jamon serrano* and *manchego*. The bar was lined with row upon row of Spanish tinto. It took her back instantly to her childhood, to waiting for her father.

Waiting. She swept around the room but short of going into the men's loos to check, Seb was right. There was no sign of Johannes. She texted Seb.

Are you sure he said here?

Yes.

Let me text him directly.

Be my guest.

Carla leant against a pillar in the corner of the bar giving the place a final sweep before pressing send.

Instantly his message came back:

I'm here!

Where?

Here! I can see you.

Well, I can't see you…

Except she could now. Carla looked up, straight into the eyes of someone she'd not noticed on entering, would never ever have noticed. Carla had assumed he was one of the staff. For their night at the opera, Johannes was dressed as Mozart himself, in full 18th century regalia, complete with wig and glasses. He was also tucking into tapas and a bottle of wine. This time, funnily enough, he was quite alone. Carla knew then that Johannes was never going to make her friend happy. Carla wasn't sure how he could make anyone happy.

In retrospect the evening was farcical with the four of them sitting in a beautiful box, in their beautiful clothes with Johannes's not so beautiful wig taking up most of the space, almost completely obscuring the stage. From time to time, he would flick his hair over his shoulders with both hands and his curls, not soft and silky had it been made of human hair but scratchy and coarse, would thwack her in the face. In the intermission, tourists asked to take their picture with him.

"To go with the 19th century opera house," Gemma volunteered sportingly after an American couple from Idaho had posed with him.

"18th century," he corrected.

"I'm sorry?"

"Mozart was 18th century."

Gemma pursed her lips mouthing *'what the fuck?'* behind his back.

"Right," she said aloud.

"We're even," said Gemma on the way back to the Hotel Sacher. "I left you in the lurch in Baume, taking off soon after the blessing was over and all because I'd broken up with Titus." Except that Carla wasn't in the lurch. She was just married after all. It would have been easy to agree, to say that Titus was a dickhead anyway and that Gemma was better off without him, but Gemma wasn't. She was alone.

'The real honour of friendship is being invited into someone's real…to the nitty, gritty, the not-so-pretty…' Well, Gemma certainly knew a thing or two about that, thought Carla now as she gathered up Gemma's presents from the back seat. They all did. *Les Girls, my girls*, she thought fondly making her way up the garden path. Late flowering wisteria cascaded over dormer windows. Honeysuckle and roses clung together in a riot of quintessential country charm. The grass needed cutting and the topiary had shot over the boundaries of its hedges, and the apples were thick on the ground. Carla felt the squidgy peel of rotting plums underfoot, the fine shell of

a tiny snail and the glossy skin of a few chestnuts bright against the fruit. How could it possibly be that time of year again?

And when she glanced up, through a gap in the trees she could see to the far end of the garden. The rest of Les Girls were already gathered under the pergola to wish Gemma a happy birthday.

21

"How was it?" asked Seb in the morning, his voice strangely distended as it penetrated her quilted layers of sleep. Was he talking to her? Carla was so surprised to hear him address her directly that she actually turned her head to see if there was someone else in the room. He followed her gaze his eyebrows in an upward bascule. She turned on her side, propping herself on her elbow. It was a while since they'd sat in bed chatting. These days he was up and out, leaving breakfast half made on the kitchen table.

How was…? *Oh, that.* She'd already forgotten lunch with Les Girls but if describing it to Seb would initiate conversation of any kind - most of which had been sorely lacking recently, then she could happily start there. Calmly. Well, it had been lovely for a few hours. Until the biscuit incident.

"Ah, like that, was it?"

Yes, like that… A disappointing reflection of these Covid times…Carla snuggled back under the duvet. Today could just be the day for a swim. She'd not been back to the David Lloyd since lockdown began. She was used to swimming four times a week, out of doors, no matter the weather but had become used to Jessica Smith dot TV for her exercise routine. Or lazy. She wasn't sure which was the stronger impulse but she no longer fancied getting into a car every time she wanted a swim. But today she felt ready. And then, she would ask Seb about Karen. She had to. Her heart did a flip at the very idea, her skin going all prickly. Stop! she told herself silently. Deep breath. Remember: *'thou hast not half the power to do me harm, as I have to be hurt…'*

"It was lovely and it was shocking," said Carla pretending in the moment that everything was good between them, that she could really just recount a day out for what it was without the weight of this other thing, heavy and solid tugging at her heart.

"Oh?" Seb had been reaching for his phone. He used to reach for me, before anything else, thought Carla with a pang. But he stopped short.

"It's just the Covid thing," said Carla dismissively. "It makes even the sanest, most measured among us afraid. We all know that."

Seb frowned.

No, don't worry! Please! I'm not going to start a Covid discussion, I'm really not! Carla willed the message to him telepathically and maybe it got through because his expression softened.

"How 'bout I make porridge and you tell me all about it," said Seb patting her knee in a friendly gesture or at least patting the duvet above her knee. Either way, it was the most affection he'd shown her in a long time and she stared at the imprint of his hand a while longer. She fell back on the pillows. Quietness is a great ally, she reminded herself. Be swift to hear, slow to speak...

And parts of it had been lovely. They'd sat outside (following the old and new rule of six) on a trestle table to eat delicious roast chicken and salads. To begin with, they'd all made suitably sympathetic clucking sounds when Carla had done her party piece and shown them her dog bite. (*'Only Carla can have a designer bruise - it even matches her dress!*) They'd chatted about their monthly Zoom meetings, their work, their friendship, the fact that they'd all known each other for over forty years. The fact that Gemma's dog had taken an aggressive and severe dislike to Hope (only because she was wearing dark glasses and a Panama hat) and barked incessantly every time he saw her, the fact that Madeleine's husband had decided to live in Scotland - *'no they weren't separating nothing like that'* - Les Girls had exchanged long glances - *'no, of course not sweetie'*. Someone else's had taken to wearing a skirt and calling himself Miranda. Christ, thought Carla, where did you go with that? *'Talking of skirts...'* said Madeleine. One of her client's had taken to dressing like one of his teenage daughters in a tutu and walking around his neighbourhood with a transistor radio balanced on his shoulder. *'Who even uses transistors anymore?'* asked Gemma. *'Where would you buy one?'*

And then it was teatime with all manner of homemade cakes and sugary, mouth-watering muffins piled high on Gemma's own pottery on another trestle table in another part of the garden. Les Girls were generally feeling drowsy after too much champagne but Carla with the rocket fuel of Karen-provoked jealousy, bounced from the house to the garden to the various tables, handing out cups of tea and slices of carrot cake or beetroot velvet chocolate or Queen Mother's Favourite Recipe (*'never to be bought or sold'*) which was a delectable mix of walnut and date. It was virtually the only cake Carla had ever been able to make as it required little effort - no electric whisk - the ingredients just chucked in and left to do whatever chemical combination ingredients did, before baking.

It was all cosy and friendly and for a while, Carla actually did forget about the Karen woman and felt grown up and in control and well able to judge the difference between an incident and a crisis. Of course, she could. The explanation was probably perfectly simple. The blonde with Seb was most likely to be... well she couldn't think of who she might be. Not exactly at this moment but someone from polo or work or - anyway, she'd think about it all later. She was needed to serve more tea. She would concentrate on that. She stood back to examine the table. The cakes really were beautifully presented on a bed of rose petals while the adorable mini fairy cakes were a confectioner's dream.

Gemma was awfully clever and her pretty dishes in blues and green perfectly complimented the scones and cakes. In mouth-watering colours of mint green, and pink and pale yellow, marzipan had been used to shape adorable miniscule shoes and handbags and a string of pearls. It was girlie and fun, and because the rest were all so decorative, one plate stood out. Someone had casually piled small packets of unopened mini gingerbread men, one on top of the other. Looking for something more to do, Carla began mindlessly opening the sachets and distributing the little biscuits evenly on the plate. Inspired by the example of the other displays, she reached behind her to tear a few sage leaves from the herb garden. Pleased with the result, she picked up the plate and turned to face Les Girls.

But far from exclamations of pleasure, there was a collective hiss, a snake-like intake of breath and sucking of teeth. Hope's eyes were positively icy behind the sunglasses and even the dog had stopped barking.

"You've touched them!" she snarled.

Carla stepped away from the table, a bit of plastic corner between her fingers.

"What?" she said following Hope's gaze to the biscuits.

"You weren't supposed to touch them!" someone else squealed.

"You mean, the gingerbread *men*? Surely we're not gender biased-"

"Not a time for jokes," said Alice grimly.

"I wasn't -" *Actually, she absolutely was. She moved her fingers.*

"Oh, you mean you didn't want me to open the packets. Because I'd touched them?"

"That's why they're individually wrapped."

"Oh, for goodness' sake!" said Carla, "I haven't touched the biscuits. Besides, I've handled more cups of tea than I have biscuits if that's what you're afraid of."

And they clearly were, because when Carla went back to her seat, Hope moved away. In fact, they all did, or rather they huddled together so that there was no space for Carla who was left standing awkwardly cup and saucer in hand. What had happened to the *'Sister I'm With You'* part of the text and the bit about *'holding space for each other'?*

"You do know that scientists now think there's evidence to suggest the virus *can't* be caught from surfaces? Right?"

Les Girls looked blankly. All except Gemma.

"It's OK," she said kindly. "Let's sit together. You and me. Over here." She took a plate of fairy cakes and grabbed another bottle of champagne. "And we can have all this to ourselves while you fill me in on Alfie. Is he really going back to school next week?"

Yes, today was a day for getting back to swimming and her relationship with Seb on track. And that meant dealing with her suspicions about this Karen woman. Or the woman at any rate Carla had seen on Alfie's drone footage. She would drift no longer. She also had to believe that Alfie really was going back to school soon and if so, she needed to order his school uniform and name tapes. Oh, GOD! The thought of sewing (never mind ordering) name tapes was enough to keep her in bed for a week. Her phone pinged just as the doorbell rang at the same time. Over the sound of the kettle, Seb couldn't have heard it. She called down to him but he didn't hear her either so grabbing her dressing gown she padded downstairs, shoving her phone in her pocket. She prized open the front door. Kevin, the DHL man, was standing on the pavement opposite having deposited two tiny, identical packages on the doorstep. He took a photo of them with his phone to prove they'd been delivered.

"Not dressed yet. Tut tut," he said. "Haven't been here in a while."

"No, I've been good," she grinned gathering up the parcels.

"Yeah, I can see."

He waved and she shut the door. The parcels could almost have been posted through the letter box. Almost.

She hugged them to her.

"One each," she said going into the kitchen. She knew what hers was. It must be the quilted cross-body bag. She dropped the packages at one end of the counter.

Seb didn't hear her at first. He was busy brewing coffee, tending to his porridge which he always did with extreme care and attention.

"Les Girls were sweet about Alfie though," she said chirpily. "Especially Gemma. Do you think she was right to break up with Titus?"

Seb shot her a 'are you mad look?'

"No, I know. But now that we're all older and she's on her own…"

Clearly Seb wasn't going down the 'what if' route. She watched him busying himself in the kitchen. He prowled the space smoothly, on bare feet, as comfortable in this domestic setup as he was on the polo field, on a dive, at the piano. Just as he had always been. At least until recently. "She's always so kind given she doesn't have children herself," continued Carla anxious to keep the tone of things neutral. Seb was right. No need to dwell on Gemma's past. There was enough to contend with at this moment, in the present. "Always seems to be completely clued up on what they do at each stage. She was asking about how quarantine was going to work."

"And what did you say?"

Seb turned to give the porridge a stir. The table was set beautifully with her Luneville china and her new block printed cloth, the one she'd bought from George Clark in Stockbridge (the *minute* it had re-opened) which had prompted Seb to be all worried that she really had fantasised about shops re-opening rather than sex. She shot him a wistful look, even joking about that sort of thing those days seemed anathema. There was a new pot of honey by her place setting and Seb had even put out napkins. He'd made an effort. She was touched.

"I said that as far as we knew the boys would be quarantined for the first few weeks in their individual houses. That they'd be taught remotely within the house but at least they'd be with other boys." Her voice faded.

"I shall miss him," said Carla wistfully when Seb had sat down and they waited for their porridge to cool. "School has always been childcare pure and simple. I dreaded lockdown at the beginning but I've got used to it. I've got used to having Alfie at home."

Seb snorted. "It's time for him to go back. It is."

"I know," said Carla snubbed. "Just saying."

Can a Leopard?

She sliced banana on top of the mixture and helped herself to a generous dollop of cream. She took a mouthful, almost purring with pleasure. Her phone vibrated in her robe pocket.

"Oh!" jumped Carla, a spoon half-way to her mouth.

"And there was me thinking you were all excited," said Seb a glint in his eye.

Carla set down her spoon and glanced at her phone.

Just parking. Number one twin, Sophie, had texted.

'Just parking?' What did that mean?

Carla did a swift scroll. She'd not heard from Sophie in weeks. Even as long as three - no, that couldn't be right. She knew her daughter had very little spare time juggling work as an accountant and riding. Sophie's Labrador Cucumber had slipped from pole position when she'd purchased a horse - Lightening Streak - with which to event.

And there were the words pulsating in fluorescent green off the page.

Be with you by 10

By 10? But today wasn't…? Oh, yes it was.

Carla glanced at the clock on the counter behind Seb's head. It was 9.30. She took a long sip of tea. It was a toss- up between finishing her breakfast and having time to shower. To shower or not to … yes shower. What if Sophie said she was a bit pongy?

"Er… bit of a mix-up," she said rapidly explaining and moving away from the able.

Can a Leopard?

"OK," said Seb. "So, when will you be back?"

Carla shook her head.

"We're only checking out the course. And it's nearby. A couple of hours. Not more. We can talk -" Seb's head reared. "I mean we can walk then. With Alfie."

Carla stood in the delicious hot jet stream, no more than seconds, heaping her skin with soap so that when the doorbell rang, she had to grab a towel wiping away suds on her way down. Again, Seb appeared not to hear it - she was going to have to install something much louder.

"Two minutes!" announced Carla to a frowning Sophie.

"Doesn't look like two minutes to me," said her daughter stepping into the hall in muddy boots. Carla hesitated between the desire to protect her stone floor and the need to hurry.

"You can do your make-up in the car," said Sophie leaning over to tighten her boots.

"Morning Miss Sophie," said Seb coming through from the kitchen nursing a mug. He held it out to her. "Coffee?"

Sophie shook her head. "No time, plus I'm badly parked. I'm completely blocking in four cars."

Seb whistled. "Better hurry, darkling."

Hardly daring to breath, Carla vaulted up the stairs, pulled on jeans, a sweater, grabbed socks, a coat and boots. She tipped moisturiser, foundation, lipstick and mascara into a plastic bag and minutes later they were walking the short distance to the car.

Sophie glanced at Carla's bare feet. "You weren't exaggerating when you said two minutes."

*

"How was it?" said Seb for the second time that day, as Carla limped home many hours later. It felt almost déjà vu from the morning. As if they were back to where they'd left off. In fact, they could well have been. The two little parcels which they'd both forgotten about were still on the counter and Seb was still in the kitchen, this time making supper not breakfast. He was grating fresh ginger onto a plate ready to add to the mixture of butter, brown sugar, honey and soy bubbling on the grange.

"Mmmn…. smells delicious," she said her stomach rumbling in response. She pulled out a chair and sat down at the table. "How'd it go…?" echoed Carla. "It was lovely to be with Sophie." She let her voice drift. And it was, although every time she got into a car with her daughter she wondered if it would be her last. It was only sitting down that she realised how exhausted she was, how Sophie was stimulating to be with and … challenging.

Hurtling out of town Carla had pressed her back into the car seat, her legs outstretched as if reaching for an imaginary set of brakes. From time to time, she stole a glance at the speedometer.

"What's the matter? You seem frightened?"

Absolutely terrified… And we were in a bad car crash once, remember?

"Of course not."

241

Can a Leopard?

They'd passed a graveyard. Carla didn't dare look. Any little faster and they'd be in it.

"Love my car," said Sophie nudging 100.

"Yes… any problems with it?" *As in it feels really lightweight and tinny …*

And when they'd arrived at the racecourse, Sophie had set off at breakneck speed, Carla trotting behind, dodging riders and horses and dogs which seemed to be aiming for her alone and coming at her from all directions. She was warm enough in her featherlight leather, fur-trimmed jacket but she'd grabbed the wrong boots.

"Do you always walk this slowly?" said Sophie as Carla lumbered behind, sidestepping cow pats and massive horse turds. Her lovely suede Tods were billed as riding boots but of course were nothing of the kind. Nor were they particularly waterproof. Instinctively, Carla rubbed her thigh where she could still feel the dog bite. The bruise which had grown into a blousy hydrangea head, had shrunk into a solid egg-sized lump that often ached.

'*How sharper than a serpent's tooth it is to have a thankless child…*' she said aloud now.

"Ain't that the truth," agreed Seb now, wiping his hands on a dish cloth. "Supper will be ready in fifteen."

"Sorry," said Carla. "I've come home a bit rattled. We were a lot longer than I thought and then Sophie wanted me to see Lightning back at the stable. It was fine. Tiring."

She stood up. "What can I do?" It didn't seem as though there was anything left *to* do, Seb had taken care of it all. She paced the kitchen, moving a dish here, tweaking the odd flower arrangement there. The morning's post and the parcels left by DHL were unmoved from where she'd left them. "Oh, I forgot about these," she said excitedly. "And this one's for you."

Seb lurched forward snatching his away.

"When did these arrive?"

"This morning," said Carla surprised at the roughness of his action. "Remember? With Sophie here so early we both forgot about them." Carla was already tearing into hers. "Why?"

The front door slammed and Alfie appeared seconds later wheeling his bike through the house. He leant it against the counter beside her and removed his helmet. His face was flushed. His streaked hair was tousled and there were freckles along his nose. He looked indignant but handsome and if Carla weren't so curious about her delivery, she'd have kissed his smooth plump cheeks.

"Have you been swimming?" said Carla. "No, don't!" she cried as his bottom skimmed one of her Swedish, gingham checked chairs. A wet patch had already formed and Carla was certain it would leave a water mark. He kicked off dripping trainers.

"Yeah, jumping off the bridge." Alfie raised his bottom. "With Jake and Bill." He mentioned two of his former classmates.

"But you only just went out, big guy," said Seb absentmindedly, carefully beginning to unwrap his parcel.

"Yeah, but this Karen - started screaming at us -"

Carla's head shot up, her heart tumbled sideways and she froze in the process of unwrapping hers.

"Karen? What Karen? What do you mean, 'this Karen'?"

"What?" Alfie glanced in her direction taken aback by her shrill tone. "It was nothing. Just some Karen screaming at us and telling us that we couldn't jump from there. That she'd call the police. You know. Typical Karen."

"Well, you can't," said Carla automatically.

"Yeah, we can."

"*Seb!*"

"Don't speak to your mother like that," said Seb robotically.

"What? What did I say?" said Alfie pushing away from the counter in disgust. He went over to the sink leaning over to drink directly from the tap.

"Could you use a glass?" Carla hated that her voice sounded so petulant.

Alfie turned off the tap and shook his head so that water droplets splashed around him.

"Chill," said Alfie coming up for air and ignoring Carla's instruction. "I'm going out again."

"No, you're not! Wait! Tell me who this Karen is! Actually, you both can. Starting with you Seb."

Alfie started giggling. "You're cross about a Karen?" he smirked.

Carla felt her heart bang against her ribs. What, so even their son knew about Karen? Her eyes narrowed. Her hands were shaking and her leg throbbed. It seemed to do that these days a physical barometer for her state of mind. *Was* she cross? Yeah, OK, she was.

Her voice certainly cracked as she said, "not cross exactly, no."

"You mean you don't know what a Karen is?" Alfie continued to stare in disbelief while Carla glowered. She hated sentences that began *'you mean you don't know...?* Obviously, she didn't know or she wouldn't be asking!

"No," she said coldly. "I don't. Why don't you tell me? Better still ..." she shot Seb an icy glare. "Why don't you, Seb?"

But Seb was frowning. Nestling in layers of tissue paper was a hint of soft-as-butter camel leather and a glint of gold chain. He winkled it out as though he were prizing an oyster out of its shell. Or the way detectives dangled a contaminated item by the end of a pencil, in police dramas

Carla ripped open the bubble wrap and the underlying paper of her own package. Had they sent *two* bags by mistake? She supressed a hysterical giggle. His and hers. What would Seb look like sporting a cross-body? Actually, he could probably get away with it. Er... maybe not. Now it was Carla's turn to look up abruptly. The packaging was slender and neat and exquisite but it didn't contain a cross-body bag of any description. The box was the same size and shape exactly, packed in an identical padded jiffy bag but that was where any semblance ended. Besides, this one was trimmed in NHS rainbow colours.

"'Welcome to you'," she read aloud. "'Saliva Collection Kit.'" She looked up almost too stunned to continue. "'23and Me?'"

22

"So, can I go?" said Alfie into the vacuum.

"Yes!" said Seb and Carla in unison. "Go!"

"Oh," even Alfie seemed surprised his parents had capitulated so quickly.

Seb pulled out two ten-pound notes from his wallet. "And get something to eat - take your pals to the Three Joes for a pizza. Then go for a walk. Or a swim."

Alfie's eyes had widened and Carla could almost hear him gulp. Not even her valiant son was brave enough at that moment to draw attention to the plump side of salmon they could both see ready and prepped on the side of the grange. Salmon with its ginger, soy, honey crust was Seb's signature dish and they all loved it but it took care and time to prepare and as a result, eating it was a command performance. Not that it needed to be - there was never a flake left by the time dinner was over. There was a delicious aroma of roast potatoes too, seasoned with fresh rosemary, cooked especially for Alfie as neither Seb nor Carla much cared for them.

"Another swim then," said Seb begging the question. Stay out! Do whatever you want but staying out was the subtext.

"Nice one Dad," said Alfie eager to be gone before Seb changed his mind, aware that the temperature in the kitchen had suddenly plummeted. He lugged his bicycle back through the kitchen, his helmet tied to the handlebars. Carla automatically spreadeagled her body against the walls as

Can a Leopard?

Alfie clipped its corners, leaving a streak of oil. She glanced at his bare feet - he clearly didn't relish the idea of wet trainers but for once she wouldn't have cared had he grabbed her Manolos.

When she was certain the front door had closed behind him, Carla took a deep breath.

"You first" she said hovering by the French doors that lead onto the patio. "Tell me about Karen. And no funny stories, no Annabel-type ex-girlfriend bull shit. Remember I saw you, Seb. I saw you on Alfie's drone. I want to know who this Karen is. The truth."

"Karen?"

Seb looked genuinely mystified.

"Yes," said Carla shortly. "Karen. Even Alfie knows about her. He said 'this Karen' told them to stop jumping off the bridge. Is she the blonde you've been meeting? Has Alfie met her? A bit low, don't you think, to take your *son* to meet your *girlfriend*?"

She realised she was shouting, that her voice had cracked.

Seb held up his hands.

"Woa!" he said. "Girlfriend? I have absolutely no idea what you're talking about. I promise you."

Carla felt tears spurt and spill, her nose dripped. She'd never been a pretty crier and she knew it bothered Seb to see runny mascara but she made no effort to stop the sobs ripping through. Before her, the garden blurred. Months of good weather had made the herb garden flourish but now it needed cutting back. Rosemary and sage completely dwarfed clumps of thyme and spindly shallots had turned chartreuse. A geometric design with balls of club moss, planted to separate rectangular areas between gravel and brick were now entirely lost beneath sun greedy Euphorbia and Silver Ragwort. But she saw none of it. Gradually, her messy sobs subsided. She'd have liked Seb to be a little more apologetic. He ought to be, given that their lives were imploding but he was standing still, studying his phone.

Carla stepped back into the kitchen, briefly calm before anger overtook her once again. The offending package was still on the table, nestled in its bubble wrap. Thank goodness, Alfie hadn't spotted it. Grabbing a fork from one of the place settings, she skewered the plastic coating, running a spoke along its edge until the plastic fell away and pulled open the box. The accompanying pamphlet was fuchsia pink with the large letters 'HI' printed in white (*Hi to you too*). There was a big white dot over the 'i' and another, perfect, round full stop. A bit too casual and chatty for her liking. Carla flicked open to the first page: *'ooooolala… what do we have here?'* No idea. *What do we have here?* She turned back to the cover. It really was more suggestive of an expensive perfume or sexy underwear than a PGS test with the purpose of determining gene variants. *'Your genetic code is 6bn and it's carved up into roughly 20,000 genes…'* There was also a saliva collection tube containing stabilizing liquid and a clear plastic bag.

Seb crossed to her, opening his arms. "I promise, darkling, I really don't know what you're talking about. I promise-"

"Don't you dare say 'promise' to me again!" she shouted, (OK, screamed). "And this?" she hurled the leaflet at him, knocking over a glass. It fell open on a cobalt blue page: *'No app? No worries.'* The previous: *'Okay, let's get started,'* was in purple.

"Sh!" said Seb reaching down to pick it up. "I'm sure the neighbours can hear you."

Carla stared at him incredulously. "Neighbours? What the hell do I care about neighbours! Let them hear me!"

Pent up frustration was rapidly getting the better of her. All the *'you can't control events but you can control your reaction to them…'* advice from all the self-help books she'd ever read, going swiftly out the window. Besides, she didn't want to control her reaction. Not at all. She needed Seb to know exactly how she felt. "Let them hear me!" she repeated.

Again, Seb tried to take her in his arms but she pulled away.

Seb sighed. "Sit down, Carla," he said quietly. "I think you've got the wrong end of the stick. Talk about picking up fag ends as the twins used to say. I don't have a girlfriend. When would I have time for any of that? Besides, there's only you, you know that."

"That's not the point though is it? Whether you have time or not. You've certainly had time to be out galivanting."

He fingered the box, pulling out his glasses to examine the literature.

"A bit girlie isn't it?" she said hiccupping untidily and briefly distracted from her upset.

"It's very … pink," he agreed. Again, he tried to touch her, reaching for her hand but she pulled away.

"Go on then. It better sound convincing."

"Don't be angry, darkling," he said which only incensed her all the more. "I find it so upsetting when you're cross with me."

She glanced at his perplexed face down to the pamphlet again. *'Let the discovery begin… 8 easy ways to get started.'* She took a deep breath.

"I'm only going to ask you the once. Is all this because you have…" Her voice broke. She tried again and this time her voice was toneless. "Seb. Do you have a love child?"

Seb whipped off his glasses and suddenly he seemed vulnerable, older and very tired. But she hardened her resolve. She would not let him slip out of this one.

"What? No! Of course not!"

"Then who is Karen?"

"Oh, my God. Not this again! I don't know a Karen," said Seb firmly. "I've told you."

"Then why does Alfie keep banging on about her? Why did her name flash up on your screen when we were in Italy? Why is her name always coming up on Alfie's Insta messages? You know that I can't read them but I get notifications. So, do you."

Seb again consulted his phone. He pulled out his chair at the head of the table and sat down, stretching his legs out in front of him.

"I'm talking to you!" said Carla calmer, although every nerve in her body tingled with irritation.

He had begun to scroll through stored images. He pushed the phone across the table, aiming deftly between cutlery and china. Carla winced hoping it wouldn't scratch the mango wood.

"Is this her?"

And when she stared at him, he nodded again to the phone.

"Take a closer look."

Carla shrugged. "Maybe. I don't know. It was quick. I wasn't paying that much attention."

Seb raised an eyebrow.

"I wasn't!" she protested. "Don't you think I would have? But yes," she pulled out a tissue to blow her nose. "Yup, that could be her."

Seb retrieved his phone.

"How about this one?"

The image again was different. But the women were all blonde, with short, blow-dried hair.

"And this?"

Carla nodded miserably. In spinning the phone across the table to her, Seb had knocked over some water and Carla mopped it up with one of the starched napkins. A complete waste of laundry but she didn't care. Their dinner *en famille* was in ruins anyway. And Alfie was out. Besides, she'd completely lost her appetite.

"Right," he said. "I think I know how you got there. You might want to read this to yourself."

He again slid the phone across the table. As Carla drew breath to protest however, he held up a hand. "Ugh uh," he said. "Read it first. I'll make you a cup of tea. Or maybe you'd prefer a G&T?"

She shook her head to the gin. He stood up to light the gas and set the kettle on the grange. She always secretly marvelled that the flame was always stable the first time he turned on the gas, but it blew out immediately when she did. It was surreal, she thought, hanging onto these trivial domestic moments in the midst of family turmoil. Maybe because of it.

'*Karen (pejorative)*' she read, '*is a term used in the English-speaking world for someone perceived as entitled or demanding beyond the scope of what is appropriate or necessary. A common stereotype is that of a white woman who uses-*'

"Keep reading," said Seb. The kettle had begun singing and he took it off the heat. He measured out a teaspoon of the vanilla flavoured loose tea that she loved, purchased from the Russian shop at the bottom of town. He carried it carefully to the table, nursing the small green iron cast pot in his hands as though it were fragile porcelain.

'*As of 2020, the term was increasingly being used as a general-purpose term of disapproval for middle-aged white women…*'

Carla didn't dare raise her head to look at Seb. The table already set for their meal was so crowded with crockery that he placed the tea pot on top of one of the dinner plates, together with a mug and jug of milk. He put a hand on her shoulder. Which this time she didn't shake off. She rubbed her throbbing leg. Was it really possible that she'd been mistaken? Had she really got this all wrong? Had she tortured herself ever since Italy over something that wasn't really there?

When she finally looked up, Seb was watching for her reaction.

"So, a Karen is a Sharon?"

"What on earth?" Seb looked so completely baffled that in other circumstances, she would have burst out laughing.

"You know, being a Sharon? Pauline Quirke slouching around Chigwell in a shell suit?"

Seb took a deep breath. "Carla," he said speaking carefully and slowly. "I have absolutely no idea what you're on about. Who's Pauline Quickfit?"

Carla shrugged. "Quirke. Pauline Quirke. She's an actress. I forgot you weren't in England then. She was in something called *Birds of a Feather* - it was a TV comedy show about two sisters, a Tracy and a Sharon who come together when their husbands are sent to prison for armed robbery."

"Never heard of it."

Carla sighed. "Being a Sharon became synonymous with someone who wasn't very bright, a bit common, displaying too much flesh."

Seb perked up. "Sounds good to me."

"I'm serious."

"So am I.

"So is a Karen a Sharon?"

"Or Sharon's daughter?" He tried to make light of it.

It was Carla's turn to google images of women. She'd forgotten how hilarious she'd found the Sharon character. She might just download a series of the sit com.

"How did I not know this?" she said at length. "I mean even Alfie bandies the term."

Seb's mouth twisted. "Don't be hard on yourself. There's been a lot going on. You've been distracted recently."

In normal circumstances she might have agreed.

"*I've* been distracted?"

"Steady," said Seb putting out both hands and making the pumping action he did when he thought she should lower her voice or was becoming over excited. "Yes, I'd say so." Another change in expression made him add hastily, "Whatever the reason, I'd agree that we've not been very … close recently."

Carla took a sip of tea and was about to contradict him again when she stopped herself. She couldn't deny there'd been a certain *froideur* between them but was it entirely her fault? He was the one disappearing at odd times and early in the morning and not being as attentive or his usual kind self. It was ironic that now that the worst of the pandemic was over, that the harshness of lockdown was behind them, they should be so at odds with each other. And themselves. And over what exactly?

"Carla?"

Carla took another sip of tea shaking her head.

"I almost miss lockdown," she said wistfully. "Everything seemed simpler. We were kinder to each other, more patient. More grateful *for* each other."

Seb was silent. He stood with his back to the grange, his arms folded across his chest. She took another sip but her mouth felt grainy, not at all refreshed. She thought of a Karen's chief characteristics 'entitlement, selfishness and a desire to complain.' Hand on heart, she could thankfully say she didn't know anyone who fitted the description.

"*Mea culpa*," she said placatory enough. "I got the Karen thing wrong. I freely admit it."

Now was when Seb should apologise to her. She waited a few minutes anticipating the moment he did and they would make up and it would all be fine between them but he was silent. He didn't say a word. Which is why, despite warning signals and a cautionary inner voice saying, *'you don't have to react to everything'* she tacked back. "I was jealous. I mean you were too of Dr. John Lee."

"Who?"

"In Italy. Of John Lee."

Seb blinked rapidly.

"Yeah, you know. The doctor who writes for *The Spectator*."

Seb sighed deeply.

"I don't want to fight," he said in his weary, long-suffering voice, the one that implied he was used to having to placate, mediate, be the voice of reason. It only irritated her all the more.

"We're not. I'm just saying. You get jealous too."

"But … this John whomever is a real person. A 'Karen' isn't - well she is in a sense; she could be every woman."

"After everything I've read about her," said Carla tightly. "I'm going to ignore that. The difference is I've never met John."

"And I've not met 'Karen'."

Seb opened the fridge and took out a beer.

"Let's forget dinner," he said. "How the hell did we get started?"

"With this." It was Carla's turn to slide something across the kitchen table and now she flicked the 23and Me box (it was surprisingly light) towards Seb's empty place setting. She barely noticed as a wine glass quivered perilously. "You still haven't explained this. Or the woman in the drone. Who is she, Seb and why have you ordered a DNA kit

23

"*What* did you say?" Carla blinked rapidly while her whirring thoughts couldn't help thinking that she wasn't the only one to have gotten her knickers in a twist recently. Unfortunate turn of phrase given the circumstances.

"So, not a love child?"

"I've never really understood that expression," said Seb unperturbed, calmly sipping his beer. "Aren't all children made of love?"

"You know what I mean," said Carla sternly.

"Well not mine at any rate. Like I said, she says she's my niece." Seb mumbled the words so quietly she had to lean forward to hear. Normally it was the other way around and Seb had to ask Carla to repeat a conversation. "Well, half-niece. At least I think she is."

"Don't be silly," she said. "At least you've not said she's your niece."

Seb paused bottle half-way to his mouth.

"That's exactly what I just said. You weren't listening."

Carla rose from the table. He was right. She hadn't been. She'd been dismayed by how far apart they'd grown during the summer for all this to have been going on and for her not to have known. All the closeness gained during lockdown for it to evaporate the minute restrictions were lifted. And to what end? For Carla to have nurtured secret jealousy feeding it, encouraging it, allowing it to grow and Seb to have harboured his own troubles, each travelling further away from each other with no bridge, bascule or otherwise, no way back?

"I think I'll have a drink too."

"No, I'll get it."

Seb put a hand on her shoulder pushing her back into her seat and set down his beer. He pulled out a block of ice from the freezer, banging it against the wood counter with both hands. Carla winced as large chunks and splinters skidded everywhere landing in a hydrangea and wetting her calendar. He ripped open a lemon, squeezing it roughly onto the cubes. The order was all wrong but it didn't matter. Next came tonic - not much of it and then copious measures of gin. The glass clinked nervously. Carla took a gulp.

"I don't understand," she said after a few moments feeling the alcohol hit her stomach. "That's not possible. There's only Dom in America. And he's gay. Unless you have another sibling-"

"Nope," said Seb interrupting. "And that's what I thought too. That he was gay. So that the child couldn't possibly be his. But he is -"

"I thought you said 'niece?'"

They looked at each other in confusion.

"I did. I meant that Dom was gay, *is* gay."

"Well clearly not all the time." Carla shook her head bewildered. "So, the woman in the drone photo is …?"

Seb nodded taking another sip. "Zoe. Her name's Zoe. She actually grew up in the same Harare suburb as we did. The mother is Shona."

Carla frowned tossing back her own drink.

"Pretty name."

Seb looked at his wife.

"Shona as in the tribe? Actually," he added thoughtfully, "more like from the Ndau group. Don't you remember anything from our Zim trip?"

Carla coloured. "Yes, of course," she said hastily. "I misheard, I thought you said Shula... as in *The Archers*..." her voice trailed unconvincingly. Sharon, Shula... Seb must think she was a closet soap addict.

"Yes, well anyway," continued Seb barring his teeth. "Zoe's mother died recently and it was only then that she revealed the identity of Zoe's biological father. Zoe always believed him to be someone else. Her mother was basically a single parent but when she knew she was dying she told Zoe that her father was a Cave, now living in England."

Carla's eyebrows did its own version of a bascule bridge. "Not exactly a lot to go on, then."

"No, and as you now know, she found the wrong brother."

Carla emitted an unladylike slurp. "And you're absolutely sure about that?"

Seb ran a hair through his long hair. "Of course, I'm sure!" he said. "But not so certain Dom is."

Can a Leopard?

Carla scanned Seb's face. Now that she really looked at it, she noticed new lines, shadows under the eyes. And he'd lost weight. She felt a flip of compassion.

"Mother's baby, father's maybe," she said to herself. "Or *Mater semper certa est …*"

"Come again?"

"It's a wise child who knows his own father…'"

Seb had been pacing around the kitchen, tidying up from the meal they'd abandoned. He covered the salmon that had been ready to be grilled with cling film, set aside the sauce. There were bowls of nibbles on the counter and he scooped up a handful of nuts but didn't eat them.

"But that's not quite right is it?" He considered the nuts. Seb knew his Latin better than she did having been educated by the Jesuits. "It's more along the lines: 'The mother always is certain…' Carla, what are you on about?"

Carla also helped herself to some nuts, the gin was making her feel pleasantly woozy. Elbows on the counter, the line of her body formed a bridge.

"Before DNA," she said brushing salt off her fingers. "There was no way of verifying a child's paternity. The only evidence was the word of the mother (who might be lying or not know herself) or the difference in skin colour - except of course if Zoe is half Shona," she added quickly, "that might not apply…" she let her voice dwindle. "It's a trope often explored in literature. Even Telemachus says he can't be 100% certain who his father is because 'no one witnesses his own begetting.'"

"Thank God," said Seb glibly.

Can a Leopard?

Carla pushed the peanuts away. "It's quite fascinating really. Of course, traditionally, a man had no legal recourse if he was married to the child's mother and suspected her child might not be his. *'Mater semper certa est, pater est, quem nuptiae demonstrant.'*

"The mother is certain, and the father is him to whom marriage points," translated Seb.

"Precisely. Bye the way, were they married? Dom and Zoe's mother?"

Seb paused, a nut half-way to his mouth. He was eating his now in a distracted fashion, one by one, unlike Carla who had tipped her head back to accommodate more.

"You know, I didn't ask. The whole thing has been... well delicate and I didn't think it mattered."

"It doesn't I suppose." Carla grappled with this new information, her own questions and doubts. They were having the longest conversation they'd had in months and she didn't want to lose the closeness she was feeling despite the uncomfortable topic. "Mmmn...." she said after a while. "There must be hundreds of Caves in England. How did Zoe find you?"

"Facebook," said Seb crisply moving to the fridge. "Another gin and tonic or Rosé?"

Carla didn't miss a beat.

"Or both."

"My thinking exactly."

Seb refreshed their glasses and together they went out onto the patio. Jutting above the wall that formed the boundary of the garden, the west front of the cathedral with its triple porch and Gothic windows was clearly visible. Carla had started going to Evensong once again sitting two metres apart and wearing a mask. In the early days of test and trace, she'd had to write her contact details on a little card and leave it in a basket by the entrance to the nave. When the NHS brought out its App, all she had to do was scan the barcode. Watching the choir enter wearing masks and seeing the head of music conduct the boy choristers from behind a Perspex screen, still made her want to pinch herself in disbelief.

"So…" she said, setting her glass on the small wrought iron table where they breakfasted. The larger teak one, under the pergola was where they had lunch and dinner. "Zoe has found you and that's great. But why isn't she on to Dom? I mean how do you know she is who she says she is. Plus, why did you agree to meet without knowing for sure? Or are you sure? Or is that what the 23and Me is all about?" *Why didn't you tell me?*

"I don't know," said Seb and for the first time in their entire time together Carla could see that he was agitated. "I mean I don't know why I didn't tell you." Seb had always had an uncanny way of reading her mind. His gaze bored into hers, his conflicting emotions palpable. "Zoe was travelling when Covid struck. She'd been staying in the West Country since March but it's only recently that she found out herself. She emailed me a couple of times but to be honest I did think she was trying it on. I mean I think to begin with she thought I was her father."

A small flutter of fear clutched at her heart, but it really was only small, dulled by alcohol.

"And you're absolutely certain you're not?" Even to herself Carla's voice sounded preternaturally calm.

Seb made a clicking sound. Carla shot him a glance. *Oh, my god! Didn't the Shona dialect sound like that?*

Can a Leopard?

"I've never been with anyone that fits the description of Zoe's mother," said Seb starchily "I was dating a girl before I went to Oxford but the relationship didn't survive the separation. That was decades ago and besides we were kids, yah." It was the first time there'd ever been a hint of an accent. "And she wasn't Shona," he added.

"So, when exactly did you agree to meet?" said Carla equally reticent wanting to believe, but not yet entirely convinced. "Why you anyway?"

Seb chased the ice in his glass. "Obviously with Covid going on, Dom couldn't travel here. Not that he was offering, mind. In fact, I think he's in denial. Zoe has had her DNA done. She said she was coming to Winchester with some kids from her course, so, I thought I'd see her and then decide. But I didn't want to complicate things with you or Alfie. I just wanted to see her. I thought that by seeing her, I'd know."

Carla took another large sip, ice knocking against her teeth. The alcohol coursing through her veins was soothing, making everything seem removed. Everything. Including Covid. Even that seemed too extreme to have really happened. As though it were part of some disaster movie, that the credits would begin rolling, the final scene played out, the music struck up in some speaker in a corner of the cinema and they would all revert to normal. Seb's mouth was moving but Carla no longer heard him. It wasn't a particularly shocking story. It wasn't an anything story. Except of course it was where Zoe was concerned. Dom, had been ambivalent about his sexuality, had unknowingly fathered a child and then 'come out' declaring his hand so to speak, when he travelled to America. Where he'd been living for the past twenty years. Nothing dramatic. Except there was in all this, a vulnerable party - a needing, innocent one.

"And what does Zoe want?" she asked at length as Seb poured himself another gin but this time leaving out the tonic.

"I'm not sure," he said carefully. "No," he corrected. "I do know. She wants a family. She never really had one. Her mother's boyfriend left them when she was twelve. She wants to know her real father, get to know him."

Carla leant back on her downy chair, gazing down the stripes of the lawn, the pretty herbaceous border with its moss balls and hydrangeas, its exotic grasses and tumbling roses. A quintessentially English scene and as far removed from a Harare suburb as it was possible to be. Or one in San Francisco, she should imagine.

"I see," she said sucking a lemon pip. "But does Dom want to know her?"

Seb's eyes were moist. He was being a whole lot more compassionate and generous than she was feeling. "Now that is the million-dollar question. And you know Dom." She did know Dom. "Zoe," said Seb, an almost pleading note in his tone. "This … woman has never had a proper family."

Carla tossed back her drink but before Carla could launch into another 'mother's baby, father's maybe', Seb had silenced the discussion by saying the DNA testing kit would resolve it all. "But you're not identical twins," said Carla. "You won't be her father."

"No, but if Zoe is telling the truth, she'll show up as kin."

"Do you mean there's a chance that you and I could be related?" said Carla flippantly.

A muscle ticked in Seb's cheek. "Not even remotely."

"I'm not. Stranger things have happened."

"Let's stick with what we know, shall we?" said Seb gruffly.

Carla moved closer to him, pushing away her glass. She felt pleasantly giddy and warm and somehow... better. She took his hands forcing him to look at her.

"Well, what I know is that we have to find that closeness again," she said. "We used to think ourselves so lucky to have found each other. To have been given another chance - well in my case," she smiled. Seb had only been married the once. "We should be able to tell each other everything. To be able to really talk. About the good as well as the bad. OK," she added hurriedly feeling him pull away slightly. "The uncomfortable. We were closer during lockdown when we had so many physical restrictions put upon us and now that they've been lifted, we've created different barriers. We mustn't allow a wall to build up between us -"

Seb stood up suddenly pulling her with him.

"Hush *grande bébé* as Alfie would say."

"*Used* to say. I'm not sure that's Winchester speak any more."

"I said that to you when we first met," he said quietly. "Do you remember? That there was a wall around you?"

Carla nodded a catch in her throat. How could she forget the excitement of their first meeting? With his cashmere coat thrown over his polo clothes arriving in the tiny Northington church, snow caking his boots, he was the most glamorous figure she'd ever seen. The stomach-churning desire she thought dead and buried had risen, unbidden, to silence her once and for all.

"This time though it was you. This time the wall was around you."

He pulled her even closer, her body the length of his. She was bare foot and she stood on tiptoes to fit in the shelter of his arms.

"And I said," she whispered, "that there wasn't a wall. And you said-"

"Prove it. I said prove it." Seb's face was close to hers, his breath on hers, his lips barely touching hers. "By having lunch with me."

"By having lunch with you."

Which she had …

24

"OK," said Ollie, the policeman who looked no older than Tom and considerably younger than Sophie. He moved the screen towards Carla. "I've not done this before so bear with me. I have to upload the photos - there are twelve in total - and then you can tell me if any - or one at least, fits the bill."

Carla nodded, clenching her fists tightly. She always felt nervous in the presence of the police even with if this one seemed so ridiculously young. But then everyone seemed young to her these days.

They were seated in not quite a padded cell but certainly a windowless one, at Mottisfont Court Police Station, at the top of town. It was a place she had visited occasionally in the past when she'd interpreted for Spanish speaking offenders. She knew there was a good size communal garden at the rear where she'd often translated statements or conversed with a defendant's council. A little further up the road on the left, was the bronze statue of a Hampshire Hog commissioned by the Hampshire County Council to celebrate its centenary. Carla remembered trying to explain (in Spanish) why as far back as the 18th Century, Hampshirites were called 'Hampshire Hogs'. The fact that for hundreds of years, wild boar had foraged the undergrowth in the vast tracks of surrounding forest had resonated with the Spaniard. To this day he'd told her, his countrymen continued to hunt wild boar. He'd been less interested in hearing that King William I had been killed when hunting in the New Forest over nine hundred years before. She wondered what had become of Sergio. He'd been accused of assaulting a man in Basingstoke. He'd pleaded guilty, been fined £89, with a £34 victim surcharge and £85 costs. At the time it hadn't seemed very much and now, a victim of assault herself, it didn't seem nearly enough.

"And you'd be happy to appear in court, if it goes that far?" Ollie shuffled some papers. He touched his mask. "I'll wear one so you don't have to," is what he'd said when she first arrived.

"Yes," said Carla rubbing her leg instinctively. "Absolutely."

Ollie continued tapping. "I have to say we never expected it to get this far. The media response has been huge."

Carla nodded. It was thanks to a friend's daughter who had created a WhatsApp group reporting the dog attack. She had a good record for finding perpetrators of petty crime. She'd tracked down a stolen bicycle, a stolen fur coat (the woman had been seen walking down the King's Road in mink, in June) and traced an errant husband to a Premier Inn in Ryde on the Isle of Wight.

"Are you OK, though?"

"Oh, you know." Carla felt for the egg-sized lump on her thigh. Puncture wounds and the dog's imprint were still clearly visible.

"You were lucky," Ollie said sympathetically. "Playing dead like that, probably saved your life."

Carla agreed.

"Yes, very brave."

Carla glowed.

"OK, here we are. Oh, first can you sign these?"

Ollie pushed a document towards her. "It's just your previous statement, the one I took from you when the attack first happened. When I visited you at your home?"

Carla took the proffered pen.

"And to say that you're OK with my showing you these pictures."

"I thought I was going to have a real live line up," she said relieved.

"Ah, no. Not with Covid. To be honest, we've not done one of these here for ages. If ever."

"Right."

"Ready?"

"Yup. Yes, ugh huh."

"Good." Ollie turned the screen. The squares of twelve (good - who knew?) men faced her - all pretty similar although there was only one redhead. She peered closely.

"Take your time," he said patiently. She tried to read his expression - he had clear, hazelnut eyes, the whites pristine not veined and pink like hers.

She scanned the faces; tried to remember the scene. Closed her eyes momentarily. There'd been two men, two women and the empty pushchair - empty at least of a child. The man closest to her was a redhead, he'd worn a white vest, was standing drinking beer. He had a belly. The other man was younger - a youth but his face was indistinct or distinct in that it could have belonged to anyone from the market flower seller, to the jeweller in the High Street, to a teacher at her son's school. OK, maybe not a teacher.

269

Can a Leopard?

"In terms of my description," she said carefully. "The redhead is closest to that but I can't be sure. I can't be 100% sure." Again, Carla tried to read Ollie's expression but if he was disappointed, she couldn't tell. Her heart was beating doggedly, not painfully, but persistently. She knew that in the absence of a positive identification, there'd be no case.

"You have to be sure," said Ollie.

Carla looked again at the screen. No, she couldn't say for certain.

"I'm so sorry," she said.

Ollie pushed the same document back to her. "Sign here," he said gently.

"I wish I could remember…"

"It's fine," he said. "I'll get back to you when I've processed all this. I can't say anything more at this stage. I'll have a chat with my sergeant but you'll hear from me in the next few days."

Carla retrieved her bag. Why oh, why, wasn't she more observant? The artist friend of theirs who'd been for dinner had sent her a thank you the very next day with a water colour of their house, drawn from memory and on the strength of having sat in their garden for the few hours over dinner. Carla couldn't have told her what the back of her house looked like after living in it for a year! Carla was unlikely to have even identified it at hers. Her friend though, would have been able to offer the police full portraits of the dogs and their owners!

Carla was thoughtful walking the short distance home. So much had happened in the last couple of months and not just in terms of living with a pandemic. There had been her encounter with Naked Man, the incident with the dog (or

270

dogs and not at midnight) her hissy fit over 'Karen' and the discovery of Zoe. So much.

Carla breathed in the wet leaf smell. There was a definite autumnal feel, the light was different, almost eerie and the evenings were colder now. It was October and after a frantic few days when Carla had had to purchase Alfie's uniform and name it all (she still went into a cold sweat just thinking about sewing names on all those socks) let alone finding him shoes (ordered online by tracing his foot and emailing the sketch), Alfie had gone to his new school and into a 'bubble'. He wouldn't be allowed home for at least two weeks if not three. The first two would be spent within his house and the boys were prohibited from mixing with boys from other houses. Autumn was usually her favourite time of year when she enjoyed the poignancy of the fading light, the anticipation of Advent to come, the thought of cosy evenings in. The thought of any evening 'in' at the moment paralysed her with horror. There'd been far too many of those. And it looked as if there might be many more to come.

Seven months on, the pandemic was far from over. In fact, it felt as if everything was going back to where they were in March. Under new restrictions ('*your mild cough can be someone else's death knell*'), Johnson unveiled details of a national curfew whereby pubs and restaurants would have to close at 10 p.m., weddings would be restricted to fifteen people and the rule of six was back in place. In Scotland it was worse: people weren't allowed to visit each other's homes. In Spain it was worse still, no one was allowed to leave the city full stop. Many millions were being deprived their civil liberties on the basis of what exactly? Unexplained hypotheticals? The restrictions seemed to indicate that a second national lockdown was looming. Restriction, restriction, restriction. It was all they talked about these days, it kept them in a heightened state of anxiety as to what was legal and what wasn't. '*We are all slaves to the law, for that is the condition of our freedom.*' Carla had had to translate that line once and it had stayed with her. Cicero. Never had it seemed more apt, never had she understood it better.

Except now, she for one, was bored to tears by it all, bored by the lack of choice, by the drabness of their reduced world, by the lack of real live music and theatre. They'd become zoombies all right. Towards the end of August, in a bid to restore a kind of normalcy as the summer came to a close, Carla had had her way and they'd gone to the Isle of Wight for a week's holiday. Friends had raised a barely disguised eyebrow in surprise. The Caves are going where? Not Capri, or Sardinia or even Biarritz but ... (deep breath) Totland Bay.

 But they couldn't risk travelling abroad and then that country being suddenly shoved on the quarantine list, and Alfie being excluded from school, not when he'd not been there for six months, so they'd rented an apartment in one of those large Victorian, seafront buildings that might have been grand once and was now pleasantly comfortable with high ceilings, situated a hand's breath from the sea. Hal (out of plaster) had come as playmate for Alfie and they'd all had a lovely, lovely time. The boys had bathed every morning come rain or shine while she and Seb looked on from the shelter of their beach house (it came with the rental) and then, come the afternoon, they'd explored the island. Carla had been captivated by romantic Appuldurcombe House, or what remained of the 18th century Baroque mansion, glimpsed at the end of the drive. The wind had whipped her hair and what stray thoughts remained until her whole being was soothed with cobweb strands of contentment.

Which hadn't lasted. There was new hysteria in the air. All hope seemed to hinge now on a vaccine. Apparently, in July, the British government had bought 40 million doses which was enough for a third of the population. Lucky third, thought Carla although she didn't want to have an inoculation whose side effects they couldn't possibly know. She didn't want to be a guinea pig and find out. Talk of 'saving Christmas' and the notion that families might not be able to gather in or out of the house was becoming a real possibility.

It was all nonsense. And she muttered that it was out loud when she got home, going into the drawing room where Seb was playing the piano. They'd been going to have dinner at The Ivy but with a curfew of 10 p.m. her friends had cancelled. They'd been offered a slot for 5.30 p.m. *'We're not Swedish!'* Her friends had protested. *'Or American,'* Seb had muttered. Besides which, Carla had had her appointment at Mottisfont Court already booked for 6.30.

The last bars of Bach's Cantata 22 came to a close. As sometimes happened, she and Seb became obsessed with a certain piece of music playing it constantly. This latest had been playing on a loop in her head pretty much non-stop over the last forty-eight hours. At least the harmony part had- the actual singing in German (*Jesus nahm zu sich die*) was a little heavy. Regardless, she had begun to hear it when she went to sleep and it woke her in the night.

"At this rate," said Carla throwing herself into an armchair by the French windows, "we're going to be plunged into repeated lockdowns just to suppress the common cold."

Seb looked up.

"Well, don't underestimate the effects of a cold."

"I'm serious."

"So, am I." He stopped playing. "I'm guessing the line up wasn't a success then."

Carla sighed. "Not entirely. I couldn't be sure. And I couldn't lie."

Seb continued to play softly.

Can a Leopard?

"No, you couldn't."

"But it's a shame the owners will get away with it. Those dogs should be put down, they'll attack someone else." Carla shivered. "They'd have killed a child. Or an old person."

Seb got up from the piano and went over her pulling her to her feet. "Or you. They could have killed you."

"Yes, well."

Carla allowed herself to be held, smelled his familiar aroma, closed her eyes and let her mind go blank, to pre-Covid days when everything was reassuringly predictable and safe. A life to look forward to, a life of colour and adventure.

Seb released her.

"Glass of wine?" he said gently. "No, I'll get it. You stay."

He was back within seconds carrying a tray of nibbles. He set it down on a little table in the corner and settled himself beside her on the window seat. The days were becoming shorter and, in the mornings, there was a frost.

"I got the results," he said.

Carla knew he meant the results of his DNA test. For fun (which definitely wasn't how Seb viewed the experience) and to keep him company, Carla had decided to embark on her own 23and me journey. Filling the small vial with saliva had been no easy exercise. She'd spat and spewed and swirled until her mouth was dry as dust.

"Cause for celebration then?"

Seb poured Carla a glass. "Depends on how you look at it, I guess. Either way I thought we could do with a drink."

Can a Leopard?

"And?

Carla took a sip of the Pouilly Fumé. Seb passed her the chili-infused olives he knew she loved.

"I did too. This morning. Only I've not yet looked at them. Pretty confident they're going to be as I expect."

Seb took a long sip and touched her knee.

"You know what I'm like with suspense. You go first."

"All right," Carla smiled pleasantly, setting down her wine glass and pulling out her phone. "Bear with me, I hate reading emails on this tiny screen."

Carla went straight to her inbox. She was pretty confident, excited even. Perhaps there was some Malay in her, or West Indian. Definitely Jewish. European Jewish obviously. She'd be happy with as much as 16%. Her father was Spanish, which should explain it. Maybe she was a Rothschild, a Sefardic Jewess? Seb often referred to her passionate nature, her temper, her high cheek bones, her highly strung nature (neurotic when he wasn't being so sweet) her elegance. She shot Seb a sly glance. Just wait *mi amor*. Just wait. All will be revealed. Maybe she was Ethiopian. Ethiopians had been Christians since 600 AD. Quite an impressive fact, they'd never been converted by conquering forces. Wasn't Bowie's beautiful wife Iman Ethiopian? Or was she Somalian? Then there was the gorgeous Thandie Newton whose mother was Zimbabwean. Oh, it was sounding better by the minute!

Carla scanned the tabs, homing in on the 'Ancestry Composition' page. She flicked to 'view your report' and the circle in blue that showed a clear diagram of how her profile was divided. And went back a page. Scrolled up twice. Then down, repeating the process. She blanched. She'd said, 'You first' glibly because she'd been super confident as to how this was all going to play out.

275

"What's the matter?" Seb had said in alarm. "What is it?"

But Carla couldn't speak.

25

"I thought this was supposed to be about me," said Seb half-jokingly.

"Of course, it is," said Carla "but I've had a terrible shock. How would you feel if your whole life had been upended? Was a kind of lie? That you weren't who you thought you were? Not remotely?"

"Yeah, well that's pretty much how I do feel. Exactly. Besides, how would you feel if you found out that a sibling you adored was … well let's just say, less than perfect?"

Carla made a face. "Isn't that what all families end up being? I mean to quote one of Alfie's favourite pop songs: *'you're only human after all…'*"

"I guess," Seb sounded doubtful. "We parents, inevitably fall off our pedestals, I know that. But I'm trying to get my head around the fact that I have a Shona niece," said Seb mildly. "A confirmed Shona niece. We talked about it before in the abstract but seeing the results in black and white. Oops - no pun intended…I wish my parents were alive, is all I can say. They'd have loved this." He helped himself to a bread roll.

"Do you think that Dom will be involved now?"

"He'll have to be," said Seb firmly. "And it wasn't an affair," he added quietly.

Carla took the end of Seb's bread and popped it in her mouth. "Ok, so it was love. Isn't that better? Certainly, for Zoe. She just needs to get to know her," she paused for effect, "gay father."

Seb frowned. "God, you can be direct."

"Yes, well, that's my," she scanned her phone, "1 % Northern European talking."

They were silent.

"So, we're both disappointed."

Carla waved to the masked waiter. They were sitting well away from other diners since the ruling had come into effect which prohibited members of different households meeting indoors. She supposed she should be grateful that Alfie was safely at school although he hadn't been allowed home for half term. Carla had been disappointed although not so Alfie. After six months at home, being with his parents virtually 24/7, he was ecstatic to be with boys his own age. Alfie's school had managed the whole Covid thing very well. Yes, mothers complained about not seeing their boys but the school had remained pretty much Covid-free as a result. She didn't need Alfie self-isolating at home and falling into depression as he had done in March. Besides which, the kind of freedom of being child free had been countered by the new restrictions placed on the country as uncertain times continued, travel was still an unknown and now this - the latest gloomy strangle hold on their socialising. It was all becoming so boring and predictable. They should be in the South of France at this very moment enjoying a romantic weekend away, instead, they were lunching at The Ivy.

Carla slurped the dregs of her Pink Gin cocktail before ordering another. 'Disappointment' didn't begin to cover what she had felt on reading her results. Only the other day an elderly woman had stopped her on the street and asked her if she was a member of the Jewish community. *'Didn't know there was one,'* Seb had said surprised. There'd been a glint in Carla's eye and it had been on the tip of her tongue to respond in the affirmative before Seb had restrained her and she'd remembered the report. Not a drop... *Nada.* Even her supposed Spanish blood felt slightly fraudulent. She thought of her elegant, six feet tall Spanish father, his aquiline nose, his dark looks. When travelling in Jerusalem he too had been mistaken for a native.

"That's what I am," she said now aloud taking a long sip from her refreshed gin. "I'm a genetic fraud.

Carla had said it lightly hoping to distract Seb but he appeared unconcerned. She followed his gaze as it swept around the restaurant. The once buzzing eatery had been adapted to meet Covid-safe standards. Tables were spread far and wide, staff wore dark Vader-type plastic masks and screens at the entrance separated the receptionist from its clientele. As in Italy, they'd had their temperatures taken on arrival. 'What's the point?' said Carla under her breath. 'This is a disease you only get when you're dead.' Seb had made that 'bottle it' gesture as she sailed past him complaining that there was no longer anywhere to leave your coat and that the mask was sticking to her lipstick. It was incredible though how quickly people adapted. Although where had all the spontaneity gone as a result?

"How do you figure that?" he said now. "By the way, are we eating? Or just ginning?"

Carla motioned to the bar code on the triangle of cardboard in the centre of the table. They had to download the menu on to their phones.

"Actually, that's a relief. I could never read it in here anyway, the writing is so tiny and the lights are too dim. What do I usually have?"

But Carla was oblivious to Seb's culinary deliberations.

279

Can a Leopard?

"I'm not really even Spanish!" she wailed.

"Well, you are. Just not as much as you thought."

"How is it possible not to be anything exotic? I just don't get it. I am 99% European. A tiny percentage is Spanish and the rest is..." Carla felt her eyes fill with tears. "British. Just British. And you know what the worst bit is?"

Seb sighed. "No, what's the worst bit?"

Carla hiccupped. "I'm not sure I can even say it," she said feeling sick at the very thought. "I have relatives..."

"Yes?"

Carla's voice dwindled to a whisper so that Seb had to lean over the table to hear her. She took a shuddering breath. "In..."

"Yes? This is sounding hopeful?" Seb began lightly fiddling with his cutlery, something he only did when he wasn't really listening. "Can't be all bad."

She slumped against the padded banquette. Ordinarily she appreciated the gold, orange and white of the art décor furnishings, the fractured light sliding from mirrors and windows. She liked dressing up and going out to dinner. These days what was the point when you had to wear a mask and could only be with your partner anyway. It was her turn to have her head in her hands. Her rings became entangled in her hair.

"I have relations in ..."

"I can't hear?"

"Wo-" Carla could hardly bring herself to say the word. Dig deep... she told herself. Dig deep... "According to my DNA family tree, I have relatives in..."

"Carla," said Seb warningly.

"Woking!" she shouted. "Woking! OK? Satisfied? I have relatives in *Woking!*"

Other diners looked up momentarily distracted from their conversations.

"You're right," said Seb. "I'm not hungry either. Let's just gin. Although apparently, the number of people drinking hazardous levels of alcohol has doubled since March. I think that's approximately 8.4 million."

"It's not funny."

"I know. It's shocking!"

"I don't mean the drink."

"Neither do I." Seb finished his and begun chomping ice cubes which always set Carla's teeth on edge. He waved an empty glass in the air. "But at least these cousins -"

"Cousin," corrected Carla. "4th cousin - 0.79% shared DNA."

"Yeah - OK, cousin then, is just that. Besides it doesn't sound as if you're in any hurry to meet any of them. I have a niece, not much older than Alfie who desperately wants to be included. Wants to know us all. With the current climate and Dom being unable to travel here I feel I need to step up. I feel responsible."

"Why? Why do you? You, don't always have to rush around being a white knight, Seb. You're not her father."

281

"No," said Seb patiently. "Her uncle."

Carla made a slight scoffing sound.

"Half."

Seb unfurled his napkin then smoothed it out once again. "I don't believe in 'halves'. Have you ever considered how divisive language can be in these situations? No, if Zoe is going to be part of the family then she's a whole."

Carla considered her husband, his calm face, anthracite eyes, the set line of his jaw.

"You really mean this don't you."

"It's not negotiable."

Carla took a breath.

"I'm sorry." And all at once, she realised just how selfish she was being as the gin kicked in and the room began to swirl not unpleasantly and she remembered she was wearing her new Temperley jumpsuit. She frowned inwardly as a weeny voice of conscience made an unwelcome appearance. Yes, yes. She'd made a promise. Yet another, yeah thanks very much, she was aware. Obviously, she'd told herself she wasn't to buy anything new for the autumn. However, it would have been irresponsible not to. The darling thing had been hanging on the wall as she went up the stairs at Moda Rosa. It was her size too. How lucky was that? What a coinkydink she'd thought, using her son's schoolboy parlance. Surely, that in itself was a sign. Plus, it had been on sale. She touched Seb's arm.

"I'm sorry," she repeated. "I've not been very gracious about any of this. Of course, we'll be kind to Zoe, get to know her. As you say she doesn't appear to be that much older than Alfie, although I know she must be. He'll love having a ..."

what was she? Cousin? "Cousin," said Carla. Great, a Shona cousin here and another in … Woking. "I didn't ask before, in case you projected something that wasn't to be, but did you like her? I mean, did Zoe feel like family? Was there any of Dom in her?"

Seb shrugged. "I don't know her. I mean, I met up with a couple of times but as I'd not had the results from the DNA, I didn't want to believe or invest until I knew for certain. I couldn't say. She's young and blonde. She doesn't look particularly…" he coloured. "Shona."

"And now?"

Seb's face clouded. "I don't know. I honestly don't know."

"Did - did you like her though?"

Seb again waved his glass in the direction of the bar. This time the waiter appeared quickly with a refill. "I suppose." said Seb when he'd gone. "She's just a kid. But she needs direction. She wants to meet Dom and won't be happy until she does. She was studying to be a vet back in Zim."

"She sounds bright. At least she knows what she wants to do."

"Oh, she does that," said Seb. "She's very determined."

They fell silent after that, as conversation drifted back to talk of Covid, the fact that a second lockdown, inconceivable only weeks before and a sheer lunacy, seemed inevitable.

"And there will only be more tears," said Carla despondently, attempting a pun on the Tier restrictions which saw parts of the country already in total lockdown. It looked as if the country was set to shut down until the second of December. "It's asinine. Children are no longer going to be allowed to play grassroots sport, golf courses and sports clubs are also

Can a Leopard?

closing. I thought the government wanted us to spend time out of doors! And its slogan of 'Staying Alert', has reverted to the old boring one of 'staying home.' I want to be out, out, out!"

Seb studied her thoughtfully.

"Yeah, I get you. I'd do anything for sun at this moment but we have to be patient a little longer. If the virus is about to resume is exponential growth, then it's only logical we do."

"But it's not!" countered Carla in exasperation. "There are a zillion reasons why there might have been an escalation in cases. Lockdowns only delay infections so long as the virus is still circulating! Plus, all this ramped-up testing has clearly turned up false positives - roughly two percent by the way. If we're constantly testing it's always going to seem as though we're in the midst of a raging epidemic. Anyway, it's death numbers we should be concentrating on not 'cases' where people aren't seriously ill or even terminally ill."

Actually, as long as schools remained open, no matter how much Carla missed Alfie, she didn't care too much.

"Mmmn... quite a passionate little speech," said Seb calmly refusing to be baited. They generally didn't agree on anything to do with Covid, could easily allow their differences to degenerate into a full- blown argument but not this time.

Carla's gaze flicked around the restaurant

"Oh, my God, am I bored!"

Seb scanned her face frowning.

"What, with me?"

"Oh, *amor mio*," she began and then remembering the less than 14% Spanish, changed it to 'darling' adding glumly, "Of, course not! I'm bored to death with Covid! Do you realise this is the longest we've ever been in one country, continuously? I feel inert with frustration at the idea of not being able to travel and go exactly where I want. *Do* what I want."

He smiled then "You? Inert? Don't make me laugh!"

And she did, start laughing or at least giggling.

"Look at us!" she said holding out her hand. Seb took hers instantly and slowly began massaging the skin on her hand, working his way along the fingers almost as though she were wearing gloves and he was smoothing out the creases. He kissed the inside of her wrist. "The thing is, I have you and Alfie. I don't need another family. I don't want one. Maybe when this Covid crap is over we can all go to Zim for a holiday. Zoe can go to America and meet Dom and you and I can go to Zim."

Travel? Carla thought of a clip Les Girls had sent her recently. The only clip that had made her smile recently. *'I can't wait to walk down the aisle one day and hear those magical words: "This is your pilot speaking."'* At this point she could even get excited about travelling to Basingstoke. But it all seemed as realistic as a trip to the moon.

"You aren't a little bit curious about the Shona connection?"

He dropped her hands.

"Of course, I'm curious! But I've lived this long without knowing about Zoe and whatever extended family she may or may not have, that I can wait. They can wait."

Carla pursed her lips. "She has a lot to answer for- their mother. Dropping this bombshell."

"Don't blame her," said Seb kindly. "It was bound to come out somewhere along the line. Zoe had done her DNA test, so it was only a matter of time before some relation or other popped up." Seb thought of something. "We didn't go up to the lakes, did we? When we were in Zim that last time or the South or to the Mozambique border?"

"You mean, Chipinge? To see your friend."

Seb nodded.

"Yes, Chipinge. It's miraculous that Karl is still there. Who knows though for how long though? We should go."

Carla remembered Karl. He'd almost been evicted when Manicaland's provincial minister wanted his land for her son. A farmer exporting coffee, Karl's produce had won international awards until Mugabe's infamous land reforms disabled his business. Despite the uncertainty, the sporadic incidents of land invasions, the idea of returning - of getting on a plane and going anywhere - filled her with hope. She felt her spirits lift. Oh, yes. It would be wonderful to feel that African sun on her face and the dust in her mouth as they headed towards the Matopo hills. Through half-closed eyes, the burnt orange and gold and the sand-colour leather of The Ivy's earth tones, easily morphed into another more exotic landscape.

Now, that Seb mentioned Zim, she remembered the long, parched car journey from Harare to Victoria Falls in particular. There'd been all kinds of pitfalls along the way - literally huge potholes (which made for lethal night driving), menacing roadblocks appearing from nowhere and most threatening of all (well to Seb), Patrick Mavros. Unwittingly, the famous artisan had almost ruined the start of their holiday.

Because Carla liked his African- inspired jewellery and Seb had mentioned he knew Patrick (something he regretted almost as soon as the words were out of his mouth), they'd dropped in on his place on the way. Like Karl, Patrick had suffered threats and home invasion but unlike Karl, his beautiful home had been seized during the land acquisition program. Patrick was magnanimously allowed to stay in a home that his great grandparents had built and rent the farm back from local government. At the time, Carla knew little of that and merely gasped at the view when they alighted.

The white, Dutch gabled mansion, nestled within a crescent of gently rolling grassland stretching as far as the eye could see and broken only by a curve of blue hills. The place too was a mini game reserve with giraffes and zebra wandering gracefully yards away from them, as casually as if they'd been a couple of ponies turned out in a paddock. Carla gaped as a couple of ostriches, with inflated necks galumphed past.

"Can you hear them?" Patrick said in a more pronounced version of Seb's faintly accented one. "Not everyone can. See their necks have inflated to three times their normal size?"

"As long as that's the only bit that does…" muttered Seb and Carla made a swatting sound to hush him.

Carla could indeed see the warbling necks shrink and expand with every strange boom, cooing sound.

"Only the male makes that sound," continued Patrick. He'd come to stand beside her, a little too close; completely ignoring Seb. Alfie was happily chasing kittens in the courtyard. He was a giant of a man - well over six feet five, broad-shouldered and of Greek extraction. Like Seb, he wore his hair long although his was quite grey. Seb subconsciously stroked his own dark locks. But while Seb was dressed for the bush, in muted khaki, Patrick was dressed all in white as if he had just stepped off a yacht moored in the Sporades. "The female…" He looked down at Carla, his eyes caressing her face. He had a deep, hypnotic voice.

"Yes?"

287

"*Hiss*," said Seb cutting in and glaring at them both. "The women, sorry the *females* - hiss."

Now, under the table, Carla fingered her silver, alligator-patterned cuff. The visit had been fun although considerably shorter than she would have liked. Seb had been almost apoplectic by the time they continued on their journey. He'd not enjoyed being shown around the rest of the farm by Patrick's sons (four in total) or the fact that these young men had thought it perfectly reasonable for Alfie to handle a rifle at the age of three and shoot it while Patrick showed only Carla his workshop - all works in progress - ready to be shipped to the far corners of the globe.

"I like your ..." Patrick had waved his hand in the vague area of her chest.

"Oh, this!" Carla glanced at her pendant: three misshapen, battered rings each with a pearl attached. In no way could it compare with the delicacy of his exquisite jewellery.

"You mix gold and silver, it's good."

"That's not all he wanted to mix!" said Seb darkly as they careered out of the drive in a cloud of dust.

Despite Patrick's invitation - insistence even - that they spend the night, they'd carried on to Bulawayo before arriving late afternoon. Rosy and pink against a band of lush forestry, the splendid Victoria Falls Hotel, with its imposing sprawling Colonial façade - whitewashed plaster and a red tile roof - was reminiscence of a bygone age. They'd stood on the terrace looking down to the Batoka gorge and the bridge that Rhodes dreamed would extend travel by steam, from Cairo to the Cape. In fact, the hotel was first conceived, Seb told her when he'd recovered from the Patrick experience, to provide accommodation for workers on the railway.

Can a Leopard?

After dropping their bags with the concierge (who mistaking Seb for an ambassador insisted on referring to him as 'Excellency'), they'd headed straight out, along the damp, sunlit drenched pathways towards the falls. Seb had carried a sleepy Alfie on his back, his head nestling into Seb's neck. There'd been a rainbow at sunset, excitement at seeing a hippo but Alfie had barely looked up, by then, only wanting to go back to their hotel room and play with his toys. Carla had seen a different Seb in the country of his birth, a proud man, a man with a deep-rooted love of his birthplace.

"So, you'll come? We'll travel and go back?"

Seb raised her hand to his lips then kept it tucked in his.

"I'd like that," said Carla now, as the black and white stripes of a zebra settled back into being merely a palm frond on The Ivy wall and a cobalt blue sky became wallpaper, against which sand and earth and white cloud shimmied into benches and a bar, and starched white tablecloths. And as the world's sediments settled with all its uncertainty, the possibility of an unthinkable, unimaginable second lockdown, with all its grief, and joy and loss; rising unbidden as flotsam, more powerful than all those negatives combined, was also a weak, pulsating beat of hope.

"I'd like that," repeated Carla. "I'd like that very much."

Printed in Great Britain
by Amazon

55151487R00172